GU00863740

RO

TIMOTHY PILGRIM

OnLine

Visit us online at www.authorsonline.co.uk

An AuthorsOnLine Book

Published by Authors OnLine Ltd 2003

Copyright © 2003 Authors OnLine Ltd
Text Copyright © 2003 Timothy Pilgrim
Cover © 2003 Timothy Pilgrim
The moral right of the author has been asserted

Paperback ISBN 0-7552-0101-9

Authors OnLine Ltd
40 Castle Street
Hertford SG14 1HR
England

This book is also available in e-book format from
www.authorsonline.co.uk

Glossary

I.R.	Infra red
O.P	observation post
Q.R.F.	quick reaction force
P.I.R.A.	Provisional Irish republican army
I.N.L.A	Irish national liberation army
Q M	Quarter master
V.I.N	vehicle identification number
R.V.	rendezvous
L.U.P	laying up point
R.T.U.	returned to unit
U.H.F.	ultra high frequency
L.Z.	landing zone
S.O.P.	standard operating procedure
P.M.C.	President of the mess committee

The war against drugs had become as International as the problem. One of the biggest difficulties those engaged in the dangerous task of combating this menace had to face was knowing exactly who the enemy really were. All manner of reasons, excuses call it what you will, have been proffered to mitigate the guilt of those involved. Ultimately it all comes down to pure, malicious greed, be it for the easy cash or, in some cases, power. Not all of those who profit from this evil trade are shady underworld figures or dubious businessmen; these types could almost be described as honest criminals, as they simply crave the easy cash. If these honest criminals are to succeed in their nefarious activities to any degree, then the other category of 'bad guy' enters the scene.

These are much more dangerous as they crave the power as well as the extra money which, for the most part, they don't need. These are by far the hardest to catch. The lengths to which they will go to protect their identities are quite incredible. The higher up the chain they are, the greater the extremes to which they will go to protect themselves. This story came to be written when a damage limitation exercise by one or more of these scurrilous characters didn't work out quite as was intended.

In the early 70's our political masters became aware of a new means of projecting power and influence, their 'in' phrases were 'low intensity warfare' and covert operations. Their 'new' weapon was 22. S.A.S. regiment. So successful was this unorthodox regiment the sheer volume of the tasks ordered by the government threatened to overwhelm it. Passing the selection course was one thing, in itself no mean feat, completing the regimental training programme which followed was something else; in theory this period should have taken twelve to fifteen months. During this 'in between' period the new members retained their rank, this was to avoid taking a pay cut, as at the time many applicants were NCOs from the corps such as R.E.M.E.

Because of the extraordinary demands made on the regiment, many of the men who should have been instructors were required for 'sensitive' operations. One consequence of this was the 'trainees', all experienced soldiers before applying, were used on the more mundane, 'safe' jobs expected of the regiment. Little risk and experience was gained, orders were complied with, (nearly) everyone happy!

Against this background, four of the newest recruits to the regiment were formed into a squad and given the call sign 'Hotel Quebec 7'. As the call sign suggests, they were attached to Regimental Headquarters, to keep them out of trouble; at least that was the idea. The four soldiers who made up this squad were as disparate a group of individuals as it was possible to imagine, almost universally described within the regiment as four misfits who happened to fit together.

B.J, the Geordie; had started his army career in the Signals before moving to the R.E.M.E., he was the communications expert. His partner was Kenny who hailed from the mean streets of the East End housing estates. He had 'graduated' via the Engineers, on through the independent commando brigade; he was an expert with explosives.

The other pair of this 'ad hoc' temporary squad consisted of a short, stocky little Welshmen, one of the last R.E.M.E. dual tradesmen. Because of the operational pressures on the Regiment, the 'boss' took the decision to commit this 'gang'; led by the wiry mechanic from the backwoods of East Anglia to the turmoil of Ireland.

The senior officers discussing this move expressed their doubts. Paul, the leader of this squad, had narrowly missed being RTU'd on several occasions. He was in many ways the weakest member of the squad, yet he had sort of 'emerged' as leader, he hadn't sought it, they hadn't encouraged it, it just happened.

Such training as they had done had gone well, they certainly worked well as a team. There was undeniably a natural understanding between them, they didn't appear to work at it, each seemed instinctively to know, not only what the others would do, but when. It was, as one veteran put it, 'spooky'.

This is not a tale of 'daring – do' behind enemy lines, I am in no way qualified to write such a book. This is merely a tale of the ups and downs of one squad of 'in between', soldiers WITH though not OF the regiment, yet to complete their training. Seen, I should point out, from my point of view, the others would no doubt remember some things differently. This is not a case of right or wrong, merely everyone would have his or her own perspective on the events described in this book.

CHAPTER ONE

"How the hell did we end up here Taff?"

"You tell me mate," replied the stocky little Welshman, "I seem to remember you said, 'what the hell, why not,' when the terrible two invited us to have a go at joining the regiment; anything to get away from 'Spud Taylor'."

"Yeah well, there's more to this lot than feeding the wild life of South Armagh hedgerows," Paul answered and squashed yet another persistent gnat.

"I suppose there must be, but even the wild life seem to have gone into hiding, either that or drowned."

"That's something coming from you. I'd have thought you'd have felt right at home in this weather."

"Are you takin' the piss, Boyo?"

"Probably," replied Paul. "Tell you what Taff lad, I'll bet this shit is going to turn to snow before it gets dark. Get a brew on mate I'm bloody freezing."

"This has got to be one of the best hides on the boarder, it has even got running water and you still moan."

"If this is the best then I'd hate to be in the ordinary one, you're right though, at least this one is pretty well weather proof, pass that cuppa up, then you can get some kip. I've got a feeling it's going to be a long night."

"Well, look on the bright side Boyo, there's only a couple more days, three at the most and then we'll be back to the comforts of Crossmaglen."

"That's supposed to make me feel better? I wish those Intel types would do their own bloody stakeouts. I sometimes wonder just how good their information is, do these operations ever catch a terrorist?"

"I dunno, s'pose this sort of op must serve some purpose or we wouldn't be here."

As the light began to fade Paul's gloomy prophecy of snow came true, just odd flakes at first, followed by .big wet ones. An hour later it had turned into one of the worst blizzards the boarder country had seen for years. Thankfully, the gnats seemed to have given up.

1

"This is definitely going to be one of those nights Taff, pass us your rifle, mate, the image intensifier on mine is totally bloody useless in this weather."

"O.K, but don't alter the settings on it, I spent bloody hours setting it up."

"Cheers mate, at least your I.R. set up should be able to penetrate this clag well enough to let us know if any one tries to sneak past."

Dawn was late, it was still snowing steadily, but at least the wind had dropped.

"I've got to admit boyo you made a damn good job of this hide. Come on you lazy bugger, your turn to watch the rabbits."

"Cheers Taff, I'd just got comfortable."

The only sign of life that day was the farmer feeding his sheep about a mile away down the valley. It was amazing how quickly so much snow could simply vanish. By early afternoon the sun was shining, there was a gentle south-westerly breeze and only a few small glistening patches of snow remained. One effect of the rapid thaw following a snow-storm was to turn the normal gentle trickle in the ditches to muddy torrents. The little stream along the bottom of the valley watched by the soldiers had turned into a raging flood, creating an audible noise in the hide.

The night was clear and cold, but as with many nights before, uneventful. Even the stream had subsided to near its normal level, following the sudden flood caused by the rapid thaw.

Paul stretched his cold aching limbs, "Want a brew Taff?" he asked, already pouring his friend a fresh cup of coffee.

"Don't know why you bother to ask, but thanks anyway."

After they finished their drinks the two men swapped places, Paul would watch the valley for the next four hours.

As his watch was coming to an end, something further down the valley caught his attention. He wasn't sure exactly what it was, but it refocused his concentration. Despite meticulous sweeps of the area, he couldn't detect anything to support his suspicion, there was someone about. The sense of unease persisted as this feeling was reinforced by the panic stricken departure of a small flock of pigeons from a couple of ivy covered oaks about two hundred yards below the hide.

"What's up?" asked Taff as he slid up beside Paul.

"Damned if I know mate. I reckon there's someone about down there, but I'm damned if I can spot anyone."

"Move over let's have a deco, see if the I.R. can pick anything up."

"Feel free."

After about ten minutes Taff turned to his friend. "Either there is someone down there and he's very good, or you're imagining things. Are you sure there's someone there?"

"No I'm not sure, call it a feeling, instinct, what you will, but something startled those pigeons."

Taff was still trying to think of a suitably insulting reply when a rabbit shot out of the little spinney and jinked across the field below them.

"You could be right old son, there's something or someone upsetting the locals."

Paul was also scanning the valley with his image intensifier on full power, "Got 'im," he muttered.

"Where?" asked Taff, "I can't see a damned thing."

"See the tree fallen over the stream, try looking at the base of the third big branch, right on the edge of the stream."

"Crafty bugger, how the bloody hell did you spot him?"

"Easy, he lit a fag."

"Keep an eye on him, I'll make a brew then have a snooze, at the rate he's moving it'll be an hour until he's in the open."

"Lazy git, still the brew isn't such a bad idea."

Paul slid back up to the O.P. with a steaming mug of coffee for his friend.

"Move over Taff, I'll keep a eye on him while you have your cuppa."

"Cheers mate."

For the next twenty minutes or so, Paul watched the man cautiously creeping up the valley towards the two soldiers.

"Here Taff, have a shuffty at this," Paul whispered.

"What mate?"

"He's carrying a 'long' of some sort."

"Can't make out what it is, looks heavy."

"Don't it just, Oh shit, we're going to lose the bastard in the dead ground in a minute."

For the next ten minutes or more the watching men waited patiently for the gunman to reappear.

3

"What do you reckon, a scout, he certainly doesn't look like a V.I.P?"

"Darned if I know. He's up to no good that's for sure. I s'pose he could be a sniper, but it doesn't help us a lot. I think our best bet is to give the other pair a shout. Let them follow him until a Q.R.F can take over the tail, see where he runs to, might turn up something useful."

"Sounds good to me Taff. I'll get on the radio, knowing that pair they'll be well wrapped up, probably fast a kip."

Paul slid down into the back of the hide and before he had chance to pick up the handset there was a loud bang. Taff fell back amid a shower of leaves and earth clutching his head, blood showing between his fingers.

"What the fuck!" Paul was back into the front of the hide in a flash. It took only a couple of seconds for Paul to find his target and gently squeeze the trigger.

On the edge of his vision through his 'scope, something caught his eye What ever it was it was out of focus, much closer than the man in his sights. It took only a couple of seconds to check. "Shit" he muttered and slid silently down to see to his wounded friend. Because the man who had fired the shot was barely forty yards away, he signalled his friend to remain silent and remove his hand to expose the extent of the wound.

He quickly passed Taff a sterile pad from his first aid kit. Typical of attention to detail, this special wrapping could be opened with little or no noise.

Paul peered cautiously out of the hide; the target was walking away, disappearing into the dead ground once more.

"You ain't goin' to believe this pal but you got taken out by the local poacher, he was only out for a rabbit for his tea."

"You what!" exclaimed the wounded Welshman.

"Like I said, it was a poacher. When he shot the rabbit, seems you caught a stray pellet, lets have a look."

The offending shotgun-pellet more or less fell out into Paul's hand. A quick clean up, a dab of antiseptic, a piece of Elastoplast and the job was done.

No sooner had Paul finished patching up his friend than the L.E.D. on his radio flashed indicating an incoming call. It was the other pair in the team, calling from their hide further up the little

4

valley. The sound of the shot had carried a quarter of a mile to the two bored, wet soldiers.

"Was it you Paul?" enquired the caller.

"No mate. It was a poacher after his dinner; trouble is he hit Taff as well. I know it's easy for me to say, but it ain't serious he'll be alright."

"Had us worried, mate."

"Me too, if I hadn't caught a glimpse of the rabbit kicking in the grass I'd have had some awkward questions to answer. I'd taken first pressure, it was too bloody close, I'll call you later, settle down for a long wait."

"It's alright for you, we're not as cosy as you pair; our hide is bloody draughty!"

Paul chuckled, "O.K. I'll call you later, out."

Once more the patient soldiers settled down to continue their vigil. The following day was even quieter, not a soul stirred in the little valley. It was hard to believe there was anyone else in the area, much less the potential of a violent confrontation with men to whom killing was a way of life. The monotony of the watching was punctuated only by the local wild life going about their daily business. Even less happened after darkness fell. "Does this job try the patience of a saint or what?" muttered Paul as he took over from his friend on the observation step. Low cloud had swept in from the Atlantic, bringing with it the horrible persistent drizzle which soaks everything; at least it was mild.

"Try looking on the bright side, two more stints each then it's back to the comforts of the barracks, sweaty feet and all."

"If you put it like that then this place has its attractions, see you in four hours."

Some time in the early hours of the morning something attracted the watching soldier's attention, maybe it was a stick cracking under a boot. He turned up the power on his scanner to maximum and meticulously searched the valley for the umpteenth time. At first everything looked exactly the same as it had on every other occasion, 'hang on a minute,' Paul thought to himself as he scanned the fallen tree. There seemed to be a extra branch on the edge of the little stream, was it just a bit of rubbish brought down by the flood? His mind seemed to be playing tricks. When he checked again, it was gone. Carefully he examined the area around the exposed roots, 'got you.' He slid silently down to his sleeping friend, "Taff, we're on."

As the waiting soldiers watched, the shape of a man armed with what was clearly an A.K 47, emerged from the cover of the fallen tree. He was carrying what appeared to be some kind some kind of scanner.

"This guy's good Taff, or thinks he is, stopping every few yards to scan the valley. I don't suppose it's crossed the dozy bastard's mind we might have seen him first."

"S'pose he isn't the brightest star in the sky is he?"

"See the rest of them down by the sluice? I make it three escorts and the VIP we're waiting for. Wake the others up Taff. This is likely to get noisy."

No sooner had Paul uttered those prophetic words than all hell broke loose.

For the first time anyone could remember the local company of the Paras had varied their time and the route of their daily patrol, they had walked straight into a carefully laid ambush. The ambush had not been intended for British troops, but for the party of PIRA and their VIP who were heading up the valley, intent on sneaking into the north with funds.

Although claiming to be republicans, the INLA hated the Provo's almost as much as they hated the Brits. Somehow they had got wind of the large consignment of cash to help fund the Provisional political wing in the upcoming elections. What ensued could only be described as a total cock up.

One paratrooper lay badly injured by the booby trap he had triggered; his colleagues called in the cas-e-vac helicopter. Before the startled INLA ambush team had worked out what had happened, the helicopter appeared with commendable promptness, only to be fired at by the INLA gang The Paras fired at the gang, who fired back. The fleeing gunmen ran straight into their intended targets, who also shot at them. Thus a three-way fire-fight ensued, right under the noses of the slightly bemused S.A.S team. Before Paul or Taff could get a shot off, the VIP had been scrambled out of sight below the sluice.

"Fuck this Taff, can you work out who's shooting at who?" asked Paul.

"Best idea would be to keep our heads down then pick up the bits."

6

"We've still got a crack at matey with the scanner."

"Give him a shout he might surrender, if he doesn't, mallet him," suggested Taff.

"B.J. and Kenny are in a good position to flank that lot and give the Paras a bit of support. Give them a shout Taff; just to make sure they know who we are otherwise they'll shoot at us."

"With any luck we should get all of the ambush team," said Taff optimistically.

"O.K call 'em up. It ain't what we're here for but at least we'll get some sort of result."

As Taff was calling the other half of the S.A.S. team Paul shouted at the terrorist below him to surrender. His reward was a fairly accurate burst of automatic fire from the AK47. The armalite cracked twice and the gunman fell back onto the bank of the stream.

A short vicious fire-fight with the ambush INLA gang now ensued. The last two gunmen fled into the night, eight of the Paras in pursuit.

Gunfire echoed around the border hills. The fleeing terrorists sought safety in the nearby republic. At the same time loosing off bursts to deter the paratroopers intent on avenging their injured comrade.

"I suppose we'd better sort this out Taff. What the fuck?" he cursed as a well-aimed burst rattled around his head, causing him to duck below ground level. "Where the bloody hell did that come from?"

The next burst from a heavy machine gun was directed at B.J.'s hide, this was followed by several longer bursts at the remaining Paras and the Wessex.

Paul fired four carefully aimed shots at the muzzle flashes, which were clearly visible through his scope.

"You're bloody hoping they're way out of range."

"I know, but it might put 'em off if they hear stuff pinging off the rocks."

No sooner had the M.G. shut up than there was another outburst of gunfire. This time it was down the valley from the direction taken by the fleeing VIP and his escorts.

"Don't even ask boyo, I'm as confused as you are," said Taff in anticipation of the inevitable question.

"What do you reckon; all the noise must have woken up the local Gardi?"

"I doubt it, might have woken the dead but not the Gardi."

"I suppose it would account for the fact that the one I dropped has vanished!" muttered Paul. "I'm bloody certain I was spot on with those shots. He went down hard enough!"

There was another burst, closer than the last; Paul swept the valley with his sight. He could just make out the figures of two obviously armed men, just below the sluice. They were firing back down the valley at some unseen target. Each was covering the other as they moved up the valley towards Paul and Taff.

To further confuse the issue, odd shots, aimed by the unseen gunmen at the two men working their way towards Paul and Taff, were thudding into the ground quite close to the hide.

"Who the bloody hell are this pair? They're pretty bloody slick, too slick for terrorists. You have a deco, see what you think."

Taff wriggled round so he had a better view. "I see what you mean. On the other hand, if they are terrorists we'll never get a better chance. It's your call Paul, you're skipper on this op."

"Cheers pal, we wait."

The two men continued to work their way along the stream until they were directly below the hide.

"Pass the communicator up Taff."

Paul switched channels, "This is hotel Quebec 7, please respond."

A familiar voice with a distinct midlands accent crackled back.

"Where the hell are you Paul?"

"Directly above you on your left, if you carry on another twenty yards you'll come to a little side stream, follow it up to the wall, turn left again and you'll find us, Taff's just doing a brew."

"Cheers, be with you in a bit, then you can tell us what the fuck has been going on."

"I would if I could. You're clear now. I can see the lot you had a brush with. They're headed up towards the rocks where the bloody M.G. opened up from."

"Hope they shoot each other."

"Me too."

A couple of minutes after John and Brummie slid into the hide the machine gun opened up again. Once more the target was the Wessex helicopter. Paul took careful aim, fired six shots in all, the gun ceased its manic clatter after his second shot.

"I don't believe I saw it," commented John. "I reckon he hit the bloody thing, the last few rounds from the M.G. definitely went way off target."

"Yeah right, at damned nearly a thousand yards with an armalite."

"Who cares it shut them up."

"We'll give it a bit to calm down then pull out. The Op to get the VIP is fucked now so I don't see the point in sitting here any longer."

"I reckon the VIP stopped one in our ruck, we certainly hit one, maybe two of them, I'm not saying they're seriously wounded, but some of them were bleeding before they got past us."

"One might have been the one I hit," said Paul, "I challenged their scout, he let fly, so I shot back. The way he went down I'm surprised he didn't stay down."

"Some of them are wearing body armour these days Paul," replied John.

"It would explain why the bastards disappeared. Fuck this lets go home."

CHAPTER 2

At about 4am one spring morning the ageing tele-printer in the sparsely furnished room deep beneath Whitehall clattered into life. The duty operator rolled out of his blanket on the camp bed muttering heavily.

To add to his consternation it was marked, 'MOST IMMEDIATE, F.A.O. DUTY CONTROLLER.' The origin had been the security section at the legation in Kuala Lumpur. After sending the standard acknowledgement, he rushed along the corridor clutching the coded message. The duty officer was no more pleased than the young operator had been at having his sleep disturbed. He should have been at home with his family, but had been called in at the last moment. The man who should have been occupying this Spartan office, deep in the bowels of the command centre, had been delayed whilst returning from holiday.

This was the first misfortune to befall the 'bad guys' as this officer was 'straight', unlike his counterpart marooned on a Channel Ferry, unable to dock until the sudden gale abated.

The duty officer's displeasure at being woken turned to concern; then consternation as he decoded the message. A young English woman had been seized by one of the drug Barons up country. The message didn't elaborate but added, 'rescue imperative'.

"What the hell am I supposed to do about it?" he asked the bare wall.

Foreign Office then S.A.S. he thought. He replaced the phone, the number half dialled. Something in the urgency of the message rang an alarm bell. The kidnap of a tourist wouldn't have provoked such a message. This was definitely out of his league; there was only one course of action. This was definitely one for his boss.

It didn't take long for the duty controller to make his decision; this was definitely a job for the lads from Hereford. Although the controller had little to do with the current U. N. operation against the heroin trade he did know of the agent in question. The location was known, his course was clear; invoke the standing agreement with the Special Air Service. This allowed him to co-opt the services of the duty squad pretty well immediately, with only the barest reference to the units commanders. Thus a team of the regiments' veterans were dispatched to a distant land to free the captive.

10

At about the same time as the duty controller had plucked up the courage to call the director of his shadowy department, the youngest and least experienced sergeant of the equally shadowy H.Q. Support Squadron of 22 S.A.S. was also getting a call.

"Typical! The first weekend leave you have for six weeks and you go to sleep in the chair."

"Sorry Luv, this damn report, the boss wants it Monday morning. I just sort of dozed off."

"Well this boss wants you, not a report, and now!"

The exact circumstances of the agent's capture were, and still are something of a mystery. After the best part of a week being entertained by the Chinese militia unit in the area, the agent was handed over to a small group of Afghans who were in the pay of the local warlord. She was to be moved to his headquarters nearly one hundred miles away, clearly there could be no direct contact between the Chinese force, supposedly helping the U.N. effort against the heroin trade, so she was handed over to the warlord's trusted enforcers, until transport could be arranged.

If the Chinese had treated her badly, then these would prove to be a great deal worse. Already badly beaten and raped, even her wildest nightmares could not have prepared her for the ordeal she was to suffer in the draughty, remote shepherds hut. The Afghan mercenaries had been warned she was dangerous and a rescue attempt was likely. Indeed one may have already been thwarted, as the Chinese had ambushed what they had supposed to have been a U.N. patrol, but this patrol shot back. The Chinese panicked, fired an R.P.G.7 at the land rover and ended up with two S.A.S. prisoners.

The Afghans were not impressed by the warnings of the dangers of holding the skinny little woman, until they were shown one dead and another dying Chinese who had been careless enough to allow her to hit them.

The mercenaries had no cage to hold the woman in They kept her naked and handcuffed with manacles on her ankles, so she could walk but not kick. They chained her like a dog, round her slender neck, then fixed the chain to a bracket on the wall to prevent her attacking them should they all be asleep. Inevitably she was raped again and again, it was just too easy, they, like the Chinese became careless, the warnings forgotten.

One evening the old radio in the shack crackled into life, she only understood part of the message, but it filled her with dread. It seemed as though she was to be collected tomorrow night and would be transported to the headquarters of the local warlord for interrogation by Fat Wan in person.

She had seen some of his handy work before; his victims had been one of his own men and a young local girl. He had suspected them of stealing a small amount of his heroin for their own use. After he had extracted confessions from both with the aid of a set of heavy jump leads and a large battery, both were killed.

As if they hadn't suffered enough with the jump leads attached to their tender parts. He then devised his own barbaric methods of execution, to serve as an example to the rest of his men should they err in the future.

The boy's arms were bound behind his back he was then hung by his elbows, which of course dislocated his shoulders. His pretty young girl friend was raped by several of the men in front of the helpless youth. The young man then had to hang there and watch as his girl was partially skinned, before being bound screaming to a stake close to a small fire, which was then built up so it literally roasted her alive. He hadn't even been able to close his eyes to the horror, as his eyelids were pinned open adding to his agony.

When the girl finally stopped moaning and was clearly close to death, Fat Wan decided to hurry the end of the unfortunate youth by emasculating him, having slowly skinned his manhood first. With typical thoughtfulness, the two unfortunates were then left where they were, as a warning to others not to get any ideas about helping themselves in the future. The agent had discovered them the following morning; she finished off the dying youth herself as he was far beyond any help. With the assistance of the girl's traumatised mother, she and a helper had rekindled the fire and it became the funeral pyre for both the young lovers. The tale of their daylong ordeal had been relayed to her by a village elder; now it seemed as though she too would soon be in the loving care of the same monster she sought to destroy.

Knowing their own private plaything would soon be taken from them, served only to make the Afghan mercenaries more determined and the next few hours would be a session to remember. In their haste they got careless, the battered English woman was bent over a bench, the handcuffs removed and her wrists bound to a

12

couple of supports. For the next hour or so she endured every kind of indignity they could think of. The only things outside the hut to hear her cries were a couple of startled goats.

One of the knots on her bleeding wrists was not as good as it might have been, as the cruel mercenaries enjoyed themselves, she was working away at slackening the knot. Even when she could have got her hand free, she waited for an unguarded moment, when the chance came she took it. A single blow killed her present tormentor instantly. In one smooth movement she had grabbed the man's knife and severed the rope holding her other arm. She then threw the knife hitting the most alert one of the others squarely in the throat. Before either of the others had time to react the A.K47, carelessly left against the bench was making its familiar clatter. Almost as an afterthought she fired a couple of shots into the crotch of the still gurgling man with the knife embedded in his throat. This not only finished him off, it also made her feel better as he had been by far the most perverted of her tormentors.

Surprisingly the woman didn't hurry, taking her time she carefully selected the most suitable items of clothing from her erstwhile captors. The final touch was the cleanest of the turbans to cover her long light brown hair, even from a few yards she would pass as a local goatherd boy. The real difficulty now was how to get out of this godforsaken place without being seen. The weapons were not a problem, one of the dead men's A.Ks was a very battered looking, light weight model of the kind issued to Russian special forces. As there was more ammunition than she could sensibly carry, the only decision was how much. She finally decided on just four magazines taped in pairs, she would have liked more, but thought if the need arose she was unlikely to use even the four mags.

Her attention turned to the ancient radio, maybe she could get a message out and get some help; it had to be worth a try. There was a small U.N force somewhere in the general area; she had been trying to reach them when she had been captured. The problem was which direction and how far?

After nearly an hour of trying she got a reply of sorts, it sounded Finnish, the batteries were on the point of packing up. She took a chance and transmitted the co-ordinates she had memorised for one of the few distinctive features in this barren wilderness, adding "in five days," then the batteries finally gave up.

Having collected two goatskins containing water, which was near enough drinkable. She had a last search of the shack for anything, which would aid her escape She hated the salted goat meat, it seemed to be the staple diet in this part of the world, but it would have to do. Then she made a discovery that alarmed her. Try as she might, she couldn't think why she should have felt unease at the discovery of a 9mm high power, it was after all a common enough weapon. It was a particularly clean pistol; even the spare clip was immaculate, right down to the piece of cling film over the open end of the magazine. The realisation hit her it was an army issued weapon, a British army issue too. The most likely explanation was the previous owner had been one of the other prisoners. She wondered if others were being held at the same fire-base; the one she had been moved from a few days earlier. All she could do now was her very best to escape with her information.

She headed steadily north west for four days, moving mainly at night taking extreme care to avoid leaving any sign of being in the area, as far as she was aware no-one had seen her.

As dawn on the fifth day broke she was still four or five miles short of the distinctive pile of rocks in the middle of a valley, which was otherwise an unbroken sea of sand.

Because of her extreme fatigue she wasn't thinking straight, or paying her usual attention to detail, normally she would have stayed alert and near cover. In her exhausted state she didn't hear the approaching truck until it was almost on top of her, by then it was already too late. The men in the truck were part of the local warlords' private army.

.CHAPTER 3

Despite the chill of the early morning, both soldiers were soaking, the sweat glistening on their wiry limbs. The straps supporting the heavy Bergen packs were showing dark patches where the sweat had soaked through their old smocks and into the webbing.

Despite the sweat and the fact eight hard miles lay behind them, the two men were still breathing easily, testament to their superb fitness.

"You know what's pissing me off Taff?" asked the taller of the two sergeants.

"No, but I'm sure you're going to tell me."

"We've been out on two ops against the 'Mad Micks' and both of those ops has been either blown or scrubbed. From what I can make out the 'funnies' have fucked up both times."

"We're not the only ones' it's happened to. I heard a couple of lads from 'A' squadron in the mess last night, moaning how they'd spent a couple of weeks setting up a pair of right nasty buggers," replied Taff. "From what I heard, they were about ready when Special Branch turned up and made a right pigs ear of the raid."

"I thought they caught one guy but missed the other two," answered Paul. "I wondered what the boss was swearing about last night. Most out of character for him, he was quite fluent."

"Makes you wonder whose side some of our super sleuths are on at times. It's what they call the sickener factor Paul."

"It's that alright, just like this poxy pack. It's getting heavier with every bloody step."

"Probably something to do with all those fags you smoke."

"Could be."

They ran on in silence for the next mile or so, with practiced ease they slipped into single file as the vehicle approached along the narrow moor-land road. Paul's hand opened the zip on his battle smock as a car came to a halt twenty or so yards ahead of the sweating soldiers. The powerful .357 Smith and Weston in easy reach if needed.

The lean, hard eyed man who emerged from the front passenger seat had noticed the young sergeants cautionary move but chose not to mention it, merely making eye contact then lowering his steely gaze to the open zip.

"Morning Boss."

"Morning lads, I've been hunting high and low for you pair, dump your gear in the boot and hop in. Something's come up a bit urgent."

"And we fit the bill?"

"You do indeed, should be right up your street."

"Sounds like ten days watching ants in a sodden South Armagh hedge row to me," quipped Paul.

"Cynic!" responded the grey haired Lieutenant Colonel. "Take the long way back to camp Gary, I can brief Paul and Taff on the way."

"O.K. Boss," replied the driver. "Twenty minutes long enough?"

"Fine Gary. How can I put this?" The C.O. paused. "A problem has arisen, or rather been dumped in my lap. We can discuss the finer points in the adjutant's office when we get back."

On arrival back at camp, Taff was sent off with both Bergen packs, and to find the other pair who made up the squad.

After sorting out the obligatory coffees, the adjutant produced a slim folder.

"Right!" began the Major, "basically Whitehall have got an operative in the shit and they want us to provide a taxi service."

"With me as chauffeur?"

"It's about the size of it."

"Call me cynical if you like Sir," Paul began. "Taking into account the fact I've only been badged a couple of months or so, and I've only done two ops, both of which turned tits up, I'm bound to ask, why me?"

"Why not? I'd have thought this mission would have been exactly the sort of thing you worked so hard to join the regiment for," replied the C.O.

"With all due respect Sir, I'm as green as the bloody grass as far as ops are concerned. I'm flattered you obviously have faith in me and you know I'll do my damnedest, but I still ask, why me?"

"Very well, put in the simplest terms. You're the most senior fit member available. You're right; normally you'd be back up on several missions first, then as a squad member on a lot more before being given the responsibility of leading one. It's also undeniable, this sort of op can easily go pear shaped or, as you so eloquently put it, 'tits up'. However, short of sending men in plaster or pulling a team off another job, the choice is limited to one - you!"

"Thanks for being straight Sir, I can't explain why but it's made me feel a lot better about it."

"Good, now maybe we can tell you what's to be done," observed the adjutant. "Basically you'll fly out this afternoon on a regular supply flight to a small U.N. base which is supporting the International efforts against the warlords in the Golden Triangle. You'll have your team, Taff, Kenny and BJ equipped with a fully gunned up Panther. It will be a drive of over a hundred miles into the mountains. Lay up at a particular spot for anything up to four days. Once you've met your passenger you'll then drive back to the U.N. base and return on the next supply flight in a week's time."

"Just like that?" was Paul's response. "What's the catch? There's got to be one or it wouldn't be us providing the wheels."

"As long as no one knows you're there, there shouldn't be a catch."

"I see."

"As long as no one else does, you'll be alright."

"Thanks Boss."

"You've been on countless escape and evasion exercises, the only time we've caught you and your Welsh cohort is when we put a tracker in his kit. Even then it still took hours to finally catch the pair of you."

"The point being," added the adjutant. "Despite your lack of operational experience, you are still in many ways, the ideal choice for this mission."

"You're hard to catch, that's if you're seen in the first place. On top of it, you're one of the best shots in the regiment. You stay cool; otherwise you'd have shot John and Brummie. How you identified them turning up at night, as they did in the middle of fire fighting and dreadful weather, is one of the great mysteries of our time, as for the poacher!"

"I was only doing my job Boss."

"Exactly my point! The only things you're lacking are confidence and experience. One will come with the other. I'm not in the habit of backing 'also rans' in this job, which is why I'm backing you in this instance. Clear?"

"Clear Boss."

"Right, find the Welsh reprobate and get sorted. You leave Brize at 13.00.hrs."

"Yes Sir."

"Good luck."

17

The four young soldiers who made up the squad with the call sign 'Hotel Quebec 7' spent the next two hours huddled over maps and some amazing recon photos, plus a couple of bundles of ordinary photos taken by members of the U.N. team on the ground.

"Bleak looking place ain't it?" observed Kenny. "Somehow you'd expect jungle clad hills in that part of the world."

"I thought the same Mate. Something to do with rain shadows and erratic monsoons."

"With our luck it'll piss down the whole time we're there."

"Shouldn't be a problem for you Taff with your webbed feet."

"Bollocks."

"Alright you lot! Let's check the route, it'll only take one of those early bearings to be a couple of degrees out and we'll end up miles off course in bloody China!"

One hour later, everyone was satisfied the route was as accurate as they could make it.

"Any questions or observations?" asked Paul.

"Not really Paul. The only thing which caught my eye was this." Taff slid one of the recon photos, supplied by the R.A.F across the table. "Just there," he added pointing to a small dark smudge.

"What is it?"

"Dunno Mate, but we pass quite close to it and it don't look natural."

"Pass those magnifiers. Ta."

Paul studied the smudge for a minute or two, adjusting the magnifying binoculars. "Looks like a burnt out vehicle of some sort, recent too judging by the scorch marks. Must have been bloody fierce to show up."

"Better take a bit of extra care in the area."

"Wouldn't hurt would it. Well-spotted Taff. Right check our kit then get some grub." ·

While the others headed for the canteen, Paul rang one of his old R.E.M.E. friends who worked on the special land rovers at Brize Norton.

"Yes Mate, what can I do you for?"

"Any chance of four extra wide tyres, preferably well worn on the front and slicks on the rear, for the Panther we're picking up today?"

"Couldn't tell you off hand Mate, if we've got any, they'll be on O.K.?"

18

"Just a thought. If those extra wides are set out, will they still fit in a Herc?"

"Damned if I know! I'll check."

"Thanks Titch, see you later bye."

"Bye Paul."

Just as he replaced the phone, the Boss walked in and enquired about the call.

"Had a bit of an idea Boss. Just checking it out with Titch."

"Like what?" asked a slightly worried C.O.

"Well Boss, by the looks of those photos, over half our trip will be over sand. The thought occurred to me, if we fitted extra wide treadless tyres, at least on the rear, then we wouldn't leave obvious tracks for any nosy sod to follow."

"Interesting. What's wrong with the usual couple of sacks dragged behind the wheels?"

"Nothing Boss, as far as it goes. With the drags it's obvious the tracks have been obliterated. The fact it's been done deliberately does, by definition, mean whoever was responsible has something to hide, true?"

"Then why bother with slick tyres on the rear only? Surely you'll just get stuck."

"Should be alright Boss, use the four-wheel drive if we have to, but keep it smooth - should just glide over it. Wide, well worn ones, on the front and the spare. No tracks to speak of - nothing to raise suspicion. The smooth rears will obliterate the fact the fronts are uniroyals."

"Sneaky sod, very good. Very good indeed, you'll do."

The trip on the Herc seemed to last for ever. First stop should have been Bahrain; somehow they ended up at Salalha. Paul crawled out of his 'maggot' cursing having been dumped onto the floor by an uncharacteristically hard landing.

"What the fuck was that all about?"

"Sorry back there, caught a down draft at an awkward moment, are you lads all right?" enquired the pilot.

A quick check revealed nothing broken.

"We'll live."

"Why the diversion Sir?" asked Paul as the ground crew set about turning the transport round.

"Not quite sure, something to do with your presence I gather."

19

"Like how? Bahrain's usually pleased to see us."

"Oh, it's not the locals, I think there's some Whitehall types waiting for you. Seems as though your boss would prefer your respective paths not to cross."

"Fair enough, some of them make my blood boil and most of the rest, my skin crawls," replied Paul. "I suppose some are O.K. but there's always cock-ups when they're involved."

Because of their diversion the next stop was Colombo. True, this time the squad had to stay out of sight on the plane. For once the turn round was swift, no problems, within two hours they were on their way again across the widest part of the Bay of Bengal, straight into an unseasonable tropical storm.

"Told you it would piss down boyo."

"You are allowed to get it wrong sometimes Taff," replied Kenny.

Eventually the Herc landed on the dirt strip somewhere near the northern tip of the 'Golden Triangle'.

"Two crash landings out of three," observed B.J. as he picked himself up.

The unloading could only be described as frantic.

"What's all the panic about?" enquired Paul.

"We were shelled an hour ago, second time this week. We're a bit worried the Herc might attract some more shit. We're sending our casualties out. I think they're sending a cas-e-vac VC10 to meet the Herc at Colombo." replied the young officer who appeared to be in charge of the unloading party.

"They'll have a bloody rough ride. There's one hell of a storm out there. I thought it was going to rip the wings off!"

"That's all they need. Look, you lads nip over to the mess tent; get some grub and a cuppa. You won't be leaving 'till dark will you?"

"Thanks Sir, we'll see you before we go."

Having parked their panther beside one of the few buildings, as out of sight as possible, the four men headed for the mess tent.

"This must be a bitch of a posting, they're supposed to be U.N. monitors."

"What are they monitoring, dust storms?"

"Damned if I know Mate."

Soon after they finished their meal, they heard the Herc start up again.

"That'll please the local Boss, one less worry."

The great plane's wheels had hardly left the ground when there was a series of loud explosions.

"What the fuck?" exclaimed one of Paul's team, as they dived behind some sand bags.

This time no one was hurt. Paul spotted the camp C.O., a youthful looking Major. "Natives a bit restless Sir?"

"They're not exactly friendly are they sergeant."

"I suppose the obvious questions are who and why Sir?"

"The who, is officially local rebels, one of the warlord's private armies. The why, is because our presence makes his Heroine trade more difficult. Our camp is right on his main road in and out of the mountains away to the north, it's also beside the best well for a hundred miles, and we've made it better still."

"They're bloody well equipped rebels," replied Paul. "That stonk had to be 155s, at least six guns."

"Quite."

"Chinks?" enquired Paul.

"Almost certainly. Although as I said, officially those guns are part of one of the warlords' armies."

"You seem to have plenty of men and fire power Sir, why not take 'em out or at least chuck some bricks back?"

"Not allowed to sergeant, the Chinese are officially allies on this operation."

"Bloody rum allies."

"They can be a bit difficult at times. We'll get a visit in a few days time from the 'liaison' officer, complete with commissar. He'll suggest we move our base fifty miles or so to the west where there's no roads, water or anywhere to build an airstrip."

"Of course the drug runners avoid the area and the terrain is ruddy nearly impossible." stated Paul.

"Exactly, then when I point out the impractical nature of this suggestion, I'll get berated for about ten minutes. Why should he make the dangerous trip to see us, and try to help us if I then ignore his advice."

"How often does this happen?" asked Paul.

"Every two or three weeks, usually two days after an 'incident'. Most of us have been 'captured' several times by the Chinese, when out on patrol."

"What a bloody farce! I hope they don't try to 'capture' us. What's the usual excuse, your patrol crossed the border?"

"Except the border is at least ten miles beyond those ruddy guns and our lads are never even half way towards the guns."

"Why put up with it?"

"Orders! Don't antagonise them, just stay put."

"You should invite a General out here, let him get 'captured' see what happens then."

"You're no respecter of rank are you sergeant?" observed the Major.

"Oh, I dunno Sir, as long as it's been earned, and I reckon you've earned yours. You must have the patience of a saint, putting up with all that shit. Or you upset someone in high places."

Half an hour before the sun set the team descended on the mess tent again. Chatting to some of the British members of the UN. Force, they tried to pick up a few tips on avoiding the Chinese.

"What's their I.R. kit like?" asked Paul.

"As far as I know they haven't got any, they just spread out in a line and wait for us to blunder into them!"

"Haven't you got any either?"

"Sure, but we're not allowed to use it on patrol!"

"That's bloody mad!"

"Goes with the territory."

"Time we were off, thanks for the info, hopefully we'll see you in about a week.. Come on you shower, time we went camping."

Ten minutes were spent double-checking all their kit and supplies, nothing was left to chance.

"Everything in order?" asked Paul. "Right mount up and let's go."

The C.O. approached just as Paul was about to start up. Instead of 'good luck' he got "Hold it!"

"What's up Sir?" Paul enquired innocently.

"Where do you think you're going?" asked the Major.

"To do what we were sent to do Sir."

"Not with the I.R. gear you not, or the radio."

"Pardon."

"You heard!"

"I'm sorry Sir, the kit stays!"

"Then so do you Sergeant, right here!" the Major was quite firm. "My orders specifically prohibit the use of any hi-tec systems, now if you would hand over all your I.R. kit and radios to my Q.M. you can be on your way."

"All I can say is we're not under your orders Sir, so the directive drawn up by some senile old git a couple of thousand miles away does not apply to us."

"I say it does apply, so consider it an order sergeant."

"Take it up with your bosses, then they can take it up with mine, let them argue about it! See you in about a week." Paul fired up the engine and drove off into the night.

"That went well Paul," observed Taff.

"What a load of bollocks, I hadn't got him down as a jobs worth."

"Me neither," replied Taff "oh no! Two sets of lights behind us."

"Don't say the muppet has sent some of his lads to fetch us back so he can smack our wrists."

"Looks very much like it mate."

"I wonder if he's let them use I.R. gear to catch us," Paul asked no one in particular.

"We can soon find out, isn't there an area of flat rock ahead?"

Taff checked his route chart. "Yep! About half a mile ahead, then there's about five miles of it, unbroken as far as we could tell from the recce stuff."

"O.K. lets see how good the boy scouts are, Taff check our bearing and distance so we can get back on track."

"Of course mum."

"Alright, I asked for that."

Half a mile onto the rock Paul turned right, then after another half a mile he turned the panther right again, back to the edge of the smooth rock. He finally stopped facing the point where he had originally crossed onto the rock surface. Paul flipped the roll of tarpaulin which had lain ready across the bonnet. This would mask the Infra red signature of the panther's engine for a little while. They needn't have worried; the two pursuing U.N. land rovers stopped briefly, then turned round and went back in the general direction of their base.

"Oh dear," sighed Paul, "is it really so easy?"

"Seems that way mate."

"We'd better get a move on we've got a long way to go."

The tarpaulin was quickly re-rolled and they were off again, everyone wearing their Infra red goggles on the lookout for trouble.

"Wasn't that burnt out wreck somewhere around here Taff?" Paul asked.

23

"Yep, about a quarter of a mile further on then a couple of hundred yards off to the left."

"We'll take a quick look, might learn something useful."

"Like what?"

"Pass, we'll see. There it is, let's have a look."

Paul stopped the panther a few yards from the wreck. There was something eerily familiar about the charred, mangled wreck bathed in their infrared headlights.

"Oh fuckin' hell," muttered Paul.

"What's up Mate?" asked Taff, "stand on a mine?" noticing how Paul seemed frozen to the spot.

"That's a panther you burke," retorted Paul.

"Hey?"

"It's one of our bloody panthers. What the fuck's it doing here?"

"No one said anything about anyone else being out here, or being missing, did they?"

By now Paul was up to the wreck, which concealed another shock, the near skeletal remains of two men. The bodies had been badly burnt then ravaged by the local wild life, large and small alike.

Paul picked up a piece of charred sandy material with a bit of a badge sewn to it.

"Oh shit, they were two of our lads," he said passing the charred remnant of the beret to his friend.

A quick check revealed the cause of death. One had clearly been hit in the head by at least one heavy calibre round. The damage to the land rover indicated a direct hit with an R.P.G.7 or something similar.

"What's to do Paul? Take 'em with us or leave them here?"

"Tell you what we must do; get the V.I.N. number of the panther then when we get in contact with H.Q. and let them know what we have found."

"Good point Mate, but what about those two?"

"We'll leave 'em as they are. I don't like it either but if we move them, and then whoever did it comes back they'll know someone's about won't they?"

"You're right I don't like it, though I'll grudgingly admit, you might have a point."

"Listen up you lot, I feel the same way as you do. We'll pick 'em up on the way back if we can O.K.? I'll get the V.I.N. plate."

Taking great care to stand on pieces of wreckage, to avoid leaving any footprints. He used a tiny shaded torch, so he could see to copy the long number which would identify the destroyed vehicle.

"Right let's go, don't dwell on it, otherwise we could end up the same way."

An hour before dawn saw them at their destination, a rocky outcrop in the middle of a sea of sand which covered the entire valley floor.

The panther was backed into a gap between two large rocks, one of which overhung the gap. The tarpaulin normally used to mask their tracks was now used as a screen across the front of the panther to lessen the chances of detection, should anyone scan the area. A strategically placed cam-net completed the job. A small piece of cam net provided shelter and cover for the duty lookout forty feet above. Access to the observation point was straight up what was virtually a chimney about two feet wide. It couldn't have been better.

All they had to do was watch and wait for their mysterious passenger to turn up and give them a lift home. Keeping a look out was mind numbingly boring and required a lot of concentration, all the time the demise of the mysterious patrol niggled away.

"We ought to have done something Paul. It just ain't right leaving those lads there."

"I didn't say it was right BJ, I didn't like it anymore than you, I still don't, but what else could we do? If we get detected, we could very quickly end up the same way. We'll pick 'em up on the way back."

"You're right Mate, I wasn't having a go. I'm just bloody glad it wasn't my decision."

"Any idea who they are Paul?" asked Kenny.

"I know who collected the Panther after I'd serviced it six weeks ago. Thing is, I know neither of those two is the guy who signed it out."

"Go on, who was it?"

"John and Brummie collected it but I'm bloody well certain those remains weren't either of them."

"I suppose it's possible the other two could either be captured or pegging it out."

"Thoughts which had occurred to me Mate."

"We ought to help them Paul."

"Agreed BJ, but someone else is depending on us. When we've got this job sorted, we'll see what we can do," replied Paul. "Before we can rescue 'em we have to know who's got 'em, or if they're free, as I suspect, then we've still got to find them."

"Tracking them would be hard enough if the trail was fresh but it must have happened two weeks ago," observed Kenny.

A soft whistle from the top of the rocks interrupted the conversation.

"Paul, up here and bring your 'scope."

Paul shinned quickly up the rocks to his friend.

"Over there about 11 O'clock, directly below the 'v' in the skyline."

"Lights?"

"That's what I thought, damned if I can make out what it is."

"Got it, what the hell?"

"What is it Paul?"

"Hang on, now let's try. That's better," he fiddled with the focus of the powerful sight. "It's a convoy of light trucks, 4X4 Pickups by the looks of it. Yep. Six of them with four heavier trucks and two armoured cars."

"Coming this way?"

"Don't think so, more to the south."

"Chinks?"

"Probably, at least the heavier stuff looks like Chinese."

"Great!"

"Here, watch 'em with this. I'll send Kenny up, he's the next one on. I'll get some kip. I've got the last stag before dawn."

The next two days were spent watching the arid expanse of the valley.

"We might as well be on the moon, there's less life here than in the empty-quarter in Saudi!" commented Kenny as he came off watch.

The only living thing seen in daylight in two days was a single bird soaring over the distant hills, tentatively identified as a buzzard by Taff or a black kite by Paul.

It wasn't any different at night, no more lights, just a single rat like creature scurrying between two of the rocks.

"This place gives me the fucking creeps, nowhere can be as dead as this!" muttered Taff as he came off watch.

"I must admit, I'd expected to spend most of the time hiding from prying eyes and general nosey buggers."

"When do we have to call in Paul?"

"Tonight 21.00. our time."

"When is this character supposed to turn up?" asked Taff.

"Tonight sometime, although it could have been last night, or there again it might not be until tomorrow night."

"In other words no bugger knows, so we sit and wait in the middle of nowhere, for as long as it takes. All for someone who may or may not turn up."

"That's about the size of it mate."

"Bit like waiting for a train back home," observed Kenny.

As dusk approached, the team were settling down for the third full night in their pile of rocks, Kenny who was on watch above, called down, "Company Paul."

Paul scrambled up to the look out point "Where mate?"

"More traffic same as before see 'em?"

"Dammed if I can, hang on, yep, got 'em."

The convoy was virtually identical to the first one except there were only five pickups instead of six. An hour or so later there was another convoy, this time heading in the opposite direction. As far as the men watching could tell this was the first group of trucks returning. Paul had taken pictures of both convoys through his powerful sight, but he didn't hold out much hope of any of the photographs showing anything interesting.

"I wonder what it's in aid of?" Paul asked to no one in particular.

"Looks like chink military escorting half a dozen civvy pickups, weird."

"Reckon it's got anything to do with our passenger?"

"Maybe Taff, time will tell."

"Personally I'll be glad to get out of this godforsaken place, gives me the bloody creeps, it's so dead."

"You and me both mate. The sooner our body turns up the better. We should know a bit more after our Sat link tonight, the boss won't leave us stuck out here longer than need be."

At the appointed time Paul opened up the Sat link to their H.Q. He was pleased to discover it was the boss on the other end, then to his consternation the link broke up in a burst of static. No matter how he tried he could not re-establish the connection.

"I like the way the boss says if no one turns up tonight give it one more night then move out, anyone would think we're on a weekend break at Bognor!"

"What did he say about the lads we found?"

"He didn't, the damn link broke down before I got the chance to tell him."

"Why?"

"What do you mean why?"

"Why did the link break?" asked B.J.

"I don't bloody know do I, our set seems alright, the satellite is supposed to be up for another hour or more."

"That's my point Paul! I suppose there's got to be a first time for everything, but those things don't just pack up."

"Well this one did, both ways!"

"Someone's found a way of jamming our signals Paul, I heard the static, it's what they call white noise," said B.J. who was the little squads' signals expert.

"You mean some bastard doesn't want us to talk to our base. What could be so bloody vital about this operation someone is prepared to go to such lengths to jam our radios? That's more than a bit bloody worrying," replied Paul.

"I'll tell you what, you obviously feel the same as I do. It's too late tonight to get anywhere safer, so as soon as it's dark tomorrow what do you say to the idea of haulin' ass out of here?"

"I'd say it was a bloody good idea boyo."

It was just after nine the following morning when Kenny, who was on watch, called Paul to the O.P.

"What's up Mate?" asked Paul as he crawled under the cam-net.

"I can see someone Paul, right up the valley as far as you can see."

Paul spent a couple of minutes fiddling with the focus on his powerful telescopic sight. "Blast this shimmer. You're right, there is something or someone there. Well spotted, you've got bloody sharp eyes, I'll keep the 'scope on it, you resume general watch!"

After a good half hour, Paul's patience paid off. He got a clear view, fleeting as it was; the figure could only have been a young goatherd from one of the nomadic groups who actually lived in this arid wilderness.

"After all it's just a local rag-head, a kid. Still, bloody well spotted Kenny. I'm glad the shimmer cleared, I was just thinking it might have been our passenger and we ought to go and pick him up."

"We'd have looked right idiots breaking cover to pick up the local goatherd," replied Kenny. "I must admit I was thinking the same thing, pick him up and get the hell out."

"I can imagine the Boss's comments, if we had broken cover for a local kid, I reckon I'd have been back to Arborfield and the joys of holding platoon and Spud bloody Taylor!"

He rolled on his back and stretched his aching limbs, a slight breeze wafted through the O.P. Paul relaxed for a couple of minutes. He must have been on the point of dozing off.

He was awake in the blink of an eye. "What the hell was that? Sounded like A.Ks, a long way off though."

He checked the scope, still wedged in the rocks. "Oh shit! A truckload of China's finest have just grabbed our goatherd. The kid's still alive, and kicking, looks like the plucky little sod got a couple of Chinks. Oh Sod this shimmering haze!" Within ten minutes the truck had vanished back into the hills.

"That clinches it, we pull out as soon as it's dark tonight."

The trip back towards the U.N. camp went without a hitch. The soldiers completed the gory task of collecting the remains of their comrades, carefully sealing the body bags.

"Fuck that for a job," was the only comment from B.J.

Halfway across the area of flat rock where they had lost their pursuers of the outward trip, Paul stopped and switched off the engine.

"What's up?"

"Listen, can't you hear it?" asked Paul.

"Shit! That's gunfire from the camp."

"That's what I thought, get those M.Gs ready, let's take a look."

There was the distinctive flat crack of odd rounds passing close by.

"Fuck this Paul, alright I know, at least it proves some of our lot are still fighting. Go on take us in, we're ready."

With the engine on tick over the big land rover was surprisingly quiet. Using their sophisticated I.R. gear, it was easy to pickup the targets. Nearly a hundred, apparently Chinese troops, were attacking the small U.N. post. The angle of the Panther's stealthy approach meant there was little danger to the defenders from overshoots.

Chance had given the S.A.S. patrol the perfect position for a flank attack; slightly behind the almost straight line of attacking troops. This meant the militiamen presented virtually one long target for the mounted machine guns on the panther. When Paul judged he was as close as he was going to get undetected, he stopped and signalled Taff to take the drivers seat. Taking all four of the squads' 66mm. rockets he gave the order, "Open fire!" as he headed for armoured cars supporting the attackers.

Three weapons, a .5 B.A.R., a 7.62mm G.P.M.G. and an M16 on 'auto', all opened up on the attackers. Using the 66mm rockets, Paul quickly despatched all four light armoured cars, supporting the attack. They were ancient vehicles, poorly made and maintained, three of them simply fell apart under the impact of the small missiles; the other blew up! In less than two minutes of the dramatic intervention, the attack was over. A single 'jeep' type vehicle made a run for it.

"Light 'em up Kenny and you B.J."

The two machine guns poured several seconds worth of ammunition into the fleeing 4X4, which duly burst into flames before blowing up, its occupants already dead.

All that was left of the attacking force were about twenty injured men and a group of four who were doing their best to creep away into the darkness, most of the rest of the force were dead, or had fled in panic.

The S.A.S. team circled round to get well ahead of the four fleeing Chinese, after switching off the engine they simply sat and waited for the panic stricken survivors of the attacking force to bump into them.

To Paul's utter astonishment one of them spoke fairly good English, to the extent he asked for a lift back to the U.N. camp he had just helped attack!

"No chance! You'll bloody well walk!"

Paul flicked a switch on the dashboard and the conventional headlights blazed into life.

"Now you can see where you're going, get moving!" He commanded the now disarmed Chinese soldiers.

The U.N. casualties were surprisingly light considering the magnitude of the attack. Pretty well all of their equipment was destroyed or badly damaged. All three of their 120mm field guns were wrecked along with most of the U.N. vehicles and over half of the garrison's supplies!

Even so there were eleven dead U.N. troops, eight of them from the small Finnish contingent who were unfortunate enough to have been on duty at the time of the attack. Over half of the remaining members of the contingent were wounded to a greater or lesser extent.

Hardly had the S.A.S team re-entered the battered camp to hand over their prisoners than the C.O appeared.

"This is all your fault sergeant, I ordered you not to leave camp. You disobeyed an order. You, and your band of cut-throats are under arrest. Disobeying a lawful command."

"Keep it up and I'll be wishing we'd have just sat out there in the dark and allowed those chinks to destroy the rest of your camp."

"Oh, so your little unit arrived in the nick of time to drive off the attacking hordes and save the desperate defenders; four of you, against over a hundred of them. I like your tactics, wait until the enemy is beaten off and withdrawing then pick up a handful of stragglers, then claim you saved the day, typical bloody S.A.S glory hunters!"

"Easy to see how you ended up here, though how you got your commission in the first place defeats me. I thought officers had to have at least one active brain cell!"

"How dare you!"

"Oh we dare, that's the fuckin' difference Pal. It's easy to see who's right, simply check the calibre of the bullets which killed most of the shower of shit attacking you. You'll find most of them were hit by point 5s out of our B.A.R. or 7.62s rather than your 5.6s and 9mil stuff," snapped Paul. "And while we're at it, as far as I'm concerned you can take all the credit, I just want to get home and find out what the hell is going on."

"We all want to get home sergeant, as long as you are here you and your men will obey my orders is that clear?"

The conversation was cut short by the shriek of an incoming salvo and a series of large explosions around the camp and airstrip.

"Fuck this! Any of those one twentys still whole?"

"They're all wrecked Paul," replied Taff.

"Have your lot got any 66s?" Paul asked the badly rattled Major.

"Err? I don't think we have, if there were any they were destroyed when the ammunition tent was hit."

31

"Oh for fucks sake! Don't they teach you anything at Sandhurst? What do they do there? Give everyone a full lobotomy."

"There's no need for sarcasm sergeant."

"This solve your problem Paul?" Kenny held out an R.P.G.7 he'd taken from a dead Chinese. "We've got a dozen so far."

"Chuck 'em in the Panther Mate. Let's go and shut the artillery up before they do some real damage."

As if to spur the tired troopers on, another salvo shook the camp, shredding yet more tents.

The 21C of the U.N. force appeared, "Have you lads got a radio that works?"

"Of course, B.J, get on the horn and get these poor sods some help. They need a cas-e-vac and loads of supplies, every thing from bog rolls to bullets."

"Will do Paul."

"Look sharp, we've got to get going, and shut those bloody cannons up before they get the range and blow this place off the map."

"Shall I leave our radio with the captain here Paul?"

"Sure B.J, we've still got the one mounted in the panther, right lets go!"

The panther roared off into the night, it's crew intent on silencing the artillery which was shelling the U.N. base.

The attack on the guns started well enough, the S.A.S. team had closed to within a hundred yards of the guns without being noticed by the sweating crews.

The plan of attack was simple, there were six guns; to initiate the attack each of the team would fire an R.P.G. at the guns. Taff and Paul would then each fire another, B.J. and Kenny on firing their R.P.Gs. would then open up with the two mounted machine guns. As soon as all the guns were destroyed Paul would continue firing rocket grenades into any worthwhile targets in the camp. Taff would use his rifle to pick off any of the opposition who had been missed by the machine guns and looked like making pests of themselves.

That was the plan, and it went just like clockwork to begin with; the first six missiles destroyed all six of the guns, according to the script. The initial bursts from the mounted machine guns silenced any developing opposition, just as it was supposed to. That was when the plot ran out, Paul launched his fourth missile at a large shape covered with cam netting, it turned out to be the fuel dump! Apart from scorching the attackers, it also blew them off their feet. Most of the camp was showered with blazing fuel; tents and huts alike quickly caught fire, as did the ammunition dump, which began to explode in truly spectacular style.

"Move!" shouted Paul, "Let's get the fuck out of here!"

As they began to pull out, one of the outlying guard posts saw the attackers and opened fire on the land rover. Several bullets struck the big 4X4 mercifully doing little more than spoil the paint job. Before any of them could fire at the sentry a rogue 155mm shell from the bonfire saved them the trouble.

"Can we get back to the U.N. lads, I'm getting peckish," quipped B.J. "All this lot have got is burnt, boiled rice."

"What's he rabbiting about?" asked Paul, "He didn't get hit on the head did he?"

"You know how B.J. likes his grub Paul, he was just about to grab a sandwich when this lot opened up."

"He is a growing lad after all."

"Bollocks, you lot are taking the piss just because I'm hungry."

As soon as they were safely away from the explosions in the wrecked fire base Paul slowed down a bit, and headed back towards the U.N. camp a good deal slower than he had left it.

About half an hour after dawn a sentry on the Eastern perimeter of the battered U.N. post reported a single vehicle approaching at high speed. It turned out to be a Panther, there were several bullet holes in it, but it and its occupants seemed intact.

"What have you done?" asked the shocked major. "You've just signed our death warrant."

"I doubt it somehow."

"Those guns will decimate this camp now."

"They'll need some bloody brilliant fitters then," replied Paul. "If you think this place is a mess, you should see their fire base. No guns, no ammo, plenty of scrap though! I think you'll find they'll leave you alone in future."

"You enjoy killing, you gloat over the demise of your perceived enemies. You disgust me." The Major spun on his heel and headed for the doubtful shelter of his shredded tent. He suddenly stopped and turned to face the S.A.S. men again. "There's something else. What's the meaning of dumping two stinking skeletons in my camp, trophies for you to prove your killing powers?"

"Far from it old son, it's all that's left of two of the bravest men I've ever met, they're a couple of our lot from "B" squadron. The rest of the team seem to be missing."

"That's why you're here, to find your friends."

"No, we were sent to meet an agent, but our body didn't show. We even waited an extra 48 hours, just in case. We stumbled on the body bags, about ten miles out. I'm surprised you didn't hear the fight, as there appears to have been one. If you'd have been patrolling the area, you couldn't have failed to find the poor sods."

"We didn't know they were in the area."

"Neither did we. Hey Staff!" Paul shouted to a tall man with three stripes and a crown.

"Yes Sergeant, what do you want?"

"Does that dozer still work?"

"As far as I know, why?"

"Why not use it to cut a trench over there and stick all the Chink bodies in it. Why knacker your fit lads digging holes?"

"Why not, then we could use it to push up some banks, give us a bit of protection?"

"I'll leave it to you Staff. We'd better make sure the airstrip is useable by the time the cas-e-vac's due."

"I'll see to it sarge, his nibs won't like it. It might provoke the Chinese."

"Then it will have to provoke them," replied Paul. "Stop me if I get something wrong. This unit was sent here as part of the U.N. operation against the heroin trade, right?"

"Right."

"The camp site was selected because it effectively blocked the easy route from the mountains, away to the north, into the 'Golden Triangle', and you're right beside the only reliable supply of fresh, clean water for heaven knows how many miles."

"Yes, I suppose this is a vital spot."

"A few patrols, if they went out about fifteen to twenty miles, could completely close this valley to the traffickers?"

"Most definitely."

"Then why the merry hell hasn't it been happening?"

"The Major didn't want to antagonise the Chinese."

"As long as they stayed on their patch, fair enough but they're at least forty miles into Burma. I don't suppose it occurred to your illustrious C.O. there just might have been a reason for their

34

increasingly violent attempts to get him to pull out from this choke point?"

"I know he'd figured out they wanted us to move, I doubt he'd even bothered to wonder why."

"What do you think Staff?"

"Bloody obvious, they're in with the warlords, or at least the local one."

"That's what I reckoned as well, a bent local commander anyway. Tonight's shenanigans should have pissed on his matches, he didn't bargain on anyone having a go at him. I still can't understand your C.O. not at least, staging a show of force. I'm sure it would have deterred the Chinese. The least sign of U.N. action against them and they'd have pulled out so damn fast, there'd have been friction burns on their boss's arse."

"I'm sure you're right Paul, let's get this sorted. I'll see to it 'dozer; you find sergeant Makepiece and see what's salvageable."

"O.K. Staff, we'll see if we can get some power on again and sort out some shelter, especially for the wounded."

By lunchtime a lot of progress had been made. The airstrip was operational again, although it would be, at least, another six hours before the cas-e-vac arrived. BJ. had received one garbled message he couldn't get a repeat on, something about, 'medics on the way.'

The generator was itself undamaged; the engine which drove it however was smashed to bits. The solution was in the shape of a five-litre diesel out of one of the Finnish trucks, the engine was fine, just everything else was smashed. At two thirty in the afternoon, the 'jenny' purred into life once more, to everyone's great relief.

Ten minutes later an American Star lifter appeared. Eight pallets tumbled from its cavernous hold, to float sedately down on huge parachutes. The great plane turned and flew back along the runway at around 2,000ft. To the battered troops on the ground the sight of thirty parachutes descending gracefully was a great tonic. No sooner had the first paratroops landed and the word was out. Get those pallets off the runway, another transport was on its way and it would need to land.

It turned out this first supply drop was made up of medics, two field surgeons and very basic equipment along with a couple of pallets of field rations. These were a medical team from the 101st airborne division, they, along with half the division had been en route to Saudi Arabia, on a rapid deployment exercise. They had be due to land at Dieago Garcia, a remote British base in the expanse of the Indian Ocean, before flying on to Saudi.

The desperate plea for help had been picked up by both the British in Singapore, and the Americans at several locations. A quick call to the Pentagon quickly resulted in a signal to the great plane ordering a new mission. The giant transport peeled out of the formation, topped up its fuel from an accompanying tanker, it then headed off on its mercy mission.

The first arrivals had just enough time to get clear of the strip, when the drone of powerful turbo fan engines reached their ears. A gigantic Antonov appeared, gleaming white. It slowly circled once, and then landed in a welter of dust and noise on the airstrip, only just big enough for a Herc.

The amount of kit it contained was amazing. The bulky part of a field hospital, including an x-ray set. There was also a field kitchen which included a new mess tent, sufficient tents for the entire garrison. Four pallets of ammunition, three of them 120mm shells and wonder of wonders, 3 brand new light weight 120mm field guns, their crews as well. Best of all was the rough terrain forklift to speed the operation. This was first off, followed by an eight-wheel bowser full of diesel.

"How the hell did they cram it all in there, never mind get it to fly?" exclaimed a trooper.

The Russian co-pilot, a woman, spoke good English. If they could put most of the wounded on board, they would be flown to Colombo to meet the R.A.F. VC10, flying hospital.

It was pointed out the VC10 could only safely carry 30 stretchers.

"Very well, give us thirty of the most serious cases as quickly as possible."

The senior surgeon quickly assessed which of the worst cases could be moved reasonably safely and returned to his makeshift operating theatre.

The arrival of this leviathan was, to put it mildly fortuitous, as the 'cold war' was only just beginning to show signs of a thaw. The Russian transport had been to Singapore with a huge generator for the new hospital, it was almost ready to leave for home when the call for help was received. A quick thinking quartermaster with the garrison, aware of the plane and the call for help, suggested the solution. The Russians eager for 'brownie points' with the U.N and any foreign currency, especially dollars, quickly agreed to help.

Everything the U.N required, was available from the resident garrison and was quickly loaded onto the plane, along with a few 'extras'.

One of the men on guard duty reported two men approaching on foot although still about five miles out. So flat and barren was the valley floor, they were clearly visible through binoculars or a good telescopic sight.

"Taff. With me in the Panther, let's go!" Paul pulled up about a mile short of the two figures and put his powerful sniper scope to his eye. Without comment he passed it to Taff.

"Fucking hell. Is it who I think it is?"

"Well it ain't Jilly Johnson and Linda Lusardi that's for sure!" replied Paul. "Let's go get 'em, keep your eyes open Taff, they could have company."

"I doubt it with that pair, still better safe than sorry."

Paul pulled up beside the two battered soldiers, having driven past them before turning back towards the camp.

"Wanna lift?"

"I thought you'd never ask."

"What the bloody hell are you pair doing out here?" asked Paul.

"You mean apart from getting' stuffed by a load of Chinks?" replied one of the battered men in a thick Midlands accent. "I could ask you the same question. Are things so desperate they're sending out sprogs on missions now?"

"We were sent out to pick up an agent, but he never showed. We're due out on the next flight."

"So were we, a Whitehall wonder operation. All we got was ambushed big time. Cy and Terry were with us but I don't know what happened to them. The explosion knocked both of us out, we've been entertained by the Chinks ever since.

Last night most of the garrison moved out, a couple of hours later there was a lot of shouting and running around, then the 155s opened up big time.

Normally they'd fire two or three rounds then shut up, not this time. About five or half past this morning, the Chinks are happily still slinging their bricks, presumably at this place when all hell lets loose, machine guns, including one which sounded like a B.A.R. There are rockets flying everywhere, explosions all over the place then their ammo dump went up. We'd hit the deck in our cage, when we looked

37

up our guard's been chopped up by flying shit. The only sounds were from the fires and from a Chink trying to hold his guts in with the stumps of his arms, so we legged it."

"I presume you were responsible for all the noise?" commented the other man.

"Ably assisted by Kenny and B.J., if we'd have known you were there, we'd have given you a lift!" replied Paul to the taller of the two men. "Oh, and we found Cy and Terry, what was left of them. They're back at the U.N. camp. We couldn't leave them like that."

"Kinda guessed they'd copped it. Cy was a good skipper, he'll be missed, they both will."

"That's the worst part of this job. Being a small family, any loss really hurts."

"Ain't that the truth."

Paul pulled up near the new mess tent; he spotted Kenny and called him over. "Sort this pair of skivers out and look after them. I'll let H.Q. know, then get us all out of here."

Two hours later the team, along with their faithful panther were in a Herc. Also on the plane were the two survivors of the ill-fated rescue mission and the bodies of not only two dead S.A.S men, but also the dead U.N soldiers on the first leg of their journey home.

CHAPTER 4

"Well my lad," the steely eyed C.O. began, "you've certainly made a name for yourself. Sit down, the Major will make the coffees. We must have a serious chat. Frankly I'm at a total loss as to where to start. You've been on one observation job and this is your second operation, all three have gone totally pear shaped. As far as I can tell none of these cock-ups have anything whatsoever to do with the fact you lack operational experience. The first two we've already discussed at some length, in my opinion there is nothing further to be gained by chewing it over again. In the end analysis no one could have handled either of those situations better.

This latest escapade however, definitely warrants a full and detailed study. You're sent on what appears to be a straight-forward taxi job. You fail to collect your passenger, in all fairness we already know your fare didn't make it to the pickup point, so that part is not down to you in any way at all. Whitehall sent us an order for your recall, I was about to call you when we received a message saying you had started world war three!"

"That's a bit unfair Boss," replied Paul, sounding hurt.

"Now we come to the rest of the debacle, I've already read the reports on disobeyed orders, which with the benefit of hindsight I will choose to overlook. I'm not sure how to react to your decision to leave the remains of two members of the regiment where they had fallen. My first reaction was one of total disgust, however, I'm beginning to get an idea of the way you think, so I will reserve judgement until I've heard your explanation."

"I must admit my initial instinct was to collect the remains there and then. Then I weighed up the options and the possible consequences.

We could have buried them in the body bags there and picked them up on the way back, but if whoever was responsible returned they would know someone else was around the wilderness. True we could have taken them straight back to the U.N. camp, again it would have alerted those responsible to the presence of friendly forces and brought about another confrontation with the Major.

The other alternative was to take them with us, which wasn't really an option. So you see Sir there really wasn't any alternative, as unpleasant as it was we had to leave the poor sods there. The best

39

we could do was collect them on the way back, I didn't like it, I'm not proud of it, but it was my call and I stand by it.

If anyone has any advice on the subject, I'll happily listen to and heed advice. I sincerely hope I never have to make such a choice again."

"I can only agree with you Paul, I'm sure it must have been a terrible choice to make. On reflection you took a very difficult decision, and I have to say thinking about it, you got it right."

In the next couple of hours the little group gathered in the CO's office, went over every detail of the operation.

"One thing I really want to hear about is all the noise with the Chinese, I can not understand why you got so close. That was against all your training. Why get in close to such a powerful force when you've got a longer reach?"

"They did have four armoured cars with soddin' great cannons Boss."

"Why didn't you take them out with the B.A.R., you know as well as I do it would have riddled them easily."

"I know that Sir, but we needed its fire power to even up the odds against their infantry. We had some sixty-sixes, it was the obvious way. We needed to get relatively close to use them to full effect. Despite their numerical superiority we had all the advantages, superior weapons, infrared gear, mobility and above all surprise. For what its worth, in this instance I believe surprise was greatly enhanced by us getting in close. A panther on tick-over, heading into a nice breeze, with all those A.Ks banging away, you could pretty well run over them before they knew you were there."

"We'll go over it in more detail later," said the Major. "If I was puzzled by your methods you employed to deal with the attack on the U.N. camp I'm totally baffled by your subsequent blitz on the Chinese support base, explain please."

"Well Sir, the fact it was a Chink camp doesn't really come into it."

"Oh?" exclaimed the C.O., "Then what did?"

"We attacked the guns, which were chucking 155mm bricks at us Sir. I really can't see we had much choice. It was a case of sit and take it; leg it; or persuade them to stop."

"You certainly did that, I realise now you were left with little option but counter attack. Have you any idea of the Chinese casualty figures?"

"No Sir, I don't really see the relevance, I know we took four prisoners and there were in the region of thirty or so wounded, which were treated by the medics who flew in. As to their fatalities I really don't know, but it must have been a lot."

"More than a lot," the Major interrupted, "The Lot!"

"Most of the gun crews must have died when their ammo dump went up, it bloody well nearly got us as well. They should have known better than to have it all in one heap right next to their fuel."

"I'm horrified by your lack of concern. A major international incident seems unavoidable as a result of your actions."

"I can't see why, Sir."

"What!" exclaimed the C.O.

"Well, it was either a deliberate attempt by their authorities to totally knacker the U.N. operation, an operation they signed up to and offered to assist with. Or, and I think this is the version of events we should stick to, largely because it's true, is to admit they were hit by U.N. troops while actively attacking the U.N. base. And the evidence suggests this was a renegade unit whose commander was in league with the warlords."

"I fail to see how it will help."

"You could add he had brought dishonour to the People's Republic by accepting bribes from the drug barons Sir."

"You know what, he just might have a point, which could well be the way out," replied the C.O. "It is accurate and gives them a way out and saves face, a vital point when dealing with Orientals."

"So how does the release of the terrible two fit into this rather shattering chain of events, we haven't been able to talk to them yet, they're still in hospital?" asked the Major.

"We didn't know they were there, if we had we would have given them a lift. It's true we knew they must have been in the area and we intended to radio you from the U.N. base about them. Our plan was to leave Cy and Terry with the U.N. lads, stock up on supplies and then see if we could find them. Our plans got overtaken by events."

"Well unless there's anything you want to raise, we'll leave it for now, I'll see you tomorrow, here at 09 00hrs."

"O.K. Boss, there are a couple of things which are bugging me."

"Very well, get them off your chest," replied the Colonel.

41

"Thanks Boss, the first point is the mysterious failure of our Sat link, any idea who was jamming it? Our boffins tell me it's virtually impossible to jam without inside knowledge."

"We're looking into it Paul. What's the other thing?"

"How come two of our teams ended up in the same area knowing nothing of the others presence? O.K. I know it is none of my business what they were doing, but we ought to have been alerted to the fact, or at least the possibility another team might be in the area. Such omissions can cause accidents."

"We couldn't tell you Paul because we didn't know ourselves where they'd been sent. Whitehall had borrowed them. As you may be aware these things happen from time to time, and our funny friends don't always let us know the ins and outs of a particular job."

"It could make things difficult, sorry Boss I didn't think of that."

"I can tell you now they were sent to rescue an agent, captured by the warlord in the area."

"Then we're sent to the same area to evacuate an agent, on behalf of Whitehall. Do those spooks know what they're doing, you must admit its a bit odd Boss."

"Working on the assumption the target was the same for both operations, it does rather suggest the agent may well have escaped in the intervening period."

"That sounds reasonable Boss, but doesn't the fact no one showed up at the R.V. also suggest the agent may well have been recaptured? Should this have been the case, it suggests Whitehall knows a hell of a lot more than they're letting on. They must have someone else on the inside to have known our passenger didn't make it to the pick up point."

"The truth is we can sit and theorise all we like it won't help the poor sod. Until, or if, we ever get any concrete information there's bugger all we can do," observed the 2IC.

"We'll have to have a more detailed chat about your two fire fights with the Chinese, your tactics warrant a closer look. There could well be some valuable lessons to be learned."

"Well, I've certainly learned a hell of a lot Boss, I'll admit I'd be a lot happier if we'd come home with the agent. It would be nice if something went according to plan just for once."

"Quite, well don't dwell on it. It has to be said you did bloody well. Maybe there's a lesson in this for us all, I suppose it's just possible we could well pay a little more attention to what you new boys have to say. There has been a tendency recently to start believing in our own invincibility, getting stale in this job is dangerous. That will be all for now, thank you sergeant."

"Thank you Sir." Paul left to rejoin his squad to complete the task of sorting out their kit.

The following morning they began the tedious task of the detailed debriefing session, which followed every operation. Every minute detail would be scrutinised, from the planning right through to the return journey. Every decision taken by the commander, in this case, Paul, would be questioned, it could be a painful process even for a senior commander with plenty of experience. For someone as junior as Paul it was, he later admitted, 'more frightening than taking on a company of Chinese boarder guards.'

Half way through the second session, to Paul's consternation, the Boss himself walked in accompanied by two grey haired men in civilian clothes.

"I'm sorry to interrupt your session, but I'm afraid this matter must take precedence. It would be easiest if Paul came with us, we can use my office, these gentlemen are from the M.O.D. they would like to interview you, to clarify a couple of points."

"Don't look so worried sergeant, we don't bite," said the elder of the two strangers. "We just need to clarify a few points, I say again it is nothing to worry about."

"So why am I worried Boss?"

"I can see why you have confidence in him Peter," was the unexpected response from the senior man.

"Of course, you won't have met our top brass yet, these officers are the director of Special Forces and his deputy. They are very much on our side, not as you obviously thought a pair of our civil service colleagues."

Paul felt as though he ought to salute, but as they were in civilian dress and he was bare headed he thought better of it.

The interview was nowhere near as bad as he feared; the senior officers were very interested in the tactics Paul's squad had used against the renegade Chinese. They raised the same concerns as the C.O. had expressed on the squad's return, and received the same answers.

"You seem very sure you got it right sergeant!" said the senior officer. "Is it possible there might have been a better way?"

43

"There is always a better way Sir, I did the best I could under the circumstances. We had to take account of the fact they were attacking the U.N. base, and it seemed likely these were the same people responsible for the demise of the earlier patrol sent to the area from here."

"So there was an element of revenge in your attacks on the Chinese force."

"I can't discount that Sir, but I wasn't conscious of it. To have adopted the softly, softly approach would have invited disaster, we had to go in hard. It was regrettably, the only way I could see which held out any realistic chance of success."

"So, how many did you personally account for sergeant?" asked the deputy director.

"I don't know Sir, I don't know what happened to the crews of the armoured cars, but most of them ought to have got out. As to their casualties at the artillery site, a lot of them must have been down to me. The explosion triggered by the last rocket grenade was not exactly predictable."

"How many did you shoot?"

"None Sir, I didn't fire a shot from my rifle the entire mission."

"Which brings me nicely to the other reason we needed to see you Sergeant," said the deputy director removing a thin folder from his briefcase. "As you no doubt know, a record is kept of all weapons used by the regiment, this includes a photograph of a fired round showing the markings left by the rifling."

"Your personal weapon is a bit of a one off I believe?" asked the director.

"It is a bit different Sir."

"In what respect?"

"It's basically an armourlite with a grenade launcher and a longer, heavier barrel. This gives it a couple of hundred extra yards effective range, as well as improving sustained fire performance."

"Which raises another question, why, if what you say is true, didn't you use your rifle as a support weapon against the Chinese?"

"Simple really Sir; Taff's rifle has a different sight, it lacks the definition of the image intensifier on mine but is pretty well immune to bloom-out. The flash from the exploding 66mm rockets and grenades would have blinded mine for vital seconds. The two systems are complimentary, if one won't work the other will."

"So the rounds from your rifle would be distinctive?"

44

"No doubt, may I ask what all this is leading up to Sir?"

"Well, this is the file photograph of a round from your rifle," the officer then produced two more pictures. "This is a photograph of a bullet removed from a body found near the boarder by the Gardi early last week."

"Assuming it is from my rifle, and it looks as though it is, I did say I definitely hit one in the ruck, although none of us saw what happened to him after he fell."

"Yes, but it was a terrorist suspect and you claimed to have fired two rounds, and I quote; both hit the central chest area."

"Sounds right Sir, he had just let fly at our position with an A.K.47 after being challenged."

"The thing is sergeant, this body was found nearly a mile away from your alleged position. Also the bullet was lodged in the victim's neck and thought to have severed his jugular, he had then bled to death."

"I don't suppose this body was near a pile of rocks, roughly a thousand yards south east of our hide?"

"You're thinking it might have been the machine gunner you mentioned in your report?"

"It does fit," replied Paul's boss.

"Except for the fact, he wasn't a known suspect."

"John was watching through his 'scope, Boss and confirmed a hit, although I didn't really believe him. The best I could have hoped for from such a range was to scare them off, to stop them shooting at the cas-e-vac chopper."

"So you could have hit a target at that range?"

"Oh yes, I'm confident all ten rounds I fired at the machine gun would have been within a couple of yards."

"We can reasonably account for that one," said the Director.

"Very well Sir," replied the deputy. "It now leaves this round, which also appears to have come from your distinctive rifle."

"Looks like it Sir, where did it turn up? Clearly somewhere unexpected."

"The R.U.C. found it embedded in a bag of heroin seized in a raid in North Belfast."

"How the bloody hell did it end up there?" queried Paul.

"We were rather hoping you could tell us sergeant."

"Apart from the ranges here, I've fired twelve rounds from the rifle. Two at the scout, and ten at the M.G., a group of four and another of six, that's it."

"Well it didn't get there on its own."

"The only possible way I can think of, is if the V.I.P. we were waiting for was carrying heroin rather than cash. He and his escorts were very close to the machine gun when I fired the second group of shots."

"So now you're saying you hit him as well at that range!"

"I'm saying it's the only thing I can think of that fits Sir. The round looks undamaged, which means it was pretty well spent when it hit something soft, like his bag with the heroin inside."

"Sounds reasonable, except for the range!"

"I have seen him hit targets consistently on the ranges Sir, with that rifle and sight" added the C.O.

"Very well, I'm satisfied by your explanation sergeant," said the Director. "It just remains for me to say well done, very well done, and welcome to the regiment!"

CHAPTER 5

Following the squad's eventful deployment to the golden triangle, Paul's boss decided to temporally suspend the team with the call sign Hotel Quebec 7 from operations. He emphasised this was in no way a reprimand, it merely reflected the fact they had been thrown in the deep end before they had chance to complete the regimental basic training program. The C.O. noticed the slightly disappointed looks on the faces of the four newest members of his command. Although one of the toughest commanders in the entire armed forces, he was also one of the fairest.

"I know how you must feel, you've been on a couple of operations which should have been straight forward and proved to be anything but! In all honesty no one in the regiment could have handled those situations better. As well as you all performed, there are still gaps in your combat skills, you have the makings of a first class team."

"Thanks for explaining it Boss, it's a bit easier to live with, makes sense when you put it that way."

"There is one other thing," the colonel continued, "Kenny is being transferred to 'B' squadron, to replace a trooper who is leaving us. A new lad who has just been badged from the last selection course will be joining you. He will, I'm certain strengthen your squad. He is multi lingual and a trained field medic, two of the weakest areas in your current structure. I know you won't be happy about the change, but better now than later."

"Fair enough, Boss."

"I know you depended on Kenny's combat experience from the commandos, but collectively you've proved you all have the vital instincts in that department. Right get yourselves off to the training cadre. Kenny, report to 'B' squadron."

"Thanks boss," the four soldiers said in perfect unison.

"Get out of here," replied the Boss, allowing himself a little grin.

As is the way of these things, a couple of days later things reached an unexpected climax in the ongoing operations in the Oman, urgent reinforcements were rushed to the theatre, hopefully to end this dirty little Civil war once and for all. Among those sent were most of the training cadre members.

"So much for our training schedule Taff," observed Paul.

"Where does that leave us?" asked B.J.

"Best guess, guard duty until someone comes home from wherever they're skiving," replied Paul.

"Everybody called me a lucky bastard when I was told I'd be joining your gang," moaned Mickey.

"You are lucky old son, if you'd gone to 'B' squadron you'd have your boots full of sand, ears full of flies and an arse full of A.K.47 rounds by now."

"That or knees scraped to the bone scrambling over those bloody rocks," added Taff.

"Right, so far I've had two days of having the shit kicked out of me by the unarmed combat training team, now you say we're duty section in the guard room!"

"That's only a maybe, I've got to see the skipper in half an hour. We'll know what's next then Mickey."

It turned out, the squad was to be spared the ball ache of an extended guard duty.

The C.O. welcomed Paul into his office, "So much for catching up with your training. Sit down."

"Thank you boss, what's next, guard duty?"

"Don't worry, it's not quite so bad. We've got to test and evaluate a new sub machine gun. It's officially designated as a machine pistol, it's envisaged as the ultimate close quarters, hostage rescue weapon. We've got four of them, collect them from the Q.M. in the armoury, see how you get on with this new wonder weapon."

The next week proved to be interesting, if a little frustrating. By lunchtime of the first day, it was already obvious this was anything but a wonder weapon. It was indeed light, strong and pinpoint accurate, as long as it fired!

The sight was a remarkable instrument; it could illuminate a button in a darkened room. It was so powerful it could even penetrate moderate smoke to provide an aiming point. On the down side it was offset, too far forward, and the final factor which consigned it to the dustbin, it weighed in four times as heavy as the gun itself! The other disaster was the case-less ammunition in its preloaded, crushable magazines. The first trial disintegrated into chaos within five minutes of arriving at the firing points on the range. It was a warm humid morning and using the case-less ammunition it proved impossible to fire more than two or three shots before the weapon jammed solid. A change to conventional ammunition didn't improve matters significantly. The modification to the ejector, unnecessary with the case-less rounds, meant the spent cases of the standard rounds were often only partially ejected, resulting in a difficult to clear jam.

"These things are fucking useless Paul," observed Taff as he resorted to a stout screwdriver to prize out the fourth blockage in as many minutes.

"As they are, I agree with you mate," was Paul's reply, "but take off the bloody abortion of a sight and it's a nicely balanced bit of kit, accurate too, even I can hit the target if it decides to fire!"

"Well I still ain't impressed."

"I didn't say I was Taff," replied the equally exasperated young sergeant. "Let's be positive about this. We all agree the thing feels pretty good, light, strong and beautifully balanced with the laser sight off?"

The others grudgingly muttered in agreement.

"Equally," Paul continued, "the laser is a complete abortion on this particular weapon."

"Bin the bloody thing," suggested B.J.

"Fair enough, but as I understand it, the idea was to give us a clear aiming point instantly in a hostage situation, without having to aim with conventional sights."

"That's a damned good idea as far as it goes, anyone any ideas?"

"Yes," replied Mickey, the new member of the squad, "My nephews were playing with a couple of toy guns when I was home the other week end. They were 'death rays' or some such space weapons."

This produced a couple of ribald comments and more than a little laughter.

"Alright, take the piss, but the point is, when they fired at each other it activated a torch inside the gun, it was bright enough to see the spot clearly at ten yards."

"How big are these torches?" asked Paul.

"About the size of a decent marker pen, they run on a couple of calculator batteries. Granted they only stay bright for about ten minutes, but wouldn't it do the job?"

"How big is the spot of light say at about twenty feet?" asked Paul.

"About the size of your thumb nail."

"And you say it's clearly visible even in good light?"

"Yep, clear as these lasers, same colour as well."

"Then why don't you get changed and nip into town and get us four and plenty of batteries."

"Sounds better than buggerin' about clearing blockages here for the rest of the day."

"Go on then, and no chatting up the shop assistants."

"As if."

"That still leaves the perpetual blockages, which looks terminal to me mate."

"Could be, but I wonder if there are any unmodified breech blocks around with the original ejectors."

"What you thinking boyo?"

"I'm not quite sure Taff, but I don't think the jams with the different ammos are caused by the same problem."

"Like what?"

"Well I reckon, in the case-less crap absorbs moisture out of the air as soon as the seal is broken and swells, hence the jams."

"S'pose so, and the others caused by the modifications?"

"So you agree?"

"Well yes, but is it worth it?"

Paul laid his last three targets in front of his friends; each target had neat little groups of nine millimetre holes.

"Yeah, quite, your point is taken Paul."

The rest of the week was taken up un-modifying the ejectors and breech mechanisms, not to mention fitting Mickey's torches.

"All right, at ease," the steely-eyed C.O. said as he entered the small workshop attached to the semi-enclosed close quarter range. "I just thought I'd pop in and see how you lads were getting on with your new toys. I presume, from the lack of a report on my desk there is a problem?"

"There was more than 'A' problem boss," replied Paul. "That thing must have been designed by at least three committees to have crammed so many gremlins into such a small package."

"Oh dear,' replied the Boss. "I take it you must have found something good or you'd have binned it by now. Is it worth any more effort?"

"I'd like another day or two Boss.. We've sorted a fair bit; it's really just the case-less stuff that's the problem. We might have cracked it also, but we won't know for sure until the new batch arrives in a day or two."

"Fair enough, I'd like to hear your thoughts so far."

"Well, it's light, tough, wonderfully balanced without the damned great laser. It is also very accurate and easy to use, it just feels right."

"Taff, what do you think of it?" asked the Colonel.

"I've fired two hundred rounds this morning boss, all standard ammo, not a single jam, there's my last target. Twenty rounds, from twenty meters, down to five, average accuracy, less than one inch."

"That's bloody marvellous, so what's the problem?"

"There isn't one as long as we use the bolt out of an Ingram Ex 19, the curved mag., off a modern arms MP3 and Sellior - Belliot ammo."

"A strange mix, please explain."

"O.K., the ejectors on the weapons we were given had been carved around to cater for the case-less stuff, we tried to get an unmodified one and we were told that one didn't exist! So we nicked one out of that Imgram proto type. Hey presto it worked, to a point. We could now fire seven or eight rounds before a jam instead of two or three. A film we took confirmed our suspicion, after a few rounds the bullets were being presented arse end up to the mechanism instead of horizontal, the Ingram and Ouzie ammo are too short, the Indian crap the army uses isn't up to speck hence the Sellier-Belliot ammo."

"And with this odd combination it works?"

"Most definitely boss, here, you try it."

"What's this?" asked the C.O, indicating a slim plastic tube clamped to the side of the short barrel.

"A torch, 55p at the local hardware store, batteries not included."

"I see, you've replaced two or three grandsworth of sophisticated laser with a kiddies toy costing less than a quid?"

"S'pose we have, but it works just as well. Better really as it doesn't upset the balance of the weapon or get in the way."

"Typical."

The C.O fired five aimed shots at 10 metres through the ordinary sights, five aimed with the torch and the rest in a couple of short bursts, again using the torch. To his immense satisfaction all his rounds were in a four- inch group.

"Not bad Sir, seeing as it's a new weapon to you and you must be out of practice."

51

"That will cost you a drink sergeant, unless of course you can do better."

"Is that a challenge Sir?"

"I suppose it is."

To the senior officer's astonishment, with no apparent effort of concentration, the young NCO promptly blasted a two-inch hole in the target at 20 metres. In less than thirty seconds the remaining members of the section emulated his success.

"Bloody hell!" muttered the C.O, "I thought I'd seen it all. That is bloody incredible, and I take it repeatable?"

"Certainly boss, double or quit?"

"Not bloody likely. Looks as though our need for a reliable light automatic has been well and truly met, brilliant."

"Not quite Boss, there's still a problem with the case-less ammo to sort. I was under the impression this was the single most important feature. No clues as to who had been and no poncing around collecting stray spents."

"Well carry on. I'm sure you'll crack that too. I must say I'm very impressed so far, very impressed indeed."

As with most problems, the answer was so simple, to the extent everyone felt distinctly sheepish when one of the team first suggested it. A 9 mm bullet with a 8mm charge, this along with a minor modification to the collector on the bolt, cured this problem. A side effect of the sub calibre charge was a significantly reduced muzzle velocity and range, but as Paul pointed out, this was not necessarily a bad thing. The principle use envisaged was after all, hostage rescue, the last thing you wanted was a bullet passing through a terrorist and killing the hostage.

The team spent the next week practicing every hostage rescue scenario the training wing could dream up. Buildings, aircraft, boats, trains, daylight or dark, equipped with their new 'wonder weapons', complete with laser pens and stun grenades they achieved consistent results far in excess of the best which any other squad had ever managed. All this with weapons which had originally, been next to useless.

As is the way of these things, a unit of what can only be described as 'Whitehall funnies' had also been given a batch of the same weapons. Their tests were, if anything, even less successful than the original Hereford tests. The different philosophies of the two units meant whereas the military evicted the gremlins, the 'civil servants' tried to work round the faults without, it must be said, any great success. Not surprisingly the reports of the Whitehall warriors arrived on the desks of their Lords and Masters before the military ones were written.

These reports coupled with the knowledge the youngest, least experienced sergeant at Hereford had been entrusted with the task of evaluating the new weapon, gave the two men discussing the recapture of the English woman, renewed hope.

As they were the two most senior civil servants responsible for intelligence matters in this area, their recommendations on what action, if any, to remedy the situation would certainly be adopted.

Their course was clear, delay as long as possible then belatedly send a rescue team on a mission which could only fail. Clearly they could not send a team of their own operatives, as failure would not do them any good at all in the constant power games played in those unhallowed halls. The solution was simple. Send out a section from the S.A.S. to do their dirty work. When the mission failed, leak it to the press to the discredit of the regiment. It would at least badly dent the mystique of the unique fighting force and at the same time destroy its image of near invincibility.

Why on earth should two of Whitehall's 'pinstripe and old school tie' brigade hold such convictions?

The English woman captured by the heroin overlords was no back-packer; she was an agent, a good one at that.

It had taken nearly three years of patient, careful work to infiltrate the dangerous world of the heroin suppliers. This woman, known as the **'English Rose'** was not only the most senior agent on the ground, she also knew the others. Take her out, better still, persuade her to talk, and the current operation would collapse. It would take years to rebuild, in the mean time the money would continue to roll in and their prophecies of failure for the operation would come true.

By lunchtime, it was clear the word was out. The canteen was a buzz of speculation as to who had been kidnapped, by whom and where. To avoid any suspicion falling on their particular 'desk', as their department was designated, the fateful call was made to the regiment whose cap badge was the winged dagger. The commander, a Lieutenant Colonel with more years of service than he cared to admit, was slightly taken aback by the phone call. On reflection it was more the tone than the actual request which made him uneasy. It wasn't unusual for sections to be seconded to all manner of strange departments, often with scant explanation. The request for a particular section was unusual, this had been explained but the fact these were the only men available, who were trained to use the new wonder weapon. As this operation would be 'deniable' it would have to be them, with the case-less ammunition, no way to trace the weapons from lost cartridge cases therefore no embarrassment for HMG!

They might have added they could also blame it on the incompetence of the military, sending such inexperienced soldiers when it failed.

CHAPTER 6

For the first few days of his overdue leave, the most energetic undertaking was a couple of hours of unproductive fishing. Paul sat quietly in the bushes, cursing his inability to tempt even one of the smaller fish out of their watery home under the over hanging tree, when he became aware of the presence of someone else on the bank. To his consternation he found it difficult not to hide from the intruder, this job was getting to him!

It turned out to be a life long friend, someone he had known since childhood, "Hello Davey, thought you'd have a go at the chub?"

"Not a lot of point after you've scared them all is there?" replied the new arrival. "How long are you home for?"

"Rest of the month with any luck."

"Why don't you come up the pub for a drink, see if you can still throw a dart straight."

"That sounds like a bloody good idea, about eight o'clock O.K."

"I'm looking forward to that pint you're going to buy me when I thrash you three nil, I can taste it already."

"Oh yeah, that'll be a first."

Friday evening came round all too quickly, Paul had been coerced into the darts team having beaten Davey three times on the trot, no mean feat as he was the team captain and had only lost once all season.

Tonight was the big match, the local derby, the White Horse against the Blue Bell from the next village, both unbeaten. The setting could not have been more idyllic, the tables outside on the village green, beside the large pond. It seemed as though most of the population of the two villages had turned out to support their teams. The domino match was already underway, the tables placed under the copper beech attracted most of the senior citizens. The rivalry was just as great here as with the darts teams; although it must be said the support was a good deal quieter.

By ten o'clock the darts match was reaching its climax, it looked as though the visitors from the Blue Bell were about to level the match at four all. Paul took advantage of the temporary lull this created at the bar to get another pint; convention was the captains played the last game of a match, tonight however this convention was waived. Because he had beaten his own skipper so easily, it

55

had been unanimously decided at the team meeting which Paul should play the, as yet unbeaten, skipper of the Blue Bell.

Paul's response was simply, "cheers pal!"

The skipper of the Blue Bell, Billy, was another old school friend, predictably Billy put his first dart into the 25, very close to the wire surrounding the bulls-eye. Try as he might Paul couldn't get the 'bull' he needed to go first, consequently he lost the first leg without even getting a shot at his double. This of course meant Paul had the advantage of first shot in the second leg and he promptly returned the favour of denying Billy the chance of a shot out. So everything now depended on the deciding leg, not only the match but the league championship itself would most likely be decided tonight. Because it was all square it would be the closest to the middle to take the first throw with all the advantages this would bring. It took three attempts before it was agreed Paul's dart was the closest. The game was finely balanced to say the least; the tension was tangible. Just as Paul was about to attempt a shot out of 101 the phone rang, it seemed abnormally loud. Ted, the landlord picked it up, "Paul, it's your missus, says it's very urgent."

"Bloody good timing," commented someone.

Paul spoke to his wife without showing the least hint of any emotion, "You did say imperative, didn't you?"

On receiving an emphatic affirmative reply, he was heard by those close enough, to mutter. "Oh bollocks, I'm on my way."

He paused only to take a quick sip of his beer as he picked up his darts from the bar.

"Ted," he called to the landlord, "look after my arrows, I've got to go, see you again."

To the astonishment of the crowd, he threw just two darts as he passed the end of the mat, the first was the triple seventeen, the second, released before the first had hit the board and slammed into the bulls eye.

He was out of the door before anyone realised what was happening, everyone heard the powerful old jaguar start up and roar off, startling the over fed ducks resting under some of the tables on the grass.

"What the fuck was all that about?" a voice asked no one in particular.

Tom, one of the local gamekeepers had stood open-mouthed, found his voice again, "did you see that?" he exclaimed. "Left handed, back handed from ten or twelve feet on the move, that ain't natural."

"You missed the best bit," observed Ted the landlord, as he held up Pauls' third dart, "he only picked up two of his 'arrows'."

Arthur, Tom's opposite number on the adjoining estate, was sitting at the bar, near Paul's barely touched pint. He picked it up and drank most of it in one go; noticing the reproachful look from Tom, he merely said "What?"

"That was Paul's pint."

"So. He won't be back, waste not, want not."

"How can you be so sure?"

"My nephew, Davey, was fishing with him the other day; he says Paul's changed. When Davey asked him where he'd been and what he'd been doing Paul just clammed up, he used to be full of stories. Young Gary, Davey's cousin is home on leave and reckons Paul is SAS, what ever that is these days.

"I was in the desert rats during the war," said Wilf, the retired blacksmith. "There was SAS out there, right mad buggers, scared the Africa Corps shitless, blowin' things up hundreds of miles behind the lines."

The debate on the legality or otherwise of Paul's last throw carried on long after Paul had reached his isolated home a mile or so outside the village.

"So who called?" he asked his concerned wife.

"Whoever it was didn't give a name, just told me to get hold of you and tell you to ring this number immediately. He was very insistent and quite rude."

Paul took the note pad from his wife, "I don't know that number, I wonder who wants me. Make us a coffee love while I find out what all this is about; please," he added.

"Glad you added that bit," she said as she headed towards the kitchen.

Paul was about to pick up the phone to dial the mysterious number when it rang, making him jump.

"Hello, yes speaking," was as far as he got before the voice on the other end of the line cut him off.

"About time sergeant, I've been waiting for nearly half an hour for you to call me."

"Well, I was at the pub for a darts match. I am, after all, on leave!"

"It is not my concern, I want you to report to the gate-house at USAF Mildenhall in exactly half an hour. Oh, and do not, under any circumstances contact anyone about this call, in particular do not contact your regiment, is that clear!"

"Sure perfectly clear, just a couple of points, like who, or rather what are you, and how the hell do you expect me to get to Mildenhall in half a bloody hour."

"I'll ignore the implied sarcasm sergeant, you've got a jaguar, get in it and drive."

Paul stared at the phone as though it was about to melt; "bloody hell," was all he could say.

"What's wrong dear?" his wife asked from the kitchen, "you haven't been recalled surely?"

"Looks very much like it I'm afraid."

"That's not fair."

"I've got to go luv, sorry."

"It's still not fair, take care."

"I will, love you."

As he predicted he was twenty minutes late, the military police two striper on the gate was very polite.

"Yes sir, you are expected sir," and relayed directions so Paul could find the building where he was to meet whoever had called him. Another M.P. appeared, "I'm your escort sir."

"Cut the sir, I'm only a sergeant, like you, I still work for a living."

The military policeman sank into the plush leather seat next to Paul. "They'll never believe this back home," he muttered quietly, almost to himself.

"What's that?" asked Paul.

"This, the little nigger boy from the back streets of the Bronx riding in a real jaguar."

"Well you're riding in one now, and unless I miss my guess you'll end up parking it in one of your hangars for me until I get back."

"Where you goin' sarge, anywhere interesting?"

"I don't know where I'll be going, it's why I'm here, to find out, it might be just about anywhere. As to the other bit, it rather depends on your definition of interesting. One thing's for sure, the shit has hit the fan somewhere, and I've been chosen to clear it up. What really pisses me off is I'm supposed to be on leave!"

"What's your unit Sarge?"

"I don't think you really want to know, what you don't know can't hurt you."

"Like that is it, O.K Boss, I'll not ask any more questions, fair enough?"

"I wasn't bein' awkward son, it's just the types of jobs my lot get sent to sort out are best not talked about."

"That's the place your friends are at," said the M.P. pointing to the annex of the Officers' mess.

"Who says they're friends?"

After the American had escorted Paul into the lobby and introduced him to the duty Security Officer, he turned to the soldier "I'll wait with your car sergeant, make sure it doesn't get towed away."

"Sounds like a good idea to me son, here catch," he threw the keys to the startled young American, "park it somewhere safe and handy, keep an eye on it for me. You'll find some tapes in the glove box, feel free to play some music while you wait."

"You trust him with your jag?" asked the security officer.

"You trust him with a colt .45 automatic."

"Just because he carries one it doesn't mean we trust him with it!" replied the officer. "Your friends are this way, I think they're getting a bit impatient."

"Why does everyone around here assume they're my friends?" Paul sat in the vacant chair facing the two Civil Servants; "This had better be good, dragging me away from a darts match!"

"You mean to tell me you've kept us waiting while you played darts!" exclaimed the senior man. "This is bloody outrageous, I'll see you're on a charge when you return."

"Please your self but I was, no, I am on leave which is why I wasn't hanging on the end of a phone. The reason it took so long to get here is, as you damn well know, the thirty or so miles between here and my home are for the most part country lanes! Now we've got that out of the way what's so damned important, one of your lot got themselves lost north of Watford?"

"We'll have a little respect if you don't mind sergeant, we selected you for this vital mission for a very good reason, it is a deniable operation, therefore your vital skills are an essential ingredient to the success of this task."

"Which is?"

"Take this file with you; read it on your flight to Frankfurt, you will travel there on a Hercules which is currently waiting for you on this base. The file contains all the information you will require to carry out your mission."

"Which is?" asked Paul.

"As I said, all you need to know is in the folder, you will follow those orders to the letter. You will not, under any circumstances contact your regiment, we will be arranging for the rest of your section to join you later. You will not do anything which might embarrass H.M.G. Now get on the plane so we can get our end of things organised."

The two men rose. "That will be all sergeant, your plane is waiting." They simply gathered their papers together, placed them in the identical cases they carried leaving a bemused soldier staring at the closing door. He decided there and then the Whitehall Warriors could take a hike, bugger their orders he was going to talk to his boss no matter what. If he got kicked out then at least he'd still be alive!

He returned to his car and his escort. "There is a Herc, a C130 to you, waiting for me I believe, it is bound for Frankfurt."

"That's out on the flight line."

"Which way do we go?"

He followed the American M.P.s. directions; typically he drove as close as possible to the waiting plane. Paul grabbed his small kit bag, "Take care of my car," then as an afterthought, "I'll be back."

"You're an O K guy sergeant whoever you are, the keys will be in the Provo's office in the H.Q. building when you get back, Good luck."

No sooner was the plane airborne than Paul sought out the crew, "Could I use your radio please, it's quite urgent?"

Once the crew were convinced it was military business they could not have been more helpful. Initially 'the boss' was horrified at Paul's disregard for his clear orders. He calmed down somewhat when Paul explained why he had called, and agreed to meet Paul as he requested.

"Yes I'll bring the rest of your band of reprobates, with your new toys. Yes, bravo zero five are available; I'll bring them with me. If you can convince me you're right, they can come with you."

"Thanks boss you're a star, see you in Frankfurt, I'll be in the U.S.A.F. goods receiving office. Oh, while I remember the Q.M. in the armoury has an ammo box full of preloaded mags of the new ammo, could you bring it as well please?"

" O.K. Paul see you in Frankfurt."

He persuaded the American C.O to send one of his men in his place on the ancient B.A.C.111. It was bound for Bahrain with more stops than a 39 bus. Paul was sure he could talk to his boss without raising the suspicions of the civil servants who had briefed him at Mildenhall.

Paul explained his doubts to his boss; his flimsy reasons were met with a non-committal grunt.

"You must admit it's a bit bloody odd Sir?"

"What you're asking for, a back up team, an RAF Herc and a couple of choppers for extraction and a VC10 equipped for crazy-vac from Kota Baru, all based on a feeling? And all in defiance of your strict orders on ingress and egress already arranged. As I understand it, even this meeting is in breach of your orders?"

"That's the point boss, you give me orders, not some nameless burke in a pinstripe suit and bowler hat. They tell us what needs doing and leave us to sort out how. After all, it's not their arse on the line."

"Damned right," agreed the C.O. "Come on, we can sort out the finer points in the air, the leer jet will get us to Bahrain well ahead of the clapped out thing you were supposed to be on. For what it's worth, I agree with you. This does stink; someone's being set up. Let's make sure we're not the ones paying for someone else's cock up."

The speedy Leer-jet did indeed arrive in the gulf long before the ageing airliner. Using its advanced satellite communications, the men on board were also able to get all the other elements of their rescue team on the move. The CO made sure his personal transport was safely tucked away out of sight of prying eyes.

"I'm still not happy about this Paul," he confided to the young sergeant. "I'll be honest with you. I think it's one of the most hopeless rescue attempts ever mounted."

"It's not exactly what I had planned for tomorrow boss, but it'll be alright."

"I wish I shared your optimism."

"Look at it this way Boss. We both agree, it's almost certainly too late to save the poor bloody agent and we, that is my team, are expected to fail?"

"True."

"Well, too late or not can't be changed. Doing it our way we won't be as late as we would have been. The way I see it is, arriving eight hours before the so-called plan put forward by our bowler-hatted friends has several advantages. For a start the element of surprise is once more with us, better still, the entire exit flight will be in darkness, both of which greatly increase our chances of survival. The idea of using a pair of stripped out Lynx's carrying the extra fuel in detachable drums means we'll be out a hell of a lot quicker than the soddin' great Chinook, suggested by the Whitehall Warriors."

"Granted it looks a lot better but, without trying to dishearten you, I still put your chances of getting out unscathed at barely 10%, and the chance of rescuing the 'English Rose' is to say the least negligible."

"But worth a try?"

"Absolutely! With the proviso we don't lose anyone or worse still, a bloody chopper."

"Don't worry boss, I might not have the experience myself but we're a good team and our support squad are the best there are, we'll be alright. Just remember, I've got the single greatest asset any member of the regiment can have in abundance, I'm totally allergic to pain."

"I had noticed," replied the Colonel. "I've also noticed you've got the luck of the devil, I just hope it holds."

"It will Sir, I'll make sure of that."

To compound the deceit, the team which left on the commercial flight to Kuala Lumpur were not the men who would go after the captured agent. The four veterans, travelling as businessmen, carried I Ds which identified them as Paul and his team. They had been picked from the duty squadron in Salalha and bore some resemblance to the men's I D they carried; to the extent one was a Taff. Such was the detail of the deception, they even carried the photos of Paul and Taff's wives and kids, as well as photos of themselves and their respective 'wives'.

One of the men carried a copy of the orders given to Paul at Milldenhall, their orders from 'the boss' were to follow Whitehall's orders as slowly as possible. "Just make sure you get the guns from the consulate and don't go any further than Kota Baru."

62

In the event the decoy team didn't get further than Kuala Lumpar. Whitehall commandeered a Chinook from the garrison at Singapore for the rescue mission, this needed some modifications to extend its range. The special long range Chinook based at Kota Baru wasn't available; it had already left on a mission and could not be contacted.

The 'civil servant' responsible for mounting the mission was so relieved at having a genuine delay to his plans, he didn't even think to check on the deployment of the 'special' Chinook. He instructed his operative in Singapore to ensure one or two vital parts for the conversion of the helicopter were incorrect or missing, anything plausible to delay for another day.

The grey haired flight sergeant in charge of the team of R.A.F fitters was nearer the truth than he could have imagined, he turned in exasperation to his head fitter "Any one would think someone, somewhere doesn't want this bird to fly!" He hurled the third fitting at the rubbish bin. "Right size, wrong bloody threads; how come? I didn't know they made fuel fittings with such coarse threads."

The men who were the supposed beneficiaries of all this work were still a couple of thousand miles away about to board their plane for the next leg of their journey.

"We're buggered if those Whitehall wankers decide to come out and wave us off themselves," remarked one of the fakes.

"I doubt they'll do it mate, I don't know what's going on but it's got to be a 'deniable' and a dodgy one an all. Nah - they won't show up 'till it's over, either to grab the glory or slag us off for fucking it up."

"'S'pose your right."

The departure of the slightly odd looking Herc provoked little interest as it took off and climbed out down the gulf. Such things were commonplace with the on-going involvement in Oman and the Trucial States. The departure of the great Victor tanker about an hour later was no more noteworthy as it climbed, presumably headed towards its usual home at Akrotiri on the island of Cyprus. The old converted bomber was much faster than the Hercules and soon caught it up.

The two planes joined up far out over the Indian Ocean, the Victor topping up the Herc. The difficult task of refuelling the much slower transport completed, the Victor headed to Dieago

Garcia to take on a full load of fuel. They met again just to the west of the Andaman islands, this time the Hercules took on every last drop of fuel her tanks would hold. The tanker headed for the safety of Singapore leaving the Herc., to head east into the gathering darkness and unfriendly skies.

The crew scanned their radarscope for the blip which would signal the appearance of the Chinese airways flight from Kuala Lumpur to Beijing. Five minutes late but right on course, the ancient Illusian freighter lumbered onto the scope to play its vital but unwitting role.

Old the freighter might have been, but it still required all the power the special Hercules could muster to get in position, just below the jet transport.

"This could get dicey skipper," said the flight engineer of the Herc. He's doing about 10 knots faster than normal, which means we're on 98% instead of 90. It could give us a fuel problem."

"Trying to make up his time I suppose," the pilot observed quite casually. "How tight will it make the fuel situation?"

"Very tight Skip, like about fifty miles short of Kuala Lumpur."

O.K., let me know if it gets worse flight, we'll just have to divert to Kota Baru."

"You'd have thought with all this modern technology they could design a plane which doesn't turn into a bloody flying deep freeze," muttered one of the troopers of the back up team.

The temperature was dropping rapidly in the un-pressurised hold of the Hercules as the plane climbed with the ancient Chinese cargo jet. The idea was to fly tucked in as close as possible so their radar signatures registered as one.

"Oxygen in three minutes lads," came the voice on the intercom.

"Final equipment check!"

The eight men wearing their parachute packs split into pairs and quickly checked every strap, buckle and clip of their partner.

"Check your personal oxygen supply before you hook up the plane's supply," said one of the men without a parachute pack.

"As if we'd forget boss."

"Stranger things have happened Taff."

"I s'pose."

The eight combat equipped men resumed their seats, fidgeting to try and get comfortable with all their bulky kit.

64

"O.K. relax. There's about forty minutes to drop zone. Then there's ten seconds between the two sticks. I'll give you the signal so you won't have to check your watches. Deploy your 'chutes at exactly two thousand four hundred feet on your radar altimeters, we calculate if you allow the wind to take you down to about five hundred feet, you should be nicely placed to see your individual drop zones. Everything is looking good at the moment. There is a little light broken cloud at about fifteen thousand feet; this should not be a problem." The loadmaster, proud of his speech, took a last look round to ensure there were no loose items of kit left lying around.

"O.K., hook up your masks to the plane's supply."

The tension was tangible, yet surprisingly the most stress showed on the loadmaster, he'd been on more than a few such 'deniable' operations, yet he could never get used to the at least outward calm of these men. The act of jumping out of a perfectly serviceable aircraft in daylight over his own airfield in ideal conditions on a warm sunny day, without his own weight in kit took every ounce of his resolve to contemplate such action, never mind do it.

"Any questions?" asked the anonymous man the soldiers called Boss. There was no reply. "So you're all clear on all the details, routes, times, who's doing what?"

They all nodded briefly.

"Well good luck. I'll see you all when you get back."

"You'll be lucky to see any of them again never mind all of 'em," muttered the loadmaster. The ageing flight sergeant had seen some of these men before but the young sergeant who seemed to be the commander of those, about to step into the blackness which concealed their objective, was a new face.

This time, he'd noticed, the normal flippancy was missing; he'd never seen a team so focused. They'd spent most of trip studying maps and aerial photos, the latter brought out to the plane by an officer from the intelligence section as they were about to take off. On reflection, they'd been ready for a few minutes before the motorcyclist had rushed out to them with the folder of pictures, which in turn meant they must have had to wait for the vital recon photographs. It was not difficult to deduce this was a rush job, add to the location and this could only increase the already high risk involved in these missions. The loadmaster, shook his head, he would never understand what made these men tick.

There were several odd things about this operation, not the least of which was the presence of one of the regiment's senior officers. The old hands present seemed designated as back ups, more moral support than anything, very strange. As was always the case when things happened, they happened fast. The eight men, one minute fidgeting on their kit, next minute the ramp was down and they were gone.

"O.K. Skipper, the birds have flown."

"Thanks flight, hang on back there."

Even as the ramp began to close, the big transport banked right round through 120 degrees, losing altitude very fast. The idea was to get as low as possible as fast as possible, hopefully avoiding any unfriendly radars on the way down.

As the flight sergeant and the S.A.S. officer headed for the relative comfort of the crew cabin, the N.C.O. asked casually, "Blooding the new lads or sacrificial lambs?"

He was answered only by an icy glare.

"Like that is it Sir?"

"It is, and you should know better than to ask, flight."

The plane sped low over the unbroken canopy headed for the Gulf of Thailand, the C.O. checking his watch at almost one minute intervals, the crew of the plane were well aware he would much rather have been on the ground far behind them; than here, headed for safety.

The radio operator turned to the army officer, "I don't know if I should tell you this Sir," he began nervously.

"Tell me what?"

"About ten seconds after your lads left the ramp, we received the 'abort' code."

"What?" said the horrified officer.

"'Fraid so Sir, I've just asked for conformation."

"Oh my God, did they say why?"

"No Sir, just the abort code from G.C.H.Q."

"Not from H.Q.?"

"Definitely from Cheltenham Sir"

"What about the choppers? Will they have been recalled?"

"If they haven't, they soon will be."

"Can we talk to them?"

"I'll give the ships a shout and get their frequency as soon as we're over the sea."

"Can't you call 'em now?"

"Trouble is the world and his wife would know where we are."

"If those choppers turn back, they won't have enough fuel to turn round and complete their mission. The fuel is absolutely critical."

"Just for the record, so is ours," chipped in the flight engineer.

"This is fast developing into a first class fuck up!" observed the army officer. "How'd we end up low on fuel?"

"The Chink airliner was late and going faster than scheduled, so we had to go flat out to stay close enough to hide in his radar shadow."

"I think we may have got a way out Skipper. I think I've got 'em on radar."

"How does it help us?"

"If we can get close enough, we can use this," he said holding up a torch.

"So much for hi-tech fangled satellite, good old fashioned Morse!"

And so it was, granted, it took two orbits to get the message across. "Ignore abort; god speed."

Receiving a simple 'R' from each chopper, the great plane banked towards the sea once more.

"Well done Sparky," said the pilot, "Now if you can conjure up an extra 100 gallons of fuel, we might just make it so I can buy you a well deserved drink."

"I wonder how the lads are getting on, any news?" asked the army officer.

"Haven't heard anything Sir," replied the radio operator.

CHAPTER 7

Far to the north, blissfully unaware of the dramas in the air, the soldiers on the ground had their own problems. Although not perfect, the drop was good enough, the support group retrieved all the 'chutes and checked and secured the landing site for the choppers. Then set up a two man checkpoint on the escape route the rescue squad planned to use once they had rescued the hostage.

Time was not on the side of the soldiers. They had been nearly ten minutes late leaving the plane. Against all their instincts which demanded a cautious approach, they had to cover most of the distance as fast as possible. Despite their faster than intended approach, they still spotted the sentries before they, themselves, were detected. Paul and Taff crawled forward, using their night sights it was, almost easy to take them out, a swift double tap from each of the Heckler and Kocks' and the way was clear.

The building before them was a solid, rectangular structure, typical of those built by the Chinese to house their small border garrisons. With typical communist desire for uniformity, they were all of identical layout. The rescue plan was based on this knowledge and a little bit of deduction as to which room was the hostage's prison.

Now it started to get a bit harder. There was no easy way, the door simply had to be opened, but the question was how? Noisy and fast or quietly, delaying the deadly moment of discovery as long as possible, the latter was definitely favourite, Paul and Taff lay down just off the edge of the steps, from here they would be able to see along the corridor but still be hidden in the darkness. B.J. carefully grasped the door handle, ready to open the fateful door on Paul's signal. Mickey, the fourth member of the team, watched their backs.

Paul nodded; the die was cast.

Although there was an element of relief in finding the corridor empty, there was also a tangible increase in tension.

They crept along the bare stone corridor, their suspicion the third room on the right was the most likely to be the room in which the captive was held, was confirmed by a strangled scream and several males laughing and a cacophony of Mandarin babble or maybe it was Cantonese. Paul slid the fibre optic under the door, what he saw sickened him. There were eight Orientals in the small room and one European. The focus of their attention was a skinny, naked girl, suspended spread eagled from the ceiling. There was a good deal of blood around, obviously from the girl. Two large car batteries with jump leads attached were being used to encourage her to talk to her captors.

With great difficulty he suppressed the instinct to kick the door in, all guns blazing. Retrieving the optic fibre he informed the rest of the team of how many targets and the whereabouts of the girl. "There's one in shirt sleeves I'd like to take back, he looks like the head honcho. He's definitely the one asking the questions."

Another gut wrenching scream, animal like, could be heard from within, a sound none of them would ever forget.

"Come on Paul let's go, put a stop to it," said BJ, already moving towards the door as the agonised scream came again.

Paul just nodded and launched himself at the door. Using the opposite wall of the corridor as a spring-board, he hit the door with such terrific force it took the frame with it, the whole thing falling flat with a resounding crash.

The silenced sub-machine guns purred briefly. Half the occupants were dead before they had time to realise what was happening. Before the first targets had hit the floor, three of the others were also dead. Only the stocky, short-sleeved Oriental and the European were still standing.

The pale suit clad man turned to see the source of the carnage, with surprising speed a 9mm Browning appeared in his hand. There was the fleeting eye contact with Paul. "You," as he ill advisedly raised his gun, not at the soldiers, but towards the captive girl. Three of the Hecklers' purred, and in the space of a couple of seconds over thirty rounds struck the man, hurling the mangled, lifeless corpse against the wall.

"Get her down and let's go; Come on. Taff, cover the corridor, Move! Move!"

The exact sequence of events is difficult to convey, so many things happened more or less simultaneously. The woman; released and barely able to stand, was supported by Paul. Mickey who was by the remains of what had been the door, was encouraging the others to hurry as the small garrison were showing signs of aggression, a couple of short bursts had sent the militia diving for cover, leaving two dead in the corridor plus two writhing their way towards the doubtful sanctuary of the other doorways.

"B.J, grab the sack of shit."

"We'd better take him with us, and you!" he added indicating the shirt clad Oriental, "Cuff him Taff. We'll take him as well."

"I don't think so sergeant," replied the Oriental. "My men will not allow you to leave." He straightened himself. "By the time my men have finished with your gang of bandits, you will wish you had obeyed that last order."

"Which was?"

"To go home," sneered the Oriental.

The renewed racket from the corridor added urgency to the situation. B J was organising his bloody load. Taff, moving to give Mickey a hand at the door, had decided the urgency demanded it.

Taking advantage of the situation, the stocky Oriental, responsible for the torture of the woman, suddenly lunged at her; there was a glint of steel in his hand. The woman; still supported by Paul's right arm and apparently more dead than alive, barely moved. The skinny right arm shot out, her fist, half clenched, connected with the side of the Oriental's head, which simply caved in as though hit with a large sledge hammer. It had all happened so fast, Paul had only managed to raise his M P 9 half way to its intended target. The woman collapsed, now only supported by Paul's right arm, had taken revenge on her tormentor.

"Fuckin' hell," muttered Paul, gazing at the twitching corpse; the lifeless hand still clutched the thick bladed combat knife.

"Time we weren't here mate," called Taff from the doorway.

"Right, give us a tick." Paul wrapped the unconscious woman in a handy jacket then swung her limp form across his shoulders in a modified sort of fireman's lift which left one hand free for his gun.

B.J. held the corpse of the Englishman in a similar position; he even retrieved the 9mm.

They moved to the door ready to go. Taff and Mickey both threw grenades along the corridor, the second they exploded Paul took off with his load, followed closely by B.J. Taff and Mickey didn't move, they fired brief bursts to keep the Chinese militia pinned in their rooms, two more grenades rolled along the corridor, exploding two or three seconds apart. Throwing two more grenades they too fled into the night, firing alternate bursts to dissuade pursuit.

Once into the darkness they stopped, their last two 'frags' ready.

The first two militia, were cut down by Mickey. Now they began to get their act together and they began to fire from well inside the door. Taffs arm whipped over the 'frag' arched through the door, silencing the AK47s. The two men waited, sure enough another squad made a break from the building, intent on pursuit. Both the Hecklers purred their song of death followed by Mickey's last grenade.

"Right, let's go Boyo."

A few yards past the fork in the path, Mickey became aware Taff was no longer behind him. Even as he turned to find out what had happened to his friend, Taff came charging along the path.

"Go, Go." Said the Welshman as he tore past the startled Mickey.

Suddenly there was an outburst of gunfire behind the two fleeing soldiers, followed by what sounded like grenades exploding. There were more shots and confused shouts, all from the other path.

"What were you doing Taff?" asked Mickey as he caught up again, "You had me really worried for a minute."

"I brought a smoke grenade with me; just in case, and a couple of thunder flashes, I chucked them down the other path, thought it might confuse them for a bit, buy us a little time."

Twenty yards from the edge of the clearing, a familiar voice came from the thick tree roots beside the path.

"You pair took your time."

"Paul and BJ. O.K?"

"Puffin a bit, get going we'll be OK. You two go on the first chopper, it'll be in any minute."

As Taff and Mickey arrived in the clearing, Kenny met them and directed them to the far side.

"Paul is over there with the girl. There's a pile of kit and the parachutes, you two make certain it all goes on your chopper; O.K."

It was a quirk of the regiment someone always took charge of any given situation. It wasn't necessarily part of the plan; it was just something which happened. If you saw something which needed sorting out, you did it, and accepted the responsibility; in this instance it was deciding who and what went on each chopper and Kenny had sorted it out.

As they reached the stack of kit, they saw Paul, squatting, holding the girl as one would hold a child. He tried to brush away a strand of hair, to see her face; it was stuck to her cheek, the blood holding it, almost dry. As it came unstuck he felt her tense up, he just had time to wrap his arms round her to prevent her lashing out at him. She struggled to get free, "It's O.K we're British soldiers, no one will hurt you anymore, the chopper will arrive in less than a minute, then we're out of here."

The skinny little woman had stopped struggling. She turned her battered face to the soldier holding her, even in the near darkness the pain and terror in her eyes was clear to see. Her voice was weak and croaky; but the words were clear, "They were going to skin me."

Taff had just dropped down beside Paul, "Did she just say those bastards were going to skin her?"

"I think they had just started by the look of her arm pit."

"Fuckin' savages."

For one horrible moment Paul thought she was dead, then he felt her move again, he could feel her breath on his neck. "Hang on girl," he murmured as he turned to shield her against the debris hurled around by the down draft of a Lynx in a hurry.

The lynx dropped quickly into the clearing in a welter of leaves and rubbish; it was down barely 30 seconds. Paul didn't move, Taff and Mickey were flinging in the kit and retrieved parachutes, before they dived in themselves. Paul passed up the desperately hurt woman to the medic who got to work on her at once, assisted by Mickey. Paul leapt in beside the pilot, who in response to Paul's vigorous signals, pointing upwards lifted the chopper out of the clearing as fast as was possible.

"What the fuckin' hell happened to her?" exclaimed the medic as he began to discover the extent of her injuries. "Better get two drips up, pass the morphine."

In the cramped confines of the Lynx it was all a bit difficult.

"This thing stinks of fuel," observed Taff. "What the hell's this on the floor, a bloody water bed?"

"Collapsible fuel cell, try not to make any holes in it, it's not empty yet and we need the fuel to get back to the ships."

Taff got comfortable behind the mini-mi, mounted in the starboard door, he amused himself by firing short bursts at the twinkling lights advancing on the clearing they had just left.

The second Lynx had only the pilot on board; it came in almost dangerously close behind the other chopper. The pilot was a real

72

expert, he never really landed his aircraft; it was more of a hover with just the tips of the skids touching the ground, just enough to stop it moving around.

B.J. dumped the body of the mysterious Englishman in through the door. Kenny and his sidekick, Stuart, leaped in. "Up front BJ. I'll man the mini-mi," shouted Kenny above the noise.

John and Brummie appeared and dived into the side door. The grenades they had thrown back along the path, exploded in rapid devastating succession among the pursuing Chinese. As soon as John and Brummie were inside, Kenny unleashed a stream of bullets which cut down everything in their path, men and bushes alike.

In less than a minute they were well away into the darkness and relative safety.

Their C.O had just climbed out into the warm night air for a walk, it seemed as though he'd been in the Herc for days. The RAF special services teams fussed round the plane.

He sat on a fuel drum in the soft tropical night gazing at the lights of Kota Baru, his thoughts were not of the bustle and lights of the fast growing town but of his men and their impossible mission far to the North. The choppers should be there soon to pick them up, if any of them were still alive to be picked up.

As soon as the plane was over the gulf of Thailand, he'd been on the radio and it emerged the 'Abort' signal had originated from White-hall, who claimed they had information the whole operation had been compromised.

This served only to confuse the issue as the operation had been mounted totally differently and much sooner than the Whitehall plan had called for. Unless the deception of the substitute team flown into Kuala Lumpur had been discovered, and he doubted, Whitehall could not have known what was going on.

The radio operator emerged from the Herc and headed towards the army officer. "Just thought you'd like to know Sir, we got a 'burst box' transmission. 'Retrievers 1 and 2 coming home to roost, with all the flock."

"Casualties?"

"They didn't say Sir, I think they'd have said if they needed help."

"Yes I suppose they would, thanks for the news," replied the Army officer. "I just hope they're better off than we were for fuel."

"At least their landing pads can go towards them, they'll be O.K."

"How long before we can talk to them?"

"About three hours, just before dawn."

"I didn't know a Lynx could stay up for six hours."

"Normally they can't. Those two were so overweight at take off; they nearly didn't make it. You know they put a 45gallon drum of fuel on each skid and a bloody great collapsible fuel cell in the passenger compartment? The Chinook which refuelled them will be back in about two hours Sir. They've got the two army air corps pilots which flew the first leg. At least that went well."

"So as far as we can tell everything is going according to plan at the moment?"

"As far as we can tell, it all seems to have gone well Sir" replied the R.A.F radio operator. "At least the most dangerous phase is over, now the hard part; the waiting begins."

"You're damned right it's the hard part," replied the Colonel.

"You O.K John?" asked Brummie.

"Just a nick mate, it'll be alright."

"It will when I've had a look, come on."

John eased his combat jacket off, then his shirt.

"Ouch, it looks painful," observed Kenny.

The bullet had gone clean through the flesh of John's right armpit luckily not hitting anything other than muscle.

"Lucky, lucky boy," muttered his oppo as he applied the antiseptic dressing.

In the leading chopper Paul called Taff on the intercom. "It was a right royal fuck up mate."

"Weren't it just."

"I have a nasty feeling the shit will hit the fan on this one."

"I don't see why, we got the girl out, we're alive; they ain't."

"What about the stiff in the other chopper?"

"What about him, he tried to kill her, we stopped him, we've got him out so H.M.G. can't be embarrassed. There's nothing to give any clue as to who raided the place, what's the problem?"

"For fucks sake Taff, apart from the stiff, there's the dead Chink with his head smashed in. From what he said, it seems as though he was under the impression we'd been recalled; which in turn must mean he knew we were on our way!"

"Don't sound so surprised Boyo this started out as a Whitehall op so anything's possible with them involved."

"And the other thing, just exactly who or what the hell is she? I couldn't do that to a bloke with one blow and I'm twice her size. The Chink must have weighed 13 stone, mostly muscle, little miss matchstick can't be much more than 7 or 8. Damn it she's nearly all skin and bone."

"I'm as shocked as you are Paul, we all are."

"Makes you curious as to how she ended up like that in the first place Taff."

"Don't it just."

"How's she doing Doc?"

"Hanging on just, who did that to her?"

"Them back there."

"I hope they're dead," replied the medic. "If they're not, take me back and allow me the pleasure of fastening their balls to the national grid."

"Really Doc., you surprise me."

"Have you seen what they did to her?" asked the angry, shocked medic.

"Not apart from the obvious cuts and bruises, and what I took to be burns."

"That's about all there is to see, it's what they've done inside that bothers me On top of every thing else I'm certain she's had several injections of heroin; now I've cleaned her up a bit you can see the needle tracks on her arms. I'm not saying she's a junkie, or she's using it from choice, I've already removed one broken off needle, I think there's at least one more but it's too deep for me to get at. I'll tell you straight, I'll be surprised if she's still alive by the time we reach the ships."

"I don't want to hear Doc."

"You want me to lie?"

"No, but let's be positive, what can we do to help her?"

"With what we've got here, not a lot."

"What's the problem?"

"The biggest problem is potentially serious shock, medical shock."

"Which if I remember my first-aid correctly is loss of fluids causing a drop in blood pressure."

"That's about right."

"Then what would happen if we put in another line?"

"We might have to, but it's not a good idea. If we pump her up too quickly it could cause all sorts of problems, usual ones are swelling of the brain or the heart simply packs up or splits under the pressure."

"So we're damned if we do and she's dead if we don't?"

"That's about the size of it. If we put the extra I.V. in she'll tense up and all sorts of things could pop."

"Then why not knock her out, then she'll relax, gently increase the I.V. wouldn't that do it?"

"It might," replied the medic "but I've given here enough morphine to knock out a bloody horse, she will just not go out. It may be due to the heroine, it could well have raised her tolerance threshold to the morphine; if I give her even a tiny bit too much, she'll O.D."

"Paul!" Taff's voice came over the radio from the main cabin.

"Yes mate?"

"Our little lady wants to speak to sergeant Paul, she says she'll only talk to you."

"Give her a com. set, I can't get back there."

Paul heard a weak, soft voice in his headset. The only words he could make out in the chopper noise were, "Thank you."

"It's O.K," he replied, "You try and sleep until we get you safely home."

All he caught of the reply was, "Not safe."

"Relax, we'll look after you, I promise."

There was a mumbled, incoherent reply, then the medics' voice came through the head set.

"Thank heavens, she's out cold. I'll get the other line in, she might make it yet."

"She'd better make it Doc, I want to know what isn't safe, preferably before we find out the hard way."

CHAPTER 8

The two helicopters sped westward, the ground was flatter now, the ride was smoother and the internal bags were now empty so things were much more comfortable all round. The soldiers carefully rolled up the flexible fuel cells, ensuring all the fuel was squeezed out into the still attached pipes.

Most of them simply settled down as comfortably as they could, the long night was far from over.

The only ones not relaxed were the medic, keeping a very watchful eye on his charge and Paul who was clearly worried.

Paul flicked a switch on his intercom so he spoke only to the pilot. "Much longer Sir?" he enquired. "I'm a bit concerned about our little lady back there," indicating over his shoulder,

"There's a long way yet I'm afraid, about an hour and a half to the coast, the ships are about one hundred and sixty miles out, any closer and they'd show up on Thai Radar, and they wouldn't like it if they knew we were here, and even less if they knew the rest."

"As far as that? Have we got enough fuel Sir?"

"I hope so, and you can drop the Sir, my name's Andy. I gather your name's Paul and you're in charge of this band of desperados."

"Fair enough Andy."

"What's wrong with the young lady, shot?"

"Other than the fact she's been very badly treated by some particularly nasty types, I'm not sure myself."

"I see, 'the mind my own business syndrome' fair enough," replied the pilot. "I wasn't trying to pry."

"I know Andy, but certainly there's an element of what you don't know can't hurt you about this one. For a start, I haven't got a bloody clue as to who she is. I feel she just has to be an agent of some kind."

"You mean she's a Whitehall spook?"

"Of some sort, but very definitely not your run of the mill 5or 6. There's something very special about the little lady, apart from the fact she's bloody dangerous; the question is dangerous to who?"

"I don't think I want to know any more thank you," replied the pilot.

"I can't say I blame you Andy," he paused. "This whole thing stinks, I get the distinct feeling the smelly stuff is going to hit the fan when we get home."

"Sounds fun."

77

"I doubt it'll be fun somehow, but it will be interesting."

"I'll bet."

"I disobeyed orders on several counts." Paul continued, "I had a bad feeling about this op., so I did it our way rather than how I was told to. I'm glad I went to the boss and got it done properly. If I hadn't, I'm sure our little miss Bond back there would be dead by now, or wishing she was."

"Well, we're equal in that respect Paul, we were ordered to abort during the run in, an order from on high as well. It wasn't long after we'd refuelled and swapped places with the two army lads who had flown the first leg We'd just begun to turn back when this bloody great Herc appears out of nowhere, no radar contact, it's suddenly there, circling us. All this at fifty feet above the trees in the hilly country, then the damnedest thing, they started to signal us in Morse, with a torch as far as I could tell. It took a couple of repeats before we cottoned on to what was happening. It seems as though you were already on the way down when they received the abort."

"Well thanks for coming to get us Sir. We'd have been in a bit of a fix without you."

"You'd have made it."

"Maybe; but she wouldn't have."

"Like you said Paul. This could get interesting, someone, somewhere is frightened your little lady there is going to say something they don't want anyone else to hear."

"You could well be right Andy. I reckon your best bet is to say you didn't receive the message and we weren't exactly talkative."

"I might just keep my pension if I follow that advice."

"Personally I'll just settle for being alive and on my way home."

Paul settled down in his seat and tried to doze off, he was feeling, 'shagged out', as he put it. He must have dozed off for a moment or two as he woke with a start.

"What the fuck happened?" he asked no one in particular. It was Andy the pilot who answered. "Some bastard took a pot at us, hit the drum your side. We're losing fuel."

"Oh shit!"

"These barrels are only tied on loosely, it's barely half full, see if you can turn it through 90 degrees."

"Hey!!"

"You and one of your mates in the back, reach out and rotate the bloody thing, so the fuel doesn't all piss out, hurry."

It was no easy task, what with the slipstream and the down draft. Paul and Taff were nearly blown out of the chopper. Luckily both had the presence of mind to attach a secure strap to their web belts. They completed their task quickly enough however.

"Fuck that for a game of soldiers," muttered Paul.

"Fuck that for any game," replied Taff.

Paul flopped back into his seat. Andy the pilot was busy punching buttons on what appeared to be a computer.

"Well?" enquired Paul.

"Well what?"

"Have we still got enough fuel to reach the ship?"

"What? Oh yes, we'll get there OK, it's just we'll have to slow down, it will probably be light before we're properly clear of the Thai coast."

"Oh dear. Won't it mean a sizable diversion to avoid being seen?" enquired Paul.

"Probably."

"Oh bollocks; I'm tired, fed up with being fucked around, I just want a bed."

"I know the feeling."

"Out of idle curiosity Andy, how far short of your ship would we be if you maintained the planned speed?"

"Difficult to say until we've emptied those drums on the skids. There's no way to tell for sure how much we've lost."

"S'pose not."

A little over an hour later they got their answer as the engine spluttered a couple of times.

Andy casually flicked a couple of switches and turned a tap. The engine returned to its previous note. "Well, now we know," commented the pilot. "As soon as we're over the sea I'll call up, get Glasgow to crack on full speed, straight towards us, we'll be on deck in about two hours, give or take a minute or so."

The medic stuck his head through the hatch, so he could talk to Paul.

"The morphine's worked at last, she's out of it. All her signs, blood pressure and the likes, are low, too low really, but stable. I'll keep her on the drips. How long before we get to the ships?"

"Andy reckons about two hours."

"Two more hours in this? Oh my aching arse!" moaned Taff, who hated helicopters more than most.

There were a couple of minor alarms when aircraft were detected nearby, but the two choppers continued unmolested. Once out over the sea, both ditched their skid mounted drums, which were promptly sunk with a quick burst from the mini-mi's.

"At least they won't be a hazard to shipping," commented Paul.

Their welcome on the ships wasn't quite what they'd expected; it was frosty to say the least. Their orders were simple, "Stay on the choppers while they refuelled, keep the doors shut." A request for a couple of saline bags was initially ignored then refused when repeated.

"That does it!" muttered Paul. "I've had enough of this fucking about."

As he climbed out of the Lynx he was met by two armed leading regulators, "get back into the chopper now!" commented the larger of the two ship's policemen, eyeing the blood-covered soldier with some disquiet.

"Get fucked!" snapped Paul. "I want your ship's surgeon, medic what ever."

One of the leading regulators pushed Paul back towards the Lynx.

"Do that again and I'll break your fucking arm."

"You're on a charge."

"Bollocks." Paul took two steps towards the hanger then the Leading Regulator made his last mistake. He grabbed at the S.A.S. sergeant, missed and was instantly laid out cold for his temerity.

"You bastard," the other leading reg. leapt at him, truncheon drawn. With no apparent effort Paul took it from him and hurled it over the side.

"Now, unless you want to join sleeping beauty there, go and get me the bloody medic. There's a very badly injured English woman in the chopper who is in desperate need of serious medical help. She's been in the chopper for damned nearly four fucking hours, being kept alive by our medic and our first aid kits."

"Sorry, Captain's orders. Apart from fuel, we're not to help you in any way at all."

"Oh is that so! Then you'd better get your skipper down here double bloody quick, - MOVE!"

Paul got the Master At Arms instead "What's all this? You," pointing at Paul. "Get back into the Lynx."

"Bollocks."

"Do as you're told soldier boy ,or you'll be in trouble."

After a heated argument, Paul finally lost his patience. "Let me put it this way, I don't give a tuppenny fuck who gave you your orders, if you won't bring the bloody stuff here, now, then I'll go and get it and heaven help anyone stupid enough to try and stop me. Do you understand?"

The Master at Arms then did the worst thing possible. He went for his gun.

"You're taking the piss!" commented Paul as he casually bent the Master at Arms' wrist to an impossible angle. He unloaded the 9mm, then stuck it back in the holster. He then put the magazine into the shocked warrant officer's jacket pocket.

"My squad has just been flown halfway round the world in a draughty Herc, most of us called off leave. Just to be dumped out, a couple of miles up into the night sky over jungle-clad hills. We got into a fire fight with about forty nutters, armed with Aks, rescued the damsel in distress, endured four hours in a lynx, then we get a welcome like this. I want to know why and I want to know now."

"We're just following orders," bleated the Master at Arms.

"Then take me to whoever issued them, so he can tell me."

"Might as well Sir, he's got at least a couple of mates in the Lynx, if they're all like him they'll turn this ship into a modern-day 'Marie Celeste'."

"Leading Regulator Webber," began the Master at Arms, "You're a bloody defeatist, but probably right. Go to sick bay and get whatever they need, and ask the Captain to come down to the flight deck A.S.A.P."

"Right Sir."

"What unit are you and your band of pirates?" asked the Master at Arms. "As if I need to ask; you lot are as crazy as your reputation," he observed, massaging his sprained wrist. "Are you injured, it's just you're covered in blood"

"I'm not hurt Chiefie but the party we came to free is, as for the crazy bit? Some of us are Chiefie, I can think of some who wear the same beret as me who would have simply shot you and your lads and chucked you overboard for the sharks."

"I don't doubt you, by the way, what rank are you?"

"Don't worry about rank, just call me Paul."

"Refuelling complete Sir, the Lynx is ready to start up Sir." Reported a leading hand in full fireproof kit.

81

"Not without those medical supplies Chiefie, we haven't come so far to lose her now - no way."

"I sympathize now I know more. Go to sick bay and find out what's holding up Webber, and take him with you," indicating the very groggy Leading Regulator who was beginning to stir.

After a frosty welcome, Paul and the skipper went to the end of the flight deck, out of earshot of the others.

"Hold on a tick before you rip my head off Sir," began Paul. "I can't tell you too much but I'll tell you as much as I dare, then you can make your own judgement."

"Very well, make it good and keep it brief."

When Paul had finished the captain's attitude had changed somewhat.

"There's dirty tricks afoot and I want no part of it. I'll make sure you all get flasks and something to eat as well as getting the ships surgeon to give your injured party a once over, see if he can help, O.K.?"

"That would be bloody brilliant Sir. Thanks a lot and sorry about your Leading Regs."

"I should think so too, understandable in the circumstances though. What about the Master at Arms?"

"What about him Sir? He's big enough and ugly enough to look after himself, aren't you Chiefie?"

The captain failed to suppress a grin. "Yes Chief, what do you want?" he asked the hovering Master at Arms.

"Signal Sir, most immediate."

"Thank you Chief."

Paul withdrew to a discreet distance to allow the Captain to read the signal in peace. To his amazement the Captain tore it up and allowed the wind to carry it away into the growing boiling wake. He noticed Pauls' enquiring look.

"You don't really want to know. Let's get you on your way A.S.A.P."

"Sounds good to me Sir, thanks for your help and sorry about your lads."

"Good luck and I hope she makes it, who ever she is."

"So do I Sir, otherwise we're all in a lot of shit for nothing. One thing Sir, I slipped up mentioning the fact our injured party was a girl, for all our sakes, especially hers; please don't let on to anyone we had a female passenger. It is very important, there's just yourself, the master at arms and the leading regulator who fetched you who know. If you could have a word with them please, it will greatly increase her chances of survival if no one else gets to know, especially civil servants! "

As Paul climbed back into the Lynx he noticed the other Lynx climbing away from the frigate matching the destroyers twenty knots just over a mile away to port.

The Skipper reached up to shake Paul's hand. "That signal ordered me to hold all of you in the brig and put you ashore in Singapore. We said you'd already left under strict radio silence."

"Thanks again Sir. Let's get out of here Andy."

The two helicopters closed to about fifty yards and dropped to a few feet above the glassy sea. Their mother ships were quickly left far astern, finally vanishing as the sun cleared the horizon.

"Only another couple of hours to Kota Baru lads," said Andy cheerfully.

"I've got some better news still Andy," replied Paul with a conspiratorial grin.

"Oh, like what?" asked the pilot.

"Try a ninety degree turn to starboard."

"O.K., you're in charge. Where's it going to take us?" He thought for a minute. "Port Blair?"

"Well done."

"I'll bet it's where the Herc which signalled us is hiding."

"It had better be!"

The other helicopter closed up on the port side. B.J. called Paul on their short-range communicators. "Our jockey's puzzled about the course change, can I tell him?"

"Might as well, he'll find out soon anyway."

"O.K. Paul. Oh by the way, we detected a ship just as we altered course, it was at extreme range but smack on our route. Our bloke reckons it was a Chink destroyer from its' radar signature."

Paul thought for a minute. "You mean he'd got us on radar?"

"Without a doubt."

"But he's lost us now?"

"Hang on I'll check."

Paul could hear B.J. and the other pilot in the background.

"He definitely lost us when we turned. Hopefully they'll put it down to us dropping to as near the sea as possible."

"Let's hope it stays that way, give us a shout if you detect anything else."

"O.K. Paul - out."

"Looking for us?" asked Andy.

"Possibly, but he'd had to have been in the area already to have got into an intercept position."

"We've been out here for three months now and he's the first Chink warship to venture into this part of the Indian Ocean. They don't just come here," replied the naval pilot.

"They don't shadow your ships?"

"Not up here."

"Well, if he's here for our benefit, he'd have needed prior knowledge. In fact he'd have needed to have been told at the same time as we were alerted."

"You're serious?"

Before he could answer, two bright explosions attracted their attention.

"Oh yeah, what the hell was all that about?"

Paul scanned the horizon with Andy's powerful binoculars.

"What can you see?" asked the pilot.

"Not a lot, a couple of faint smoke trails from the rough area the Chink destroyer must be, and the smoke clouds of two explosions where the trails end."

What he couldn't see were the charred bodies and feathers, all that remained of a couple of flocks of sea birds which had been flying in a couple of tight V's on the same course the helicopters had been taking prior to their turn.

"I'm getting the distinct feeling, some sod doesn't want you lot to succeed," observed Andy. "The sooner this mission is completed the more likely I am to live to enjoy my pension."

"If, and this is a big if, those missiles were fired from the Chink destroyer with the intention of shooting us down then someone's getting pretty fuckin' desperate to make sure she doesn't talk to anyone, and it appears, includes us!"

"Any idea what this earth shattering secret is Paul?" asked the disconcerted pilot.

"No idea mate, damn it I don't even know her name, much less what she is, I'm not even sure I want to!"

CHAPTER 9

Twenty minutes later they were on the ground at Port Blair, welcomed by their very relieved boss. Their faithful Hercules had arrived an hour before from Kota Baru and relief at his men's safe return and apparent success was greatly re-enforced as Paul related subsequent events.

"Good god!" exclaimed the C.O, "are you alright, you're covered in blood."

"I'm O.K Boss. But we have got one hell of a problem. Some bastard is ear wigging into our signals. Who ever it is seems hell bent on stopping us at all costs."

"You what? Anyway; how the hell did you get into such a state?"

"Carrying the girl out to the chopper Sir."

"Girl! What girl?"

"The girl we were sent to get, she's only a little slip of a thing; I doubt if she's even twenty years old. She's one hell of a mess; the medics reckon she's stable for a bit, poor bloody kid."

"You mean to tell me Whitehall are using kids against these bloody warlords! What happened to her; hit in the crossfire?"

"No Sir, it's all as a result of the treatment she was getting from those barbaric bastards. Anyway Boss we've got a lot bigger problem. You do know this whole operation was a set up?"

"We sort of worked that much out, which is why we did it your way rather than Whitehall."

"No Boss, they knew we were coming, they also knew we had been recalled, and if they knew, then may be the near miss from a couple of anti aircraft missiles from a Chinese destroyer, wasn't the accident it would have been portrayed as, had they have hit!"

"What the hell are you on about?"

"I'll explain later Sir; the thing is why should a Chink destroyer, in the Anderman Sea lock on to a couple of Lynx helicopters, which had just left a pair of Royal Navy warships. The Whitehall plan called for a Chinook, in and out of Kota Baru. Who, apart from us knew about the switch? Someone just has to be monitoring our signals, to and from the 'Kremlin'; it's the only way Boss."

"How did you know about the 'abort' signal; you must have been half way to the ground when we received it?"

"The head honcho of the lot which were holding the girl told us. He said we should have done as we were told, which was to go home. Andy, our pilot confirmed the abort."

The medic came running over from the Lynx.

"Hello Sir, do you know what medical gear is on the Herc?"

"Not off hand, the rest of the medical team are on board, probably asleep in the forward compartment. There are a couple of boxes of supplies, if you need anything else let me know as soon as possible and we'll beg it from the local hospital."

"Thanks boss, it's plasma and saline drips I need, it's taking two an hour just to keep her alive!"

"Gangway, mind your backs," called Taff, as he and Mickey approached the ramp of the Hercules carrying a stretcher between them. Paul grabbed one of the handles from Taff, without being asked the 'Boss' helped Mickey with the other end. Together the four men carried the stretcher to the forward cabin and placed it on the floor as gently as they could.

"When do we rejoin the V.C.10?" asked the senior Medic. "We've got a lot better kit on there."

"As soon as we can, we've got a few things to sort out then we'll be away."

Having handed the terribly hurt woman over to the medical team, the Boss led the way back out into the sunshine. They joined Andy, the pilot of the first Lynx, who relayed his version of events to the Colonel, as they waited for the rest of the team from the second chopper.

First out was B.J. To the C.O's consternation, he too was soaked in blood, if anything he was even worse than Paul. The sight of Kenny and Lofty, lugging what was an obviously occupied body bag increased his concern. He turned to Paul, the concern changing to confusion as he noticed Brummie helping an agitated John out of the chopper.

"Get off, stop bloody fussing it's hardly a decent scratch."

The C.O fixed Paul with a withering glare, "Alright; who?"

"Don't know his name Boss, I only know him by sight. He is a Brit, I think he's a Whitehall 'funny'. Can we save all this for the debrief please Boss, it's all a bit complicated to discuss here."

"I rather think we ought to get the hell out of here. You get back to your ships and thanks again, bloody brilliant. If you ever fancy a change, just put in for a posting to our attached air corps squadron, just put 'pluck the rose' on your CV. You'll get in, no problem."

"Thanks for the plaudits Sir. Next time I'm bouncing around in an arctic gale I'll consider the offer. We're actually shore based at the moment, at Kota Baru. I might be navy, but these choppers are actually army kit, hence the skids, proper ones, like the ones I'm used to, have wheels, so we can move them around on ships."

"'Scuse me Boss," Paul began, a bit unsure of himself when dealing with the legendary Commander of his unit.

"Don't look so worried Paul, I don't bite."

"Just a thought Boss, supposing those missiles were meant for us, then won't it rather give the game away if they detect the choppers returning to the ships?"

"It might at that, what's your point?"

"Well, if they were to wait here for an hour or so then we could be out over the Anderman Sea by the time the non-arrival of the choppers at Kota-Baru began to cause concern."

"What about our guest, she needs proper medical care, sooner rather than later."

"Mickey and the medics agree she should be stable enough now to survive a flight to Sri-Lanka or Southern India, we could transfer her to the Vickey 10 there in safety."

"You think there's a risk at Kuala Lumpur?"

"Damned if I know Boss, but personally I wouldn't like to chance it."

"Yes I see your point Paul. The timing is important but it shouldn't be too difficult to arrange, once we're airborne. If our naval friends can give us an hour or so start, we should be out of harms way."

"Why not wait a bit longer Boss, as soon as we're overdue at Kuala Lumpur the Vickey can take off, headed for Bahrain or some such plausible stop over then develop an engine fault causing a diversion to wherever we land up.

Let the choppers wait here until the Vickey's out of Kaula Lumpar's radar range then they can sneak back to their ships to refuel. Before they return to Kota Baru it might be an idea if they were to lose their long range fuel bladders and attachments. Not only would it piss on the matches of anyone out to do us any damage; it would also remove most of the evidence they'd been on a covert job."

"You are a devious bugger Sergeant, you don't trust anyone do you? the C.O asked."

"That's not quite true Sir, I trust you or anyone else with a sandy beret."

"You're only a Sergeant!" exclaimed Andy. "I thought you were at least a Captain on such an operation."

"Well I reckon we were supposed to fail so it's Sergeants to the fore."

"Cynical sods" exclaimed the C.O. "We'd better get going and thanks again Andy, and your mate in the other chopper, we'll be in touch in an hour or so, watch yourselves, thanks again and good luck."

"Thanks Sir, been an education and a privilege. Good luck Paul, you and your lads take care."

"We will, bye Andy and thanks again!"

Ten minutes later they were in the air once more, this time in their faithful old Herc.

"You and I have got to have a serious chat my lad," said the steely-eyed C.O to Paul. "Come on" he motioned towards the kit bags near the rear of the planes cargo hold.

The two men sat down facing each other, leaning forward so they wouldn't be overheard.

"First of all are you alright?"

"I'm fine Boss, a bit knackered, but intact."

"I didn't mean that!" exclaimed the C.O "I mean are you feeling alright? I know you've fired for real before; but this is the first time up close and personal; this is different."

"You're not kidding it's different," replied Paul. "The part which will stick in my memory is the bloody awful sound a bullet makes when it hits home. It's worse still if it hits a solid bone, one of the drawbacks of our silencers working as well as they do I suppose."

"Are you O.K with it?"

"I reckon I can live Boss."

"What about the others; anything different about them?" asked the C.O sounding concerned. "It's simply a fact you know them better than anyone else, so you will be more likely to notice the first signs of a problem."

"Mickey's a bit quiet, but then he has been helping the medic keep her alive for the past four or five hours. It must have been a bloody hard job. I think we're simply knackered, but I will keep an eye on them Boss. Thanks for the tip, it's one aspect of this job which hadn't occurred to me."

"Right, now will you please explain to your C.O, exactly what is going on, because to say I'm confused would be to understate the case!"

"I'm not sure I can Boss, it's difficult to know where to start."

"Let's try at the beginning, when you broke your first order and came to me about this operation."

"We've already been over this part before Sir, you agreed with me it wasn't quite cosha. Which is why we mounted the op in the way we did, just as well too as events turned out."

"O.K. what would have been the likely outcome had you gone in at dawn from a Chinook, which would have landed three miles away to pick you and your rescued hostage up, then fly you all back to Kuala Lumpar via Kota Baru?"

"Based on what their head honcho said, before she killed him."

"What do you mean; she killed him?"

"Exactly that Boss, I was holding her up, he drew a knife. Before I could bring my weapon to bear, she'd hit him; just once, he was dead before he hit the floor."

"Good Lord. So what would have been the likely outcome of the original plan?"

"They would have been ready and waiting; I can't see how we could have succeeded, in fact we'd have been lucky to have survived, much less escaped. I'm certain initially we were expected and also he was aware a signal had been sent recalling us."

"It is a serious allegation Paul, then there's him," he added indicating the body bag containing the body of the English man.

"I don't know his name Boss, only his face. I've seen him around a couple of times. He was in the Whitehall team which came down to promote the MP9 before we started to evict its gremlins. I think I saw him in our London office once, just before the raid was mounted in Wandsworth which came up empty. He certainly twigged me."

"Exactly when did he draw his gun?"

"We'd taken out the Orientals apart from the one our little lady killed. Taff and BJ were moving to release her, then matey over there pulls out a 9mm high power and points it at her. There is no doubt in my mind he was about to shoot her, not any of us, definitely not the Chink. He was focused totally on her."

"So you shot him!"

"No choice, Taff and B.J reacted exactly the same as I did; no orders, all three of us couldn't have been wrong Boss."

"You took a hell of a risk bringing him out, it reduced your combat effectiveness by an additional 25%."

"I know Boss, but we were instructed to leave nothing which would embarrass HMG."

"You could be accused of being selective as to which orders you chose to obey."

"I suppose so, by the way, that was a bit of quick thinking, signalling those choppers with a Morse lamp. It must have knackered up any eaves droppers monitoring your transmissions."

"Touche. So now you're saying someone's passing on our signals to the opposition!"

"Looks that way to me Sir."

"I can see why."

"You know the skipper of our refuelling ship, the Glasgow, was initially told fuel only. As we were about to leave he received a signal to 'throw us in the brig' until he reached Singers."

"What?" exclaimed the C.O. "So why didn't he?"

"We'd had a chat, I told him what we'd been up to; well just the very bare bones of it, I didn't include where or why."

"I should hope not! But it convinced him to help?"

"More or less, he ripped the signal up and threw it overboard, wished us luck and told us to bugger off. I inadvertently let slip we had a female on board. Three of the crew heard it, the Skipper, the Master at Arms, and a leading regulator. The skipper gave me his assurance they would plead ignorance to anyone, should they be asked and none of them would mention it again. He was under the impression we were headed for Kuala Lumpur, as was Andy, the pilot, until I gave him the new course."

"That was when this mysterious Chinese destroyer turned up?"

"Well, the other Lynx had more avionics fitted than the one we were in, or at least different gear. They had just detected the ship or at least its radar scanning us. Apparently most radars' have a signature as distinctive as a finger print. The pilot of the other Lynx is certain it was a Chink."

"They're usually right, then you say there were two explosions on the horizon about ten minutes later, probably missiles fired by your mystery ship?"

"The position of the explosions was pretty well where we would have been, had we carried on our course to Kota Baru. The smoke trails came from the direction where the Chink must have been."

"What do you reckon he shot at, a flock of birds?"

"It's not as daft as it sounds Boss. We saw several flocks of cranes, I think. They were all headed the same way as us, low over the sea, it is possible Boss. Andy, our pilot reckons there hasn't been a Chink warship this far north all the time he's been out here."

"So, on the basis of all this you're assuming there's some sort of welcoming committee at Kuala Lumpur, intent on doing the young lady further harm?"

"Not assuming Boss, just allowing for the possibility."

"You know what I think Paul?"

"I'm cracking up? Or just neurotic?"

"Neither actually. I agree with you, and like you, I want to know why and more importantly who? You are under my command and it makes me responsible for your health and general well being. It therefore follows I take more than a passing interest in any party intent on causing harm to any of my flock."

"So how do we get the Vickey to meet us wherever we're going without nosey buggers finding out Boss?"

"We don't, I'll call Hereford on the burst box, they can call the VC 10 via the Sat link the four decoy lads have got with them, they can come home on the plane. We're bound for Tricomalee, we've got an 'arrangement' with the Sri-Lancan government for such eventualities."

"The real fun will start when we get home. Whitehall will go ballistic, I'm bloody certain they picked me because of my inexperience, we were supposed to fail Boss."

"Well, you didn't and you're not going to."

"Thanks Boss. What have you got planned?"

"We'll direct the VC 10 as soon as she's well clear of Malayan air space, she's based a Brize Norton, so we'll get them to file a flight plan via Bahrain."

"The question is, what do we do with her when we get her back to the U.K.? because if she's so big a risk to someone then she won't be safe in the Woolwich."

"Oh yes she will, because a couple of lads will stay with her. Until we find out what the hell all this is about."

"Cheers Boss," replied the tired sergeant.

"And all based on one of your bloody feelings," muttered the C.O.

"Sorry Boss, I didn't catch that."

"I said, 'and all based on one of your bloody feelings.' To hell with training, logic and orders, it makes you bloody wonder," replied the C.O. "Go on, get some kip and well done."

"Thanks Boss."

Paul returned to the rest of the squad, the C.O went forward to the flight deck.

"What was it all about Boyo."

"He just wanted to know who did what to who, how, why and when?"

"Yeah right!"

"Well, what did you expect? I know the regiment is used to sorting out other peoples fuck ups, but this is a different league."

"Paul," called the medic from the cabin in the front of the plane, immediately behind the flight deck and cockpit area.

"Yes Mate, what's up?"

"You're wanted."

Paul got wearily to his feet and headed towards the medic.

"Who wants me?"

"Your lady friend."

"I thought you'd put her out for the trip?"

"So did I, she's a tough little bugger. I daren't give her any more, I've pumped enough into her to knock out a bloody cart horse."

Paul entered the small compartment, "Hello, you're looking a lot brighter than I expected."

"Stop lying sergeant, I feel and must look like shit."

"Seeing as you're supposed to be asleep, I presume there's something you either want to know or to tell me which won't wait."

"Where are we going?"

"As soon as we swap to the V C 10, straight to Brize and you'll be whisked away to the Q.E at Woolwich I should think. Why?"

She shot an almost frightened glance at the medic.

"Alright, could you excuse us for a few minutes please Sir?" Paul asked the senior man of the medical team on board.

The officer signalled his team out. "Just five minutes Sergeant, no more, and keep it calm."

"Yes Sir," Paul waited until the door clicked shut. "Well?"

"If I'm taken to the Q.E, the only way I'll leave is in a box."

Paul was not totally surprised by the content of what she said but the strength of the conviction in the voice left a profound impression.

"If you could tell me why and who, maybe we could prevent it."

"Even you couldn't stop them Paul; it is your name isn't it?"

"Who the hell have you upset; E.T. and his little green friends? And yes my name is Paul. By the way what's your name?"

"I think it's safer for you and your friends you know as little as possible about me."

"From what little I do know, we're about the only friends you've got, so come on, at least give me some idea of what we're up against."

"Thank you for getting me out of that hell hole, don't take this wrong, but it's a pity you're so good at what you do. It would have been simpler if I'd have been killed in the cross fire," she hesitated. "At least it would have been over and done with, the only thing I don't know is how they'll kill me, I do know it will be soon."

"Now hang on a bloody minute. Who's this they, Whitehall funnies or their minions?"

"Probably, how do you know?"

"Because of this operation, the way it was supposed to have been mounted, the presence of a Whitehall slime ball at your 'interrogation' for the lack of a better word."

"Then you can guess the rest, assuming you knew who the others in the room worked for."

"O.K., try this for size. You're an agent of some kind working for some sort of International anti-drug operation, targeting the heroin barons in the Golden Triangle. How am I doing so far?"

"Pretty close, go on,"

Paul thought he detected a glint of her battered, sad grey eyes and he was certain he saw a flicker of a smile.

"You've found a bloody link, a high ranking Whitehall - warrior in the pocket of the drug barons."

"Not quite."

"Alright, one of our bowler hat and pinstripe brigade is one of the bosses or there's a bent section in Whitehall using the situation to further their career or cause. No - it can't be so simple, it's got to be a combination of a lust for power and influence and plain old fashion greed for money."

"Now you're getting the idea."

"The whole thing, so serious they'll kill you, so you can't tell what you know?"

"Bet on it."

"There's a flaw, a factor no one has taken into account."

"What's is it?"

"Me," replied Paul. "I didn't risk my neck just for some spook to bump you off to save his."

"You don't know what you're up against," she said, sounding tired.

"One thing before I let you go back to sleep. Are you sure they'll try to finish you off once you're in hospital at Woolwich?"

"There's no doubt, they might not wait that long. A plausible accident is the preferred method."

"O.K., I'll have a word with my Boss, we can be devious buggers. You ain't dead yet young lady, not by a long chalk. Now get to sleep."

He quietly closed the cabin door behind him as he left the girl to rest, the medical team gathered around him, one of them creeping back into the cabin to watch the patient.

The senior medic stood facing Paul, "I want a word with you Sergeant," he began. "Are you sure you rescued the right target; it's just you appear to have brought us a damned junkie to look after. I was led to believe your target was a captured agent, not some itinerant hippie on a trip of a lifetime. I will grant you she has been tortured, if her injuries don't kill her, her addiction will."

"Hang on a minute doc."

"Don't tell me to hang on! And you address me as Sir!"

"Like I said," Paul retorted sharply, "Stop jumping to conclusions, we got the right target, of that there is no doubt; did you ever stop to consider she might not have been taking that shit voluntarily. The medic who came in on the chopper pulled at least one broken needle out of her; I seem to recall he thought there might be more."

"You mean to tell me the people who were holding her had forcibly injected her with heroine. That's terrible!"

"From what I've seen of her injuries it's the least of the poor little bugger's problems. Personally I'd have been surprised if they hadn't tried to break her that way. If they could use electrodes and bare wires, they certainly wouldn't bother about her breaking the odd needle if she struggled would they?"

"So she really is the agent?"

"Without a doubt; we've done our bit, we're supposed to be the best; now it's up to you Doc, and I'm told you're the best, now if you'll excuse me I need a kip; I'm knackered."

Paul sought out his boss and related the gist of the conversation he'd just had with the rescued hostage.

"It is not a pleasant scenario Paul. If it's true what are we supposed to do about it? You know as well as I do our interest in her has technically finished!"

"But?"

"But nothing! You've done your job, and I'll grudgingly admit pretty damn well as far as I can tell at this stage. De-brief should be very interesting."

"A thought has just occurred to me Boss."

The Colonel shuddered deliberately, "Oh dear, sounds ominous, go on get it off your chest."

"Is there anyway Whitehall can know we rescued her or she's still alive?"

"Other than from the ships, I don't suppose there is. Dare I ask why?"

"I know it's nothin' to do with me Boss, but couldn't she be given a new identity and simply be 'lost'."

"You've been reading too many American F.B.I stories."

"Have I Sir? I bumped into a certain body a couple of months or so ago who used to be on of our skippers."

"Nothing unusual in the fact, people do retire from the regiment, and live long and active lives, not all end up in a wooden box with their name added to the clock!"

"So does the fact his name is on the clock, plus I was part of the honour guard and I am at this moment wearing his old boots, bought at the auction at a greatly inflated price, mean I was mistaken?"

"Oh my lord! I take it we're talking about a certain Captain?"

"We are Boss, I know it was a freak occurrence, but are you honestly going to tell me he's unique. In some cases it has got to be the best option, like this case. The only alternatives I can see is indefinite round the clock guard which is neither practical or one which offers any real chance of her ever leading a normal life."

"And the other alternative?" asked the officer.

"Do nothing. If she's right we might as well have sent one of those new Tornado super planes with a load of bombs and levelled the place. Ended it all there and then, quick and clean."

"You could have a point, it may, or may not be possible to do as you suggest, but is it any of our business?"

"It became our business when we were asked to rescue her Boss, and no-one specified who she was to be rescued from. As I recall I look on oath to defend out country and citizens from enemies within as well as foreign powers."

"Carry on, you're convincing me."

"Well Boss, if what she hinted at is right, then we've got some right arseholes in high places."

"I thought it was accepted as common knowledge anyway," retorted the C.O.

"And you always call me a cynical sod Boss! But it's not what I meant and you know it. These bastards are dangerous, they'll quite happily put the lives of security forces at great risk to protect themselves and their evil little empires. Don't forget, we were supposed to use the weapons supplied by the 'funnies'; are you going to tell me they've made theirs work?"

"O.K. we'll see what we can do, I'm not making any promises, but we'll try. You'll be heavily involved, and to be perfectly frank, I'm not happy about. There is, as you are aware, a side to the regiment of which you know little. I would prefer it stayed that way. However, clearly you have previously said nothing to anyone about your chance encounter and to a degree it qualifies you for the task ahead."

"We just might have something else in our deception plan Boss."

"Like what?"

"Him," replied Paul pointing at the lonely body bag on the floor of the Herc.

"How does it help us? I'd have thought he was a potentially serious embarrassment!"

"The thing is Sir, no-one other than us know we've got him."

"So?" asked the C.O. failing to follow his Sergeant's train of thought.

"We simply say we got there too late and he was dead when we got there."

"Paul, what about ballistics on the bullets, what about the woman?"

"What about her, we never found her – only him, dead."

"The bullets!"

Paul flicked a bullet out of a magazine and passed it to his Boss. The officer looked at the bullet.

"What this?"

"We were ordered by Whitehall and yourself to ensure there was absolutely nothing to indicate the operation had any connections to Britain."

"True, but these bullets, for Christ's sake, they'd explode like a mini nuke!"

"And have nothing bigger than a couple of millimetres long, they're not dum-dums, they're a modified plachette round. Only thing is they not only split longitudinally, they're constructed to snap in half laterally as well."

"American origin?"

"Probably, although this particular lot was I believe liberated from some Colombian drug runners."

"But you were using case-less rounds."

"Simple really, the charges for the case-less stuff are self adhesive and remove the bullet from its case, peel off the protective patch on the charge and stick the two together."

"We are supposed to operate to a set of rules Sergeant" said the C.O. "Who knows about the special ammo?"

"Only us Sir."

"How much is there of it?"

Paul tossed him the magazine from which he'd removed the round. "That's it, we used most of it, B.J and I were the only ones with any left, we stuck it all in one mag. I was going to fire it off, but never got the chance."

"What a bloody mess!" Sighed the C.O. "Do you honestly think you can cover this up? Killing an S.I.S agent, using illegal ammunition, now planning to lie to the authorities about the success of your mission. Words fail me! What's your next trick?"

"Give us the mag back Boss, thanks, and the loose round!"

He returned it to the magazine, which he casually stuck into the sub-machine gun and walked to the rear of the plane. There, to the horror of the loadmaster, he pushed the button to lower the ramp, as they were only at four thousand feet, pressure wouldn't be a problem. He stopped it slightly open and simply emptied the magazine contents into the air over the Indian Ocean.

"It solved one problem Boss" he grinned as he returned to his seat.

"Sometimes I despair," sighed the harassed officer. "So let me get this straight. When we get back to the U.K. we'll spirit your little lady away; then tell Whitehall the bad guys got this bloke before you got there."

"It should do it Boss."

"It should do it Boss! And just how the hell do we get her the necessary medical attention without the spooks finding her?"

"I suppose the easiest way is if they ain't lookin' for her in the first place. They're bound to check all military and M.O.D. medical facilities just in case I suppose. They will no doubt be arranging a welcoming committee for us even now. I'll think of something Boss, don't worry."

"It is exactly what's worrying me!"

The trip was a great deal more pleasant after the switch to the V.C. 10 at Tricomalee. The flight onward to Bahrain was almost luxurious compared to their normal mode of travel.

The gentle old transport landed as light as a feather and taxied to an isolated pad to be refuelled.

Paul sat at the open door watching a squad of British soldiers loading equipment onto a massive American transport plane.

"What are they up to Boss?" he enquired.

"Headed home, they're sappers from the Engineers airfields regiment, some of their kit is too big to fit in a Herc so the Yanks are flying it home for us."

"Oh yeah, I think it's just solved our problem Boss. Those squaddies are based at Waterbeach aren't they?"

"Damned if I know Paul, how does it help us?"

"The Yanks will help us out, I'm sure of it. They've got a bloody great hospital at Lakenheath which is exactly where the Galaxy is going."

"Even I know Lakenheath is a fighter bomber base, those things are at Mildenhall!"

"Normally yes, but they're resurfacing the runways there at the moment, so they're using Lakenheath."

"How do you know it?"

"Easy, those civil servants briefed me at Mildenhall. Only the short take off planes can operate there at the moment."

"There's a flaw in you plan, assuming the Yanks will play ball."

"What Sir?"

"Your car is at Mildenhall isn't it?"

"So?"

"So, they'll be waiting for you and will inevitably discover the girl."

"Not if I'm on the plane which lands at Brize with the rest of you." Paul replied. "They'll be watching us, not some sappers with sand in their shoes. We've got another advantage, I know R.E.M.E. Sergeant Major, he's a good bloke, he'll help us."

As darkness was only an hour away the deception was not difficult to engineer. A minor 'fault' was discovered on each plane. A request for some medical help saw the R.E.s ambulance which still stood on the tarmac nip across to the blind side of the V.C.10. A fuel tec had got a face full of aircraft fuel, "as if" commented Paul's C.O.

The now unconscious woman was quickly transferred to the ambulance along with some notes and letters to the Base Commander at Lakenheath and another for the Chief medic.

By the time the woman woke up, she was in the recovery room at the base hospital having undergone surgery to stop her internal bleeding once and for all. The security around her was discreet but tight.

CHAPTER 10

The old V.C.10 landed light as a feather at Brize Norton, the weary squads relief at being back on home ground tempered by the knowledge a civil service welcoming committee was waiting on the tarmac.

"This could be interesting," observed the C.O. as the plane came to a halt, "Stick to what we agreed, it'll be alright."

"As long as they don't try to keep me awake more than ten minutes boss, I'm too knackered to put up with their haverings."

"Keep calm Paul, now is not the time to lose your temper."

To the astonishment of the returning S.A.S. team, the civil servants were unusually civil. The senior official thanked the team for their efforts, congratulated them for getting back safely and bringing the body of the dead agent home. To the astonishment of the senior officer of the medical team, one civil servant even apologised for the medical teams wasted trip!

"All I can say is, may we have many more such trips Sir," replied the medic. "A wasted trip for us means a successful trip for these lads."

"Shame the woman wasn't there, I think she must, regrettably be listed as missing, believed dead. It is an extremely unpleasant part of the world, but then you'll be all too aware. Thank your men on our behalf Colonel, they must be exhausted after such a trip with little chance to sleep."

"Thank you Sir," replied the slightly bemused C.O. "What woman would that be Sir?" asked the Colonel, "I don't recall any mention of a female operative in the briefing documents."

"Have you still got those papers Colonel?" enquired the senior civil servant.

"Not with me Sir, but I can get them for you tomorrow."

"If you could please, by the sound of it they could make interesting reading."

They took charge of the body bag containing the bullet riddled corpse of the crooked agent and left, again thanking the squad for their efforts.

Paul threw his bergen pack into the waiting mini bus.

"As welcome as it was, why did it make me feel uneasy all over again Boss?"

"Wasn't quite what we expected was it?"

"Let's get home and get sorted, I don't suppose there's any chance of having the rest of our leave in the immediate future is there Boss?"

"Sorry Taff," replied the C.O "This operation has such wide implications we must ensure there are no loose ends on this one. There is no room for any mistakes, not even little ones."

Before the minibus reached Andoversford all the team were asleep, which was about the time the Boss began to suspect they might have grown a tail. By the time they reached Ross on Wye he was certain they were being followed. The problem was what to do about it. As they approached Hereford he had a bright idea, he woke the sleeping soldiers, "Fancy a coffee lads?" he asked innocently.

"Sure Boss," replied Paul, "What's up, we're barely twenty minutes from the 'lines'."

"Who say's anything is wrong?"

"You might as well have done Boss, I've never known you stop at a caravan before."

"It's obvious is it?"

"To us; what's up, some nosey sod following us?"

"I think so, if I'm right they've been with us since Brize."

"What are we looking for boss?"

"I think there's two of them, a white astra and a red escort."

"Well I haven't seen either go by since we stopped," said Titch, the driver.

The men out of the minibus stood drinking their coffees in the lay-bye at the bottom of the hill, when a grey ford Granada cruised in. A familiar figure got out and walked to the group. "You were right boss; they're both stopped at the top of the hill. I've got their numbers, I'm waiting on a P.M.C. check."

"Well done, we'll be off, see you back at the ranch, watch yourself Mick."

"I will boss," replied the squadron sergeant major. "Hang on a minute, the vehicle check is coming through. You ain't going to believe this, both numbers are blocked."

"Oh for fucks sake," Paul cursed, "What does it mean, bloody Whitehall warriors?"

"Almost certainly," replied the Colonel.

"Hang on a tick boss, if they're at the top of the hill, how the bloody hell did they know we had stopped here?" Paul asked.

"Despite your understandably low opinion of the 'funny' brigade some of them are very good at their job Paul."

"It's over a mile to the top of this hill boss, high hedges, trees and banks, not to mention three blind corners, there is no way they could have known we stopped here if there's just the two of them."

Paul walked over to the mini bus and quickly checked the bumpers and wheel arches, "Chuck us the keys Titch."

He deftly caught the keys, let himself in and started up the ageing Sherpa.

"What's he doing?" asked the boss, as Paul put two wheels up on the curb.

"Making it easier to get underneath," replied Taff, "I've seen him do the trick before."

Paul slid easily under the bus he was only under there for a couple of seconds before he emerged again. He walked over to the rest of the men, "Here you are boss, one M.O.D. tracker."

"How the hell did it get there?" asked Titch, who looked after their vehicles at Brize Norton.

"You tell me mate," was Paul's response, "I thought your section was in a secure compound!"

"So did I. Hang on a minute Paul, this is the spare minibus from the R.A.F. M.T. section, our own packed up this morning, there wasn't time to fix it so I borrowed this one from the blue jobs."

"If they want to play silly buggers with us why don't we return the favour boss?"

"I don't like the sound of this, but go on, what are you planning?"

"Why don't I stick their tracker to the tea wagon, Titch can take us home, then give them a wave on his way back to Brize?"

"How childish and petty, I like it though, sod it go on."

"Just a thought Boss."

"Oh no, go on Paul," groaned the Colonel in mock horror, "What devious scheme have you contrived now?"

"Why not leave Mick here until Titch goes home, then he can lift the tracker, it's easy to deactivate. Even he can do that!"

"Cheers pal, I'll remember when I'm doing the duty rosters," retorted the S.S.M.

"I was going to add, it might be worth while taking their pictures. You never know when it might come in handy. It would be nice to know exactly who is following us and why, 'cause I for one object to some nosey bastard following me."

"It's not such a bad idea," replied the Boss, "O.K with you Mick?"

"Sure Boss, no problem."

As Titch neared the top of the hill on his way home, he spotted the two cars, still pulled over on the verge, he flashed his lights, pipped his horn a couple of times and waved vigorously. This caused a good deal of consternation to the occupants, and curiosity on the part of the two traffic cops who where trying to establish exactly why the cars were stopped in a spot with no view, right beside a sign indicating a lay-bye was ahead.

The debrief was painstaking, even by normal standards, for a start 'Whitehall' demanded a detailed report, in fact two separate departments were demanding information on the operation. It was easy to tell which department were the 'good guys' just from the tone of the requests.

The requested reports were duly compiled, great care being taken to make no mention of the girl.

The soldiers who had been involved sat round a couple of tables going over every detail of the reports being compiled for Whitehall to ensure there were no clues to suggest the woman had been rescued.

"This is a ball ache of a job," grumbled Paul, "but I suppose it's worth while."

"Morning skip," said Taff as the captain who commanded their troop walked in.

"Paul, Taff, with me, the boss wants you."

"Oh shit, what have I done wrong now?"

"Nothing new, as far as I know. A little job has come up, and you happened to be handy."

"Oh nice one," commented B.J., "You get a trip and leave us to sort out the paper work."

"Sit down lads," said the C.O. "We've located Sean McStephoin, he has arranged a meeting at a remote little pub in the republic."

"Oh good, can we put our drinks on the expenses?" asked Paul suddenly sounding enthusiastic.

"No you cannot!" retorted the C.O., "Blast your sense of humour, you are bloody impossible. This is serious, it is vitally important you are not seen, they have a knack of spotting undercover security people. Their information and intelligence is damn nearly as good as ours, this operation could go some-way to plugging a leak."

"We're bloody plumbers now."

"Well we are supposed to be multi-skilled Taff," replied Paul.

"Will you pair pack it up," scolded the C.O. "Right, you'll need surveillance gear, movie and stills cameras, with low-light capability. You'll also need a parabolic microphone and a cassette recorder. As you may know he has been 'black flagged', means he is a top priority target."

"In other words we are authorised to shoot him if the opportunity arises."

"Exactly, however there are conditions, no witnesses, no risk to anyone else and it must be a clear shot. Also, in this case, as it is in the south, your escape route must be approved; any such action must be totally deniable. This time shooting him is not a priority; it is the intelligence which is crucial, who he meets and what they're doing. Clear?"

"Perfectly clear Boss. Is this going to be civvies or combats Boss?"

"The original idea was drive in, you both fish I believe?"

"Sounds good to me, a bit of fluff chucking on an Irish Lough, just the job." Paul noticed the enquiring look he got from the C.O. "Fluff chucking, fly fishing to you Boss."

"Ah, not this time I'm afraid, you'll never get there in time. Right, McStephoin, what do you know about him?"

"Thirty two years old, sadistic bastard. Prefers shooting his victims in the back, failing that a couple in the guts. Never attacks anyone who might shoot back. Escaped from the lazy 'K' last year in unexplained circumstances, last heard of shacked up in the south with an equally mad whore."

"Would you recognise him if you saw him?"

"Probably."

"Describe him."

"About six one, fourteen stone, thick, wavy, almost black hair, beginning to recede. Blue, very blue eyes, bushy eyebrows which meet and long side burns."

"Build?"

"Athletic, but beginnings of a beer gut."

"You've done your homework, I'll give you a recent photo to study in a minute."

"Thanks, it'll help a lot."

"I cannot stress the importance of not getting detected too strongly, you will leave no traces. This must be kept totally deniable, clear?"

"So far Boss."

"Good. A lynx will fly you to Lynham, be ready at 0900, there will be a Herc waiting for you. You will then join H.M.S. Antrim approximately one hundred and eighty miles west of Galway Bay. As soon as it is dark she will close with the coast, when in easy range her Lynx will fly you in, you will be dropped off five miles from your target. You will then observe for as long as possible, establish the purpose of the meeting, and photograph all those attending. You will also photograph all their cars. A video will be made of the coming and goings. These are the vital parts of the mission. If after all this an opportunity arises to eliminate McStephoin, then you are authorised to do so. You will exit on foot."

"Just like that," exclaimed Paul.

"Just like that," replied the Colonel.

" Why can't the Herc drop us in Boss?" asked Taff.

"There's a good chance the radar at the local air strip would pick it up. Believe me if there was an easier way we would use it."

The two soldiers exchanged glances, both hated water drops.

The next half was spent frantically acquiring and checking the kit they would need. Time for a coffee! They sat in an office studying the file on their target and a map of the remote area of the Conemmara coast where they were to land.

The moment the pilot fired up the engine of the Lynx to take them to Brize Norton, Paul began to get a sense of foreboding.

"What do you mean Brize bloody Norton, the Boss told us our air taxi was at Lynham!"

"It is, but there's a Herc at Brize going your way, so the powers that be said you've got to use it in the interests of economy."

"Nice of the boss to let us know," commented Taff.

"I doubt he's seen the signal yet, he's with a couple of visiting brass hats."

"I love last minute changes of plan."

Ten minutes short of Brize Norton, the pilot universally known as Paddy to his face, or the 'Mad Mick' when out of earshot, dumped the clattering, smoking Lynx into a field in the Cotswolds.

"Fuckin' great!" muttered Paul "What's wrong with the bloody thing?"

"A main rotor bearing is screwed by the sound of it."

"How the hell did you manage to land the thing the right way up?" asked Paul.

"Luck of the Irish, mate."

"For once I'm bloody glad it was you, most of our chopper jockeys would have nose dived!"

The police turned up fairly quickly and arranged a car to take Paul and Taff to the airfield. As they boarded the aircraft they got another shock.

"This is a bloody 'elint' plane, how the hell are we supposed to jump out of the little bloody hatch with all our gear," cursed Taff.

As they reached the top of the steps they were met by an officer, a Squadron Leader, Paul thought by the combination of bars on his shoulder tabs.

"Where the bloody hell have you two been! We've been waiting for you for half a bloody hour, get your gear stowed in the aft storage compartment, get a move on."

"Yes Sir."

Having stowed their kit, they then had to manoeuvre between several operators crouching over strange humming boxes and screens. There were two spare seats, on the rear of the cockpit bulk-head they would have to sit here for the trip.

To get to their kit they would have to scramble all the way back.

"This is fucking marvellous, a crash landing in the chopper, now this." The flight took six long hours, over the south-western approaches out as far as the Fastnet rock and then over the grey expanses of the Atlantic. The same abrupt officer disturbed their fitful sleep.

"You chaps had better get a move on, we'll be over Broadsword in five minutes."

"Then you'd better put the brakes on, it will take at least ten minutes to get our kit on. Anyway you're supposed to drop us near H.M.S. Antrim."

"No can do Laddie, now get a move on."

106

In the event the great plane did three orbits over the little flotilla of anti-submarine ships. It took as long to get into their freezing wet suits and double check all their gear.

The squadron leader was becoming very agitated, but Paul refused to be rushed. The constant nagging was getting to Paul, eventually he turned on the officer "Do you want to put this lot on and go in my place? I'd be happy to swap."

Not surprisingly the offer was declined. It was when Paul discovered the plane was less than one thousand feet above the sea. The two soldiers were equipped with freefall 'chutes, anyway there were no anchor points for static lines.

"Then you'll just have to climb, I take it this thing can climb to six thousand feet, eight would be better. Oh and I suppose we are expected down below?"

"I presume so Sergeant."

"Don't presume, bloody well check. It's a big pond down there, like I said, want to go in my place?"

"No thank you but I will check." It was as well he did because no one on the Broadsword, the flotilla leader, knew anything about the two soldiers.

By the time they were finally ready and the plane at a safe altitude above the barely visible ships below, the two soldiers were already two hours behind their original timetable.

The exit proved to be just as difficult as they feared. Being a specialized electronic surveillance aircraft it had only a small escape hatch at the rear. They had to use this hatch, as it was the only door which could be closed again in flight. The drop was one of the hairiest either of them had ever experienced, the great tail plane passed far too close for comfort. Tossed around by the turbulence it took longer than normal to stabilize, they deployed their parachutes as planned at four thousand feet. As the two friends floated down to the uninviting grey sea they ignited the smoke candles on their ankles and lowered the radar reflectors to help the waiting ships to track them more accurately. All they had to do now was stay close together and await the questionable safety of a 'wet' landing. The two soldiers hit hard, the heavy suspended packs dragging them deep before the self-inflating life preservers and automatic buoyancy aids on their packs overcame the downwards momentum and brought them gasping to the surface. Paul bobbed up to find Taff sorting himself out, using his pack as a mini life raft.

"Nice evening for a swim Boyo."

"I hate the fuckin' sea," spluttered Paul as he coughed out a spout of water, "Bloody hell this waters something cold."

"Then you'd better get a flare out, those ships are a couple of miles away and none of them have turned towards us yet."

"Useless bastards were 180 degrees out with the bloody wind direction, don't you just love it! What else can go wrong?"

The red flare soared into the evening sky and burst with a soft 'plop'. The soldiers could see the signal lamps flashing on the ships, although both knew Morse, neither of them could read the messages. Just as Paul was considering firing his second flare the middle ship of the little group turned purposefully towards them. To the utter dismay of the soldiers the destroyer looked like racing straight past a couple of hundred yards away. As soon as it became obvious the ship hadn't seen them Taff ignited a hand held magnesium flare brought along for just such an eventuality.

"Are they fuckin' blind!" exclaimed Paul as there was no sign they had been spotted. In desperation he fired his second flare, right over the bows of the ship.

Ten minutes later they were being introduced to the bearded captain of the De Rytter, flag ship of the Dutch Navy's contingent on the Nato exercise. Captain De Vries was sympathetic with their desire to get to H.M.S. Broadsword but his own helicopter was unserviceable, a multiple bird strike had almost caused a disaster. Anyway Broadsword was over a hundred miles away and he had no idea where H.M.S. Antrim was.

"Bloody great," muttered Paul.

By the time Broadswords Lynx was hovering over the stern of the De Rytter, Paul and Taff had discovered how they had ended up as guests of the Dutch Navy. The crew of the 'elint' Herc had been talking to Broadsword shortly before they had dived out into the void. Broadsword had confirmed the sound of a Hercules above them and had radar contact with the plane, trouble was no-one bothered to cross check their positions.

The pilot of the lynx had some more bad news for the soldiers. He was going to have to refuel on Broadsword before he could take them ashore.

"Can't you drop us of on Antrim on the way?" Paul asked hopefully."

"Maybe, if I knew were she was." Replied the navy pilot.

"Give her a shout on the radio," suggested Taff.

They tried, but got no response.

As soon as they landed, Broadswords captain went some way to solving the mystery of Antrim's disappearance.

"She has been detached on some hush - hush assignment and is under strict radio silence."

"This is fast turning into one of the biggest cock-ups of all time," observed Paul.

"I presume you two are something with Antrim's temporary detached status, I can guess the rest so I won't even ask." said the Captain.

"We'd better speak to the Kremlin Paul. Something's gone well adrift, I should think they'll order an 'abort'," said Taff.

"May we use your ship to shore radio Sir." Paul asked the Captain.

"Of course my boy, this way," he responded leading the two soldiers towards the radio room. "She's all yours Number one."

Paul talked not to his Boss, who had been called away to a conference, but to his 2 I.C.

"It's up to you Paul, you're on the spot."

"Cheers Mike, you're a real pal, wrong plane, wrong ship, Paddies' chopper, someone doesn't want us to get to where we're going"

"Can you still get there on time Paul?" asked the Major.

"Barring further fuck ups just about." Paul replied, "I suppose it has to be tonight?"

"I'm afraid it does, it's strictly a one off chance."

"O.K we'll give it a spin Mike, but no promises."

"Fair enough, abort at any time you feel compromised."

"Cheers Mike, out."

Broadswords lynx dropped them off barely three miles from their target, as it was head wind there was little chance of the sound carrying. There had been one alarm on the run in, three loud thumps shook the helicopter as it approached the coast.

"What the hell was that?" asked Taff.

"Bird strikes, starlings I think." replied the pilot sounding unconcerned.

"Thank fuck they weren't swans!"

After taking a quick 'nav sat' position check from the helicopters instruments the two soldiers melted away into the soft Irish night.

Thanks to the helpful pilot they were only an hour or so late arriving at the little inn. Paul quickly scanned the area through his powerful night sight and found a vantage point with a clear view of the door.

"Someone else is interested in this place Taff, see 'em up on the little ridge, directly above the place we were told to set up our gear."

"Got them, any ideas?"

"Other than they're not there for our benefit. Tell you what they can be the subjects of our first holiday snaps. You never know, if this new gear is as good as it's cracked up to be they might be identifiable in the pictures."

He quickly set up the two cameras and settled down to watch, the position he had chosen was at the base of a stout post. Taff was sorting out the rest of their gear, ready for a quick getaway should it become necessary. Paul's muttered curse carried through the sensitive mike to Taffs' earpiece.

"What's up mate?"

"Even the local insects are against us now."

"All this fuss over a couple of mozzies!" chuckled Taff.

"Mozzies my arse, they were soddin great black ants!" replied Paul rubbing the back of his hand. He had hardly settled into his new position when a car pulled into the car park.

Taff had now completed his sorting out, while Paul filmed the new arrivals, Taff took the still photographs, not only of the men but the car. The man out of the front passenger seat walked towards the little inn carrying a brief case, it was obviously heavy. He was escorted by one of the men out of the rear seats, the other passenger stayed beside the car, nervously looking round as though on watch. He was carrying a weapon Paul could not identify but it looked similar to an American M1.

"I don't know about you Taff, but I don't like the look of this, matey is far too nervous for my liking."

"Look up someone's coming out."

Two armed men emerged from the inn followed by Sean McStephoin, carrying a case, probably the one taken in earlier.

110

Then to the soldiers' consternation there was a burst of gunfire; both of the armed men with McStephoin fell dead. Then he casually retrieved the dead men's guns and walked to one of the waiting cars. There was more gunfire, this time from inside the little inn, two more men emerged, one ran to the car which had recently arrived, the other, also carrying a case ran to the car McStephoin was getting into. In his haste, the case caught the car door and fell open, spilling several packets of something onto the gravel. Clearly one of the packets split, there was much frantic scrabbling around before the car sped off into the night, followed by the other car.

"What the fuck was it all about?" Taff asked.

"Damned if I know mate, best guess a drug deal which went wrong. The audio might tell us."

Taff rewound the tape a little bit then pushed 'play' and waited.

"Not a fucking cheep mate, must have got some water in the works. It says it's recording but it ain't."

"Oh great, let's just hope the cameras are working."

"They'd better be, what a fuck up."

Paul scanned the area, "Our friends have gone, seems like they legged it when the shooting started."

"While you were fannying around just now I heard another car start up further down the road, probably them off the ridge."

"I've just had a thought Taff, why don't I nip down and grab a hand full of that stuff they dropped. At least we'll know what it was which cost the lives of those two."

"You're mad! Go on then look sharp, it's time we weren't here."

"Give me a shout if you see anything coming."

Ten minutes later they were packed up and headed for the border. Just as they were leaving their O.P. the radio crackled. Taff took the message, "Abort, 'red, red' from the 'Kremlin'."

"Who's on the Sat link Taff?"

"Mike, want a word."

"Damn right!"

"Just get out Paul, fast as you can, use your second option route. The operation has, I think been compromised. Do not, repeat do not respond, out."

Three days later the two weary soldiers sat down five yards from a permanently manned O.P., half a mile on the Republic side of the boarder. It was concealed in a dense clump of brambles overlooking the main road from Crossmaglen into the republic.

"You awake B.J.?" Paul asked softly.

"I am, along with everyone else for miles, noisy bugger."

"Thank you for those few kind words, mate!"

"You're welcome, you two took your time, trouble?"

"Sort of!"

"There's a lot of Gardi and army about, follow this hedge to the end of the field turn left. The terrible two will meet you where the stream comes through the hedge. Get your skates on mate you might make it back before dawn."

"Cheers B.J., happy watching."

By tea time Paul and Taff were back at their base, having been flown back by helicopter. Later in the evening the two soldiers, now cleaned up and fed but desperately tired, were ushered into the C.O.'s office by Mike the 2I.C.

"Evening Boss."

"Good evening Paul, Taff," he gestured to the two chairs facing his desk. Paul detected anger in the steely grey eyes of the Lieutenant Colonel; he hoped he wasn't going to be the target for the wrath which lurked.

"Right, what happened?"

"I can't make much sense of it all Boss. It seemed like a hell of a lot of trouble for a few pictures. Mind you the bloke who arrived with one of the cases; the one which dropped what I presumed to have been heroin, looked bloody familiar."

"You know him?" asked the boss

"I think so."

"You think so, well you bloody well should know!"

"From which I can conclude it really was the civil servant from Mildenhall."

"So you did recognise him?"

"All I said was he looked familiar, I wasn't certain. It's a lot easier sitting here looking at the pictures than through a low light view finder Boss."

"You are aware of the significance of what you filmed?"

"Not really boss, other than the fact the entire op was a complete fuck up from the start."

"I know all about the lynx, it was sabotage, the lubricant in the bearing had been contaminated with valve grinding paste. I also know about the change of plan and the 'elint' plane and the subsequent abortions."

"We did our best Boss," said Paul.

"You are the most stubborn, persistent individual in the regiment. On this occasion, I am eternally grateful."

"Just doing our job Boss."

"If you stay with the regiment until you're pensioned out because of old age you will never go on a more important mission."

"It's a bit strong Boss, all we did was take a few pictures. Granted, they show a rather confusing scene."

"You forgot the other evidence, you brought back, nice touch being filmed collecting it."

"I still fail to see what is so earth shattering Boss, alright, we always took it for granted something was wrong in Whitehall. All those pictures prove is someone from those unhallowed halls met McStephoin during a drug deal which went tits up."

The C.O. shook his head, "We've identified everyone in those shots We also know the Granada they used had false plates, I know exactly where the real one was, I was supposed to be their alibi if things went wrong. A special branch commander, at a conference I had to attend, drove the real one. But you got through, despite all the attempts to stop you arriving in time to witness the meeting, you brought back the final pieces of the jigsaw which will get them out of our hair for good. They spend most of their time trying to discredit the regiment, not any more, now we can get on with our job without looking over our shoulder all the time."

"Is it possible McStephoin is an agent?"

"Amazing as it sounds it had been considered, he is one hundred percent bad." said Mike.

"Pity I didn't get a real chance to nail him in that case, there were too many people about. Sorry Boss but I simply didn't see a chance which met the conditions."

"From what I've seen, you made the correct decision Paul."

"Well I suppose it is reassuring, but what about the abort. As usual it was too late to have stopped us."

"It was issued when we found out about the sabotage on the lynx and exactly who ordered you to use the 'elint' Herc. There was in our opinion, every chance of an ambush."

"There was boss, look at the pictures again, you'll see they are taken from a different angle than they should have been."

"What do you mean?"

"I took my 'scope as well boss, there were four armed men covering the outcrop specified as our O.P."

"Words fail me!"

"Try good night, see you tomorrow afternoon sergeant," replied Paul, "I am absolutely knackered Boss."

"O.K. but before you go, pity about the audio gear, which was also fixed before you left, very cleverly done. It would work for a few seconds then stop recording."

"So it would check out alright then be useless when used for real. Let me guess, borrowed from Whitehall?"

"He's a fast learner Mike." said the C.O. "Go on, bugger off to your beds before you go to sleep on my chairs. Bloody well done."

"Thanks Boss G'night."

"See you tomorrow, you've got some reports to finish."

"Thanks Boss."

CHAPTER 11

The day after Whitehall received their reports on operation 'English Rose' two car loads of 'Whitehall warriors turned up in Hereford, typically one lot got lost as there were no signs up for the barracks. After convincing the local police of their identity they were escorted to the gates.

The occupants of the first car to arrive were only interested in how Paul's squad had succeeded in making the new wonder weapon work, when their own operatives had failed.

A demonstration was arranged on the close quarters range and the regiments' version of 'sten alley'. They were very impressed when all four members returned 100% scores. One of the senior civil servants turned to the C.O., who he obviously knew well. "Where have you been hiding this squad Peter, I was told they were new lads."

"They are new, they are the newest members of the regiment Alec."

"Well I am very impressed, very impressed indeed, I look forward to them working with us again. We must be off I'm afraid, thank you for the demonstration sergeant, and I look forward to reading a copy of your report on the new weapon. Goodbye and the very best of luck in the future."

"Fuck me gently, if I hadn't been here I wouldn't have believed it, some Whitehall staff are actually on our side!" muttered Paul.

"Do you want the good news Paul?" asked the Captain in charge of the debriefing.

"Go on skip, we've got another week of debrief?"

"No, it's almost done. Two more visitors have arrived, I think you know them."

"Oh no" groaned Paul "Not the pair of pin striped pricks from Mildenhall?"

"The same, you will no doubt be amused to hear they were escorted here by the local plod, having got lost."

"Well this place is west of Oxford skipper."

"Come on, they're waiting over at the Kremlin."

"Bollocks to them, I ain't hurrying, let 'em wait."

"I don't think it will help very much Paul," observed the Captain.

"With any luck he'll piss them off so much they'll be glad to go."

"Don't you encourage him Taff."

115

"Have you ever seen him when he's really pissed off Skipper, trust me it is not a pretty sight?"

"I didn't know he'd got a temper, he won't do anything daft will he?" asked the now worried Captain.

"I doubt it," replied Taff, "but those Whitehall wankers are in for a hell of a shock if they think they can bully Paul. He's more than a little upset with those two as it is."

"I think I'd better let the boss know, the shit is likely to hit the fan if what you said is true."

"They've got it coming skip, why cramp Paul's style?"

"You're as bad as he is."

"With those bastards; any day."

Paul didn't rush, he took his time, to the extent he made himself a mug of coffee. There was even a little extra unplanned delay, Paul was concentrating his thoughts on what he intended to do to the very uncivil servants, to such a degree he forgot his folder containing various photographs and papers he needed for the interview. Eventually he ambled into the room where the two men waited for him with growing impatience.

"About time too sergeant, this is the second time you have kept us waiting. Your total lack of respect is appalling and has been noted."

"Good."

"I demand you show us respect."

"Respect is something you have to earn, if you don't show respect, how can you expect to be respected?"

"You are in a lot of trouble sergeant, I demand an explanation as to why you disobeyed your very specific orders. Had you obeyed them things might have turned out better."

"Better for who? Those bastards knew we were coming, we sure as hell didn't tell them, so the choice is fairly limited."

"What are you insinuating?"

"You work it out, you're supposed to be the intelligence service."

"I'm warning you sergeant, do not push your luck!"

"Or what? You ordered my lot to prevent one of your operatives talking to some pretty nasty individuals."

"You certainly did, he was hit by thirty two rounds, I suspect out of your weapons."

"Prove it."

"You know we can't," one of the civil servants snapped back. "You made sure of it, I don't know where you got your ammunition from, the fragments cannot be reassembled."

"Sounds good stuff, can you get us some?" asked Paul.

"Your flippancy appals me sergeant. You disobeyed your clear orders as to how this operation was to be carried out."

"As far as I am concerned, I take orders from the officers of this regiment. I do not take orders from nameless individuals who refuse to identify themselves. You may well be senior pen pushers in an obscure office in Whitehall; it does not give you the right to give soldiers orders. You make requests, even tell us what needs doing, but you do not tell us how to do it, give us the parameters within which we must operate, then let us sort it out."

We were nearly twelve hours ahead of your original so called plan, yet we were still too late to save your man. In fact we were even further ahead than we would have been had we have waited for your Chinook; have a bit of trouble with fuel fittings did we? As it is we are all back, nothing to indicate who called, so you see no one could have done more. I'd say the operation was as successful as it could have been."

"It's only your opinion sergeant, I am very unhappy about the outcome, there are likely to be some serious ramifications."

"Well if you aren't happy, all I can say is next time one of your lot gets in the shit you'd better go and get them yourself." Paul leaned back and lit a cigarette, knowing full well this would aggravate the civil servants.

"Your target was the woman, what happened to the woman?"

"What woman, I didn't see anything even remotely shagable, not even by Taff's standards. I'll grant you the 'English Rose' tag someone put on the operation suggested a female target, but as I recall no-one mentioned anything about any woman to me, either verbally or in your so called plan."

"Something is very wrong about this sergeant."

"There certainly is, your informant must have got it wrong, because we certainly hit the right place."

"There are a great many questions you must answer for us sergeant, and you will answer them, all this fencing around will stop, right now. Do I make myself clear?"

"Perfectly, but before you start asking questions, I've got a couple of my own," interrupted Paul. "Like who is in charge of your department, who calls the shots?"

"I do," replied the elder of the two civil servants, "and I demand you call me sir!"

Paul ignored the demand, he simply carried on as though the man hadn't spoken. "Your 'department' is known as the south west Asian desk!"

"What's the point of this sergeant, we're here to interview you, not the other way round."

"Well seeing as this entire affair has been one gigantic abortion from start to finish I think we're all entitled to some answers, don't you?"

"Answers to our questions, not yours!"

"Well I see it a bit differently. Now, unless I miss my guess you have already cost the lives of two members of this regiment. A couple of months or so ago your department seconded a section from here to mount a rescue attempt, supposedly to free the same agent we were sent to rescue. Granted it wasn't you personally sent them, you were I believe stranded on a ferry at the time." Although he didn't say it he wanted to add 'I hope it was rough'.

"How could you possibly know about the operation?"

"Easy, I found their bodies, or what was left of them. They drove straight into an ambush, someone told the bastards our lads were on the way, they were set up."

"What were you doing out there, you were only badged a short time before?"

"Again there is a simple answer. My squad was the only one available for the collection job you lot requested when your agent apparently escaped."

"So you were responsible for that mess as well."

"I suppose it was a bit of a mess if you happened to be one of the warlords' lackeys."

"It was a total failure on your part sergeant. The incident set back relations with China to Korean war levels."

"Oh I don't know, we rescued two members of the regiment, retrieved the bodies of the other two, malleted the shower of shit knocking seven bells out of a U.N. team and returned home intact. I'd call that a result. As far as relations with the Chinese are concerned, the damage was done by so called diplomats, more interested in their own self esteem than facts."

"So you are an expert in diplomacy now," sneered the junior of the two men.

"Mercifully no, but there wasn't a problem with the Chinese until you lot stuck your oar in. They were quite happy to accept the fact it was a simple case of a renegade commander in a remote out post on the take. Then you lot come along and upset everything. What on earth does this missing agent know, is it so important it's worth risking world war three over?"

"But you didn't bring the agent back."

"We spent an extra day at the rendezvous, no one showed."

"You should have waited longer."

"Why, we now know the agent was recaptured while we were waiting. At least it's what we've been told."

"Who told you?" asked one civil servant. "I demand to know."

"Demand all you like, it won't help, I'm only a sergeant, nobody ever tells me the source of such information. Although I believe it came from Whitehall."

"We still want an explanation for your total disregard of explicit orders on your last mission."

"Again, before I answer yours, you will have to answer mine. Specifically how did the bastards know we were coming? More to the point; how the merry hell did the evil bastard in charge know an 'abort' had been ordered."

"Someone here must have talked, I'm sure this camp isn't leak proof."

"I'm sure it's not, but the point is, the only people who knew exactly where we were going, were on the bloody plane we dropped in from."

"Anyway; if you received the 'abort' code why did you continue with the mission? That's another order you disobeyed."

"As for complying with your order to abort the mission; it would have been a might difficult. Once you're out of a plane, on the end of a parachute it is, as far as I'm aware, fucking impossible to get back in!"

"So you were actually committed before you were recalled. As to your other point; I'm sure it wasn't the case sergeant, someone else knew your target, they must have."

"No chance; the tanker crew didn't know, neither did the decoy squad. The crew of the recon plane thought we were only planning a possible escape route from the general area, they were totally unaware of the operation."

"What are you insinuating, we warned the Chinese you were on your way."

"Who said anything about Chinese being involved in this latest raid? According to your plan, it was to free your agent from a local warlord."

He rummaged through the file he had almost forgotten to bring with him. "Here we are," said Paul as he found the sheet of paper he was looking for. "This is the document you gave me at Milldenhall. It states; and I quote. 'You will enter the building, at', then it gives the map reference, 'and secure the release of the agent with the call sign English Rose. If rescue proves impossible you are to ensure the agent does not pass on any information whatsoever, to the warlord who is holding the agent captive'.

No mention of Chinese or of the fact the agent was supposed to be female; as I said before the 'English Rose' code name suggested a woman but so would Pansy or Petal." To Paul's mild annoyance this insult passed unnoticed. "Then there is your insistence we use the weapons you provided. You knew they would jam after two or three rounds, especially with the case-less stuff.."

"The M.P.9 is a fine weapon sergeant. Your safe return is testament to the effectiveness of your weapons."

"The point is the ones you had were fucking useless, they were going to be sent back, I've seen the reports."

"You modified yours successfully, we changed ours in a similar fashion." Replied a now sweating civil servant. "We've seen the reports on yours."

"O.K. then who sent the abort signal?"

"It's highly classified, not for mere sergeants."

"He's losing it Boss," said the Captain in the next room listening through the head phones attached to the tape recorders.

"You see it hasn't helped me understand one very vital point."

"What's that sergeant," sneered the sweating civil servant.

"Just how the bloody hell did Wan Fat Tit, what ever his name was, know we had been recalled!"

"They must have heard your radio traffic."

"Oh right, so now every Tom, Dick and tuppenny halfpenny drug dealer can read our encoded U.H.F burst transmissions, even if they are outside the signals footprint."

"I don't understand your point sergeant."

"You might at least do us the courtesy of being familiar with our systems if you're going to lie about them."

"I resent your implication sergeant."

"And I resent being used by some bloody slime ball with a hyphenated name, to save his arse at the expense of my neck."

"If you are insinuating what I think you are, then you are in serious trouble."

"You said it before, the other thing I need to know is why a Chinese destroyer, in the Indian Ocean, should test fire two anti aircraft missiles, which happened to explode precisely where our choppers would have been had we not changed course."

"The obvious reason is they didn't know you were there."

"Yes they did, they illuminated us with both search and attack radar, luckily our pilots were good enough to avoid them. But again you have missed the vital point."

"What vital point?"

"Who told the Chinese to look out for a pair of Lynx helicopters, according to the abortion you called a plan, we would have used a Chinook. The only way anyone, outside of those directly involved could have known was if they were listening to our signals.

Now; we know exactly when the Chinese destroyer left the exercise it was taking part in and passed through the Singapore channel, then headed up the west coast of Malaya, flat out!"

"All very interesting Sergeant, but what is the point of all this?"

"The point is the timing, the ship headed for a position to intercept us within twenty minutes of our signal, which moved the navy ships to a position to refuel our choppers."

"Then clearly your signals are insecure."

"I agree with you, the question is who is reading them? Not the Chinese, I doubt they even know the particular system exists!"

"You are accusing us of passing signals and information to the Chinese! It is outrageous!"

"Someone is, every part of those operations who used radios, in any form, were compromised. The only parts of the operation which were not known, were the alternative arrangements we made. None

121

of these were compromised, it therefore follows it was some nosey sod rather than a leak from within, surely even you can work it out?"

"This is getting us nowhere," said the elder civil servant; "I will have words with your Commander. I will ensure your career is finished."

"Fair enough, oh, by the way, why did you bother to put the tracker on our mini bus at Brize? Don't bother, I think I know the answer, seeing as how you had to be escorted here by the local plod. Get lost did we?"

"I have no idea what you're talking about sergeant."

"I don't suppose you have. Equally; you could have seen our reports on the M.P.9s."

"I've seen them," insisted the junior civil servant.

"Utterly impossible mate."

"How can you be so certain sergeant?" asked the senior man.

"Easy; I haven't had chance to write them yet, thanks to all this poncing around after you pair of pillocks."

"Are you insinuating we are telling you lies?"

"It's just for intelligence officers you seem to be incredibly ignorant. Next you'll be telling me you don't know anything about the drug deal with Sean McStephoin three days ago in a little pub in southern Ireland."

"How could I possibly know anything about a heroin deal in the Irish Republic."

"Who said it was heroin, I didn't."

"I'm warning you sergeant."

"Or else what, you're the ones who are finished mate, I can prove you were at the drug deal with dear Sean, I've got it on film. It might have been at night but it wasn't dark enough to stop our cameras. I can also prove it was heroin, I brought a sample back from the bag which split when the case fell open, just before you got back into the car."

"You have no idea what you're getting into sergeant," the older man was showing the first signs of being rattled, "You'll need a lot more than that."

"There's loads more, finger prints on the tracker we took of the minibus."

"It was nothing to do with us."

"Bollocks, I've seen the pictures of both of you sitting in a white Astra which had been following us along with a red Escort, we have

122

identified all the other occupants, one of them is a known Provo terrorist and a close acquaintance of our friend Sean."

"Have you anymore supposed evidence of our crimes Sergeant?"

"Loads more, logs of signals from G.C.H.Q. not to mention film of you two shooting McStephoin's body guards, but the best bit, from my point of view is lying on the table next door."

"This room is bugged?"

"Of course it is, idiot!"

"You mean to tell me a trap was set for us and they allowed a new boy like you to act out this charade. It's unbelievable."

"So is your arrogance, it was your undoing, along with the lies."

"What lies? You'll have to prove we lied."

"This is all on tape, as well as video, the best bit, like I said is next door .You claimed to have modified the weapons we were supposed to have used on the abortive attempt to rescue your agent. I can prove they are useless, and you therefore knowingly ordered British servicemen into a situation they were unlikely to survive. You both knew the weapons would not work, we have copies of your departmental report, both of you signed it. We also have the weapons, our decoy team brought them back, the serial numbers match those in your report, they are totally bloody useless, with no modifications visible. Put simply, we were sent to fail and you did everything in your power to ensure the failure."

"So what are you going to charge us with, signing a report without reading it. You'll get laughed out of court."

"You never cease to amaze me, the copies of the report we have are the originals, they contain hand written alterations even I can see are in the same hand as the signatures."

"So I suppose you're feeling pretty pleased with yourself, it's a clear case of entrapment, none of it will stand up in court."

"Who said anything about courts, all we want to know is who's pulling your strings?"

"Do not be so absurd!"

"Oh come on! there is no way on this earth a couple of thick, self opinionated pillocks like you could have set up something as elaborate as this."

"I am not saying another word until my lawyer gets here."

"Now you are taking the piss, get in here boss, I'm drowning in slime."

A moment or so later the door opened and in came a procession of senior officers; the lowest in rank was the C.O. of Paul's regiment. They were accompanied by the directors of both M.I.5 and 6 as well as four other elderly men who could have been almost anything!"

"Bloody hell boss," exclaimed Paul. "I thought there was only you and my skipper listening in. Still I understand why, I'd have died of bloody fright if I'd have known."

"Exactly, you did well my boy," said one of the anonymous grey men, "very well indeed. He's a good lad Peter look after him."

"Go get your dinner Paul, I've got a nice job for you this afternoon."

"Like what Boss?"

"Delivering two packages to an address in the home counties, you've earned a little perk."

"Cheers Boss."

"By the way Sergeant," asked one of the grey men, "just what did happen to the girl?"

"What girl Sir?"

"The 'English Rose' of course, you can tell us where you've hidden her, she'll be perfectly safe now we've caught these two treacherous devils."

"I say again Sir, what girl?"

"You can trust us Sergeant, just how did you spirit her back home? It would make a good novel, as you appear to have outsmarted the entire secret service."

"As of this moment in time I have no idea where she is, or if she's even alive, I don't even know her name. As far as I know she might have escaped from whoever is 'looking after' her and is lost in the forest. I can't tell you what I don't know Sir."

"She is a very important agent sergeant."

" The only agent we brought back was the dead one. That's it Sir; as to this girl everyone keeps on about, who knows?"

The grey man fixed Paul with an enquiring look which would have frozen hell itself. Paul merely shrugged.

"Like I said Sir I can't tell you what I don't know."

"Damn it Peter you train your lads well," he said to the C.O.

"Thank you Sir James."

"O.K. if I get my dinner now Boss."

"Go on."

"Thank you sir."

124

In the afternoon, just after lunch a slightly battered plain white van left the main gates of the camp for the long drive to the government rest home in the home counties.

Paul and Taff were in the cab, both in civvies but armed, just in case. In the back, out of sight were the two disgraced civil servants each with a combat clad soldier on either side.

Paul followed the big old chauffeur driven rover, his boss was in the front passenger seat, two of the 'grey men' were in the back.

The other vehicle in the little convoy was a grey Granada with four more members of the regiment, 'just in case' as the boss had put it.

"This would have been quicker if they had simply given us directions," moaned Paul as they trundled gently east on the A40. "This is getting on my bloody tits, call them up Taff and tell them it's the number of the bloody road not the speed limit!"

"You do it, I ain't upsetting anyone in the motor."

One of the soldiers in the back called through to Paul, "This thing has got five gears Paul!"

"I know, I can hardly stay in fourth, behind this bloody rover."

"It's all the brass in the car who are slowing it down Paul."

"You could well be right mate."

An hour later they were only just past Gloucester. As they passed under the M5 Paul picked up his hand set, "Do you want me to lead until we get to Hemel Hemstead Boss?"

"If you like, I presume you know the way."

"I certainly do."

"O.K. go for it," the boss chuckled to himself, he too was a bit surprised at the slow pace of the little convoy.

Paul knocked the van down into third gear and cruised past the car, at least it gave him a good run at Bird Lip hill, leading up to the round about where the road from Cirencester joined. Apart from the short stretch of the 'rat run' south of Cheltenham which had a speed limit he maintained a steady 60mph.

"Your boy doesn't like hanging about does he?" Observed one of the 'grey men' in the rover.

"The van is turbo charged, he'll be doing seventy on the motor ways," replied Paul's boss.

As Paul approached the roundabout at the end of the M10 he slowed down and waved the Rover past. They almost lost the escorting Granada on the roundabout as a lot of traffic was heading north onto the M10. To the annoyance of one of the men in the back of the Rover, Paul had slowed down to wait for the escort car, order was soon restored however and the little convoy continued into the lanes of rural Hertfordshire.

The lane they were in was virtually single track, it then split into two. The left hand fork had a sign with M.R.S. Fox Covert on it, the right hand track was unmarked, it was little used, to the extent there was grass growing between the wheel tracks.

This track ended at some imposing gates manned by two armed M.O.D Policemen. After checking the I.D.s of the occupants of the Rover and a brief conversation, the convoy was admitted. Paul stopped directly outside the doors of a forbidding red brick building; the prisoners were whisked inside with the briefest of formalities.

Paul's boss wandered over, "Are you O.K. for the trip back?"

"Sure boss."

"Good, Taff, would you mind riding in the back please, so I can talk to Paul on the way home."

"Sure Boss, are you sure your nerves are good enough to stick his driving?"

"Taff," replied the C.O. "In the back! But thanks for the concern."

"Everybody ready?" Paul asked.

He hadn't even reached the fork in the little lane when a car came screaming round one of the bends towards them; quite how a serious collision was avoided Paul never knew. The car lost its driver side mirror on the side of the van before sliding out of control into the Granada following Paul.

"Who the hell is the fucking idiot?" exclaimed Paul as he leapt out of the van. Amazingly no one was hurt although both cars were wrecked, two more cars slid to a halt blocking the lane To the astonishment of the soldiers, one of the occupants identified himself as a Commander in the Special Branch and announced they were all under arrest for kidnapping.

Paul sat down on the bank and burst out laughing, "Who the hell said so Sir?" he asked.

"We are armed, do not resist," ordered the Commander.

"So are we Sir and intend to remain so. I don't know who fed you such a load of bollocks about kidnapping, but I strongly suggest you go and arrest the lame brain for conspiracy."

"Exactly what are you doing here?"

"All we've done is ensure the safe and timely arrival of a couple of big time drug dealers to a government rest home for the deranged."

Paul's boss climbed out of the driver's door after struggling unsuccessfully to get out of the passenger side, which was tight against the bank.

"What are you doing here Sir?" asked the Commander, who clearly knew Paul's C.O.

"Trying to ensure there weren't any cock ups like this." Replied the angry Colonel. "Take the advice of my sergeant, arrest the idiot who told you to stop us and have him thrown into the bloody rubbish bin where we've just delivered a load of trash."

"What about the cars?" asked the Commander.

"You wrecked them, you sort it out," snapped the C.O. "Now if you would be kind enough to un-block the lane we'll be on our way." He signalled the men in the wrecked car to join him. "Jump in lads there should be plenty of room."

Everyone was relieved when the van stopped at the main gates of their camp.

"And so ends another exciting adventure in the lives of our intrepid heroes" commented one of the troopers as he emerged from the van.

"We even lived to tell the tale," added another.

"Are you alright Boss, it must have been terrifying up front, I mean you could see everything."

"You take the piss out of my driving again and you'll walk next time. At least I missed the prat in the Granada."

"All right you lot," said the C.O. "bugger off and get your tea. I will meet you in the canteen in one hour."

CHAPTER 12

As soon as all the reports were completed, Paul and the rest of his squad left to complete their interrupted leave.

On their return they resumed the detailed training which should prepare them for whatever the future might hold. All this training however, was totally irrelevant to Paul's next assignment.

The summons to the boss's office wasn't a surprise. The woman they had rescued was now well enough to leave hospital and be de-briefed. However, to the annoyance of the designated officers she steadfastly refused to speak to anyone other than "Sergeant Paul."

"Aw c'mon Boss, how the hell can I de-brief her when I haven't got a clue what she is? Frankly I don't think I want to, I don't even know her name!"

"As far as I can discover neither does anyone else, so you'll be starting from the same position as everyone else Paul."

"Why me?"

"Because she asked for you. I know obeying orders is not one of your strong points, but this is one you will obey and the paper work, which I know you hate, will have every I dotted and T crossed, it will be perfect, is it quite clear?"

"Yes Boss" Paul replied sheepishly "Crystal bloody clear!"

"Good, this has got to be better than perfect."

"You've made your point Boss, I'll do my best."

"It's what I'm worried about!"

"Thanks a lot, I know my paper work is lousy but I really will try."

"I know, look," the C.O. paused, " I'll be here to help in anyway I can, alright?"

"I know you will Sir," replied Paul "but I'd still rather you could find some evil bastard for us to sort out!"

The Colonel shot his newest sergeant an icy glare

"Alright Boss, I'm on my way."

Just after dinner, an anonymous silver grey Granada swept into the main gates at Bradbury lines. The frail looking woman in the back was quickly taken into the 'Kremlin'. To Paul's considerable alarm she showed more than the expected 'pleasure', at being reunited with her rescuer.

It quickly became the talk of the camp, she stuck to Paul like glue.

The first little session was bit awkward to say the least.

"Look, this is silly, I don't even know your name, I've got to call you something!?"

"It's something you don't need to know," she replied.

"I need to know a hell of a lot more than your name."

"Why? I'm told you're going to arrange a new I.D. for me, use the new name, it'll help me to get used to it."

"Good idea, except for one small point, we haven't even started to think about a new name, much less anything else!"

"Well, you'd better think of one hadn't you?"

"I'm damned if I can figure you out, you refused to speak to anyone else and asked for me. Now you're playing hard ball with me!"

"I'm sorry, I'm not used to telling anyone anything about me, the job I suppose, the constant fear of discovery. It is very difficult to trust anyone at all after what happened!"

"But you trust me?"

"I think so," she hesitated, "You broke all the rules to get me out and to keep me safe when you succeeded. You've obviously worked out there's a severe problem at this end for me, to have ended up as I did, I have got to trust you, it was your thanks to your squad I'm out. You've got to be alright, but it's difficult."

"'S'pose it must be. The code name was the English Rose. I was going to suggest calling you Rose English, but it somehow lacks, how can I put it, class I suppose is the word I was looking for!"

The young woman managed a weak little laugh, Paul also noticed a distinct glint in the still bruised eyes.

"Try Roana English."

She laughed again, "Yes, I like it."

"Well that's the first problem solved!" said Paul, "At least I can put a name on the paper, I have got to write down absolutely everything, I can't remember my boss saying 'or else' but the consequences of not doing as I'm told this time don't bear thinking about. Believe it or not I haven't got a bloody clue on how to conduct a de-brief like this without turning it into an inquisition." He paused, "on top of which, between us we've got to build you a new life with a provable past!"

"You'll do it."

"No I won't," Paul interrupted the woman, "we will."

"O.K Sergeant, we will."

129

"Good, now we need to work out how, 'cause I ain't got a bloody clue."

"You expect me to believe it?" she chuckled.

"I asked for it!"

"You did!"

"Look, let's use this first session to work out what we want to achieve. If we can define clear objectives then we might just do a bit of good."

"This should be interesting."

"Shouldn't it just, I suppose our ultimate aim should be to identify and remove those with, what shall we call it, dubious loyalties? We've managed to identify those two arseholes who sent my lot to get you; however proving anything worthwhile against them is another matter. You know they'd set things up so we would fail in our rescue attempt."

"Hence your boss insisting on you obeying orders. It's a miracle you managed to identify any of them."

"At least we must try to ensure others, like yourself, are not betrayed, then our lads won't be put at risk having to operate against a forewarned enemy."

"I think you're shooting at stars sergeant," she said sadly.

"Well I agree with you, but we ought to be able to nail some more of those evil bastards. Also by collating all you know and passing it on to the right people we should be able to do some damage to the drug barons."

"There's a problem with that as well, who are the right people?" she asked.

"Like I said this ain't going to be easy, but we must achieve something positive, if only so you didn't suffer in vain. No one should be subjected to what you had to endure. We've got to find a way to make these bastards pay!"

"What are you going to do, attack Whitehall with your fancy new guns?" She laughed again. "I have this vision of you and your men rushing along corridors kicking in doors and shooting half the people in most of the offices."

"Now there's a thought!" Paul replied with a grin, "wasn't quite what I had in mind, look I've got to go, I'll be back later on, give it a bit of thought. We're going to have to get things in some sort of order. I know you're not happy about telling anyone about yourself, if we're going to be successful in setting up a new identity for you, we're going to have to know a great deal about your old one."

The door opened and two men in civilian clothes came in, the woman looked uneasy.

"It's O.K they're a couple of our medics, one of them is the guy who kept you alive until we could get some proper help; they'll look after you and sort out your quarters and anything else you need. I'll see you at about five. Relax you're safe here; no one, but no one will hurt you again! See you later."

For the next six weeks much of the planned training program intended to continue Paul's progress was kicked into touch. Although the lady now known as Roana passed on a veritable mountain of information about the massive anti drugs operation against the warlords of the 'Golden Triangle' she steadfastly refused to disclose anything of significance about her personal life.

One thing which did emerge in their conversations, shook Paul to his boots when the implication of what Roana had said sunk in.

It soon emerged she had been held by the rebel Chinese army unit and their warlord allies, for much longer than he had supposed. It was during this time the warlords began to inject her with heroine; this was just the first step to try to break her, so she would betray the other agents in her network. It transpired she had been subjected to several months of ill treatment, abuse and outright torture.

"Why the merry hell did they leave it so long before trying to rescue you?"

"They didn't, apparently a team from your regiment were sent to get me within twenty four hours of my capture."

"It's the first I heard of it," replied Paul.

"Apparently their operation was compromised and they were ambushed by the Chinese and killed!"

"When was this?"

"About three months before you turned up, it was much further north in a semi desert area, the extreme north east of Burma, maybe just into China."

"Oh shit!" muttered Paul, "we lost one of our skippers and a trooper there about the same time, my team brought what was left of them back, the other two were with us on the operation when we got you out!"

"They were your friends?"

"Of course, this mob's too small for them not to have been."

"I'm so sorry."

"Weren't your fault Ro. Goes with the territory." Paul thought back to the ill-fated sortie of his squad to the barren valley. "How'd you know about it?"

"The lot who were guarding me told me, they even showed me a blood stained beret to back up their story. I managed to convince myself it was all bluff to try to break me."

"For once, it was all too true, but it begs the question how did the Chinks know the team was on the way. Whitehall again?"

"Almost certainly, the ones holding me certainly knew you were on your way. They'd assembled an elite team to deal with you but you were early."

"I had actually figured that much out, now I know why the boss went along with my revised schedule so readily. We'll go into more detail later. I'm interested in what happened around the time of the first failed attempt to get you home."

"A couple of days after your friends were killed, my captors moved me to a remote mountain hut. I think the guards were Afghan mercenaries. They were some of the cruellest men I've ever met, they were truly evil. They seemed to enjoy humiliating me and making me scream just for fun."

"You'll have to introduce them to me and my mates, sounds as though they could do with a few lessons in manners!"

"Happily it's not possible, they're dead," replied Roana, "one made a mistake. I was due to be 'collected' by the Chinese soon after, so I used their radio, I think the message got through, a pick up point was arranged, the problem was this point was thirty miles further away than I thought. I was a day late by the time I reached the valley, the pile of rocks in the middle of a sea of sand was visible in the distance when the Chinese caught me.

Because I'd stolen some of the dead Afghans clothes and one of their turbans, the Chinese were unsure if it was me or a local goat herd, unfortunately I dropped the gun and they were able to jump on me." She seemed to notice Paul's expression had changed and asked "What's wrong Paul?"

"I watched through my 'scope, we were in the rock pile waiting for you. We'd been watching you for half an hour before the Chinks appeared! I know we were too far away to stop it but it doesn't make me feel any better."

132

"Oh my god, you'd waited just in case, even though you knew your friends had died in the first attempt."

"We waited, but then we didn't know what the other section had been doing in the same area." He paused, "The other thing we didn't know was the identity of the agent we were to pick up. We spent five nights there before we pulled out, just in time as it turned out."

"Why what happened?"

We picked up what was left of Cy and Terry and got back to the U.N camp just in time to clobber a load of Chinks who were attacking the base.

Not long after we'd sorted them out, their mates must have realised something had gone wrong and started shelling the shit out of the camp. I got pissed off with dodging 155mm bricks so I grabbed my lot and shot the shit out of the Chinese fire base, inadvertently freeing the two captured lads from Cy's squad in the process!"

"I think it's the place they held me before they moved me to the mountain hut with the Afghans."

"So if we'd have hit it a week earlier we'd have found you?"

"Looks that way, I know they had two British army men there. I thought they were probably from the U.N force just over the mountain."

"Some bastards got a lot to answer for," muttered Paul.

"I think you're a bad enemy Paul."

"Bet on it? Some bastard, probably in Whitehall, must have known your whereabouts, Cy's team were sent by Whitehall 'funnies' to get you. So they had to have known where you were. My lot went from here but the request and location was from Whitehall. I'm fairly new around here and therefore a bit of an unknown quantity, I think our mole in London told his red mates where you'd be heading, so they could intercept you but stay out of the way!"

"I should think you're right Paul," she sighed.

"The other thing to occur to me is you must have stumbled onto something bloody vital for them to take so much trouble over you, what was it? The identity of our mole?"

"Possibly, I'd made the connection between the one you killed when you rescued me, and the drug barons. I'd also discovered how they moved the heroin down from the north, since the U.N camp blocked their original road. The new route is much longer, two to three days longer, the Chinese escort the pickups through the area to prevent the UN interfering."

"What?" exclaimed Paul, "Not on a mountain road at the head of the valley where we were waiting for you!"

"You know that Paul, how for heavens sakes?"

"Easy, we saw the pickups and army trucks when we were waiting for you."

"You must have sharp eyes."

"Not really, they use their lights at night. I've just had another thought, your known, identified mole is dead, right?"

"Right, so?"

"So if we find a way to make the road unusable then your 'vital information' will no longer matter and you'll be a little bit safer than you are at the moment."

"I doubt it, they'll still try to kill me if 'they' get the chance."

"Do you know who 'they' are?"

"I've got a damn good idea Paul."

"Then tell me, maybe we can remove 'them'."

"You're hoping, 'they' are far too powerful to be quietly removed, even by you."

"Come on let's get some grub."

It was, as Paul put it, 'bloody annoying'. "Look, Roana it's obvious you're not going to tell me anything about yourself, I guess I'm going to just have to accept it, but there is one thing I absolutely must know, to enable us to give you a new identity and it's your age. I know it's something a lady should never be asked, but I do need to know, the year will do."

"I'll think about it."

"Well don't take too long. We need to get started on building a new persona for you!"

The other problem Paul encountered was, she wouldn't say a word to anyone else, she simply totally blanked people. The only way to get an answer of any kind from her was to ask a question which required a yes or no answer; this usually elicited either a nod or shake of the head.

The medics were also concerned. Her internal injuries had been much more serious than at first thought. She'd had to have one kidney removed along with her spleen and most of her reproductive system. As bad as the physical injuries were, those who claimed to know about such things were much more worried about the psychological damage.

The involvement of the heroine served only to complicate matters further; apart from the obvious difficulty of de-tox, the presence of heroine greatly complicated the task of the medics trying to ease her pain. The American doctors, made aware of the problem, got round this difficulty by keeping her heavily sedated for as long as possible. The medical team at Hereford now had the problem of managing Roana's pain levels without being able to use any of the usual heroine derivatives. One went as far as to say she was like a ticking bomb, ready to explode at the least provocation.

Paul handed over his report to his boss. "Basically I've run out of questions Boss, at least ones she'll answer!"

"O.K, so what now?"

"Damned if I know Boss, but it does seem as though those two not so civil servants weren't quite the master criminals we had them pegged for."

"I think you had better elaborate on that sergeant."

"I'm not sure I can Boss, but from bits and pieces Ro has let slip they don't seem to be more than a couple of gophers. There's the suggestion, no more than a suggestion; there is a very rotten egg high up in the corridors of power."

"Any ideas on who?"

"Not really, Sir."

"Yes you have or you wouldn't have called me Sir!" retorted the C.O.

"Well there is one who comes to mind, but you're not going to like it Boss."

"Who?"

"One of those 'grey men', the one you called 'Sir James'. I can't offer a single shred of proof. Don't worry there's absolutely nothing in the report to indicate even a suspicion of what I've just confided Boss."

"I should bloody well hope not!" exclaimed the Colonel.

"The report is in triplicate Boss; just like you wanted. This one is the only copy; it contains all those little snippets I was on about, plus a few observations of my own. If you think it's all rubbish then bin it by all means, but I'm personally convinced there's something in it."

"O.K. Give it another day or two. What's next with Ro?"

"I haven't got a clue Boss, we've got to get her talking to someone other than me. It's very flattering, but I'm not sure I'm cut out for this, frankly I'm completely out of my depth."

"From what I know you've done bloody well, give it another day or two see how it goes, try taking her to the mess. You never know, she might get chatting to one of the others."

"O.K Boss, I'll stick with it, see what happens."

The following days Paul and Ro spent pouring over maps, carefully pinpointing the major sites used by the various warlords as process and storage sites for their heroine. It soon emerged there were three major sites; between them they accounted for more than half of the evil trade in the area. These were all heavily protected by what amounted to private armies.

"I can't see the Thai army getting sufficient men near enough undetected to sort them out, can you?" Paul asked.

"You're hoping," replied Ro. "The way they defend those sites, I doubt even the whole of your regiment could get in to destroy the bits which matter. The areas controlled by the gangs extend out for miles, nothing gets in or out without them knowing. The animal who controls that little empire is the worst of the lot, you met his twin brother when you got me out."

"Nice family! And you say this one is worse; I daren't ask what the father is like."

"Even if you got the R.A.F to nuke the place you wouldn't get him. He's hardly ever there. He lives in a luxury house near the Chinese border, it's like a fortress. The biggest problem in getting at him is, he has so many officials in his pocket and always knows about any operation against him long before it's mounted. The authorities have tried several times, every time a few key commanders are murdered before the operation is launched."

"Sounds as though he's worthy of our attention."

"You won't get near him, he has contacts everywhere. He'll be even more paranoid now you've killed his brother, even more so as he will know you got me out. I remember hearing one of them say he was on his way to ask me a few questions."

"Suddenly a few things are beginning to make sense," sighed Paul. "The pair we banged up were doing everything in their power to delay our strike. They knew what was going on, the evil bastards were in touch with the one we shot. If my guess is right, they were trying to time things so we arrived too late to help you. I assume this arsehole travels with a small army of his own?"

"Oh yes, anything up to a hundred heavily armed men, add them to the ones you hit and I think you would have been in trouble."

"I think you're right, the plan appears to have been to catch us as well, if only to find out what we knew. I'll bet, had the raid failed, it would have been all over the media, which in turn would prevent any response from here. Devious bastards, they seem to think of us as rivals and expendable assets. However; I think you're wrong about one thing Ro."

"What?"

"I don't think Wan Fat Tit mark two is the one who pulls the strings, I think he dances to someone else's tune. He might control things on the ground, think about it, they couldn't have screwed things up as they did from a jungle hideout. The whole thing must have been orchestrated from this end; it just had to be that way round. A 'straight' section head knew about your demise and tried to help. The real head honcho just has to be a very senior officer, probably the boss of those two pinstriped pillocks. You won't know about the Irish connection, but the same two were also involved."

"You mean they actually went to meet McStephoin themselves?"

Paul was gob smacked. "How the bloody hell did you know about it!"

"The link has been known for ages; why else has McStephoin been untouchable? He's been protected, supposedly as a source; you've obviously worked out the reality of it all."

Dissident elements in the States collect the money, buy heroin from the warlords, usually the one you call 'mark two'. It's then shipped out to the west by all manner of means, to swell their funds still further."

"With Sir Kipper in Whitehall taking a cut; swelling his already overblown bank account."

"No doubt, but who is 'Sir Kipper?' and why kipper?" Ro asked.

"A kipper is two faced and gutless, just like our mysterious Mr Big."

Ro chuckled, "I like it, I must remember the expression."

"Right young lady, whether you like it or not you are going to have to talk to my boss. Just remember, he also stuck his neck out for you. I disobeyed my orders just as much to save my own arse as yours, the Boss risked his reputation and career backing me He did it

137

because he believed it was right, he had nothing to gain, but everything to lose. I think you owe him trust, let him hear the information from you, not second hand from me."

"I find it hard enough to open up to you, Paul, I'm not sure I could talk frankly to your boss, he has this 'aura' about him. He is a bit of a living legend among the security forces, everyone respects him; many people are intimidated by his reputation."

"There is no need to include yourself in it, just have a word with him, he's okay, he doesn't suffer fools gladly, you'll get on great with him, all I'm saying is give it a try."

"Maybe I will," she replied with a grin.

"Right, lets go over those maps again and pinpoint every site you know those bastards use. Let's see if we can't get a few good kicks of our own in for a change."

Over the next couple of days the maps of the area developed measles, safe houses, stores, all manner of locations used by the drug barons to support their evil empires were marked and given numbers. Each dot was of a colour to indicate what it was, red was factories, green the safe houses and so on. A file was opened on each site, in which everything known about the particular location was carefully collated. More than half of these files were thin, little more than the location, its purpose if known, and what it was for. Others became quite substantial, all sorts of snippets of information emerged as they compiled the individual files.

By the end of the week the task was complete. At Paul's suggestion the Boss and Mike, the 2IC, came over from the 'Kremlin' to review Paul and Ro's handiwork.

After half an hour the boss sat back from the table. He leaned back in his chair, hands clasped behind his head, staring at the ceiling as if searching for divine inspiration.

"This is all good information, much of it very useful, the question is what to do with it all. I have no doubt you have some ideas Paul, I might as well hear them now, rather than spend the weekend worrying. This way my blood pressure should have returned to normal by Monday."

"Cheers Boss. You'll be delighted to know I'm not champing at the bit to go and kick the shit out of some of the nastiest people on earth. I do have one idea I think is worth a try, you will also be delighted to know it doesn't directly involve the regiment."

"You are full of surprises; go on lets hear it."

138

O.K. What do you think the reaction of the drug barons would be if they suddenly lost one of their most trusted link men?"

"Like who?"

"I don't know his name Boss, but I do know where he lives, Ro knows what he looks like, and he will be receiving about twenty kilos of pure, uncut heroine next Thursday at about three p.m."

"How do you know this, and where will this happen?"

Paul produced another file and passed it to his boss.

"While you're reading, is it O.K if I nip over to the Kremlin Boss, I think there's a picture of him on file. The penny has only just dropped, remember the pictures Mick took of the people in the Astra which followed us home?"

"I do indeed, you think this is the one which was misidentified; why?"

"The description given by Ro fits, it's all a bit muddled at the moment, but there's a connection somewhere which we've missed."

"Mike, go and get his photo, lets sort this out now, I'm getting one of 'those' feelings as well."

"Will do Boss" the Major replied as he got up to leave on his errand."

"Could we have those stills Taff and I took at the pub as well please?" Paul asked.

The C.O shrugged expansively; "Why, but then why not?"

"Would it be alright if I asked Taff to join us Sir."

"I'm not going to ask why; you've remembered something and you want to bounce it off your gang to see if they come up with the same answer. Am I right?"

"Pretty well Sir."

"That's twice you've called me sir, now I know it's bad," replied the Colonel. "O.K. Get them in."

"Thanks Boss."

This left the Boss and Ro alone together. It was the first time she had been left with anyone, apart from the medics since she had arrived at the camp.

Surprisingly it was the Boss who was stuck for conversation, it was Ro who broke the awkward silence.

"This is the first time I've had the chance to thank you for all you've done for me Colonel. Paul pointed out just what a risk you took by doing things your way."

"It's quite alright young lady, it was the least I could have done in the circumstances. How ever I will admit since your return you have presented a quite unique challenge. I have the distinct impression this whole business is far from over. I am guessing now, but somewhere along the line one of you; probably the bloody maverick who has just left to get his gang, has made a connection."

The pair chatted happily for twenty minutes or so before the penny dropped both Paul and Mike should have returned from their errands. It was the Colonel who noticed.

"You do realise you and I have just been set up by a devious bloody sergeant?"

Ro thought for a moment, "Now you mention it, he's been trying to get me talking to some of the others for ages, without much success. It's not I don't want to, most of them seem great lads; it's just I feel so insecure. The crafty devil got me feeling comfortable talking to you, wait till I see him!"

"I assure you there was no connivance on my part, but my 2I.C appears to have been in on it," the Colonel chuckled. "Still conspiracy victims or not I've enjoyed our little chat. We've got a 'do' in the officers mess tomorrow night, I would regard it as an honour if you would be the guest of myself and my wife."

"Thank you Sir, may I give you my reply in the morning?"

"Of course you can. Now where the hell have those reprobates got to."

The C.O was about to rise when Mike returned with a folder containing the required photographs; he was closely followed by Paul and his squad.

"I will deal with you pair later," said the Colonel glaring at Paul and the 2I.C in turn. "Right let's see if we can sort this out before my tea gets fed to the dog."

The photographs were spread out on the table; Paul shuffled through them, searching for one in particular. Ro was leaning on his shoulder, her chin resting on her hands, scanning the pictures.

"There, that one," she indicated a picture of the junior of the two civil servants. "I know him, he's always turning up like a bad penny, as soon as he leaves something always goes wrong. Ah! That one is this one's lap dog," she stabbed her finger onto the picture of the other incarcerated civil servant. "This pair couldn't organise a kiddies party in a tuck shop!"

Paul chuckled, "I wouldn't have been quite so polite, but it's comforting to know our opinions coincide."

"I presume they are the two you managed to catch."

"The same, it's a start I suppose, will it make a difference to their set up?"

"If you can catch that one," she pointed out another picture. "He's the one who handles things at the Irish end. You will have to catch him red handed, he's a squeaky-clean businessman. He has a large trading company, importing oriental artefacts and textiles, he's the one who will pick up the drugs, the last Thursday in every month."

"Got it!" exclaimed Paul.

"Got what?" asked Taff.

"Got the connection!"

"Kindly elucidate," said the boss, "then we can all go home for the week end."

"O.K. He was at the pub, granted in a different building, the restaurant, hence the picture. We know his address from the P.M.C. check on the cars. Now this is maybe coincidence, do you remember who the character in the Astra was originally identified as?"

"The mystery man in the back, wasn't his name Donaghue? Or at least we thought it was until he turned up dead, and must have been dead when the picture was taken."

"That's the fellow Mike, now look at the picture again and compare it with this one taken at the pub."

"I do believe you're right Paul, bloody well done," said the boss.

"I know him too," said Roana. "He hosts a monthly get together, usually on his luxury yacht, he also has his own private jet. It gets better, I know who he gets it off and when."

"Then we are in business. Let customs know, they can handle it."

" I've got a couple of points boss."

"Go on, what devious scheme have you thought up now?"

"Clearly, we cannot raid these places ourselves; why don't we quietly tip off the Thai authorities about a shipment, making certain it's the good guys' we tell. Keep an eye on things and see what develops."

"Any particular reason Paul?"

"Oh yes; with bodge it and leg it out of the way, we must take care tipping off the powers that be, only about an operation the pair must have known about. If we are careful we should be able to roll up a lot of their operations without giving the game away about Ro."

"It is a good point Paul," replied the boss, "one we will have to keep in mind."

"I think we should make our objective the exposure of the main player in this country. There has to be a link between Donaghue, the two muppets we caught and the next one up the chain."

"You called the Irish man 'Donaghue' as though it is his name. I thought we established he was dead."

"We got the name from the P.M.C. check Boss, it's also the name of this arsehole.

"This is a bit of guess work, they could well turn out to have been brothers. They certainly looked very similar; think back to when the other was killed. Thanks to the stray bullet from my rifle turning up in the bag of drugs in Belfast, it is a pretty safe bet it's what the V.I.P. was carrying."

"Now I'm beginning to see the links developing between all the bits. Mike, I want you to run this operation. Enjoy your weekend; then get to work on it Monday. With the information Ro has and Paul's devious mind, there appears to be the possibility of getting a really big fish."

"We won't catch him that way Boss, the only way I can see is by planting information which he cannot ignore, then proving he leaked it to the bad guys."

"I told you he was devious," said the boss as he got up to leave the room.

CHAPTER 13

By Monday evening the plan to catch Donaghue was beginning to take shape. Surprisingly Paul had contributed little to the discussions, he seemed deep in thought. For almost an hour he had been studying some old files.

"You're quiet Paul," said Mike. "What's bothering you?"

"I don't know, something isn't right; we've missed something. It could be we've picked the wrong target to start with. You carry on, I'll work it out."

"Any idea what it is?"

"Not really, I'm not bothered about that prick of a Paddy. The one we should be after is the evil bastard in Whitehall. He has cost the lives of at least two of our friends and if we're not bloody careful we'll lose more. I have the nasty feeling the same individual was ultimately responsible for your demise Ro. I also think you have a bloody good idea who it is."

"You mean the one you christened Sir Kipper?"

"That's the fellow. If we go after the bloody bog hopper we'll scare the really evil bastard off. Can we find a way of setting up this arsehole with what we've got?"

"I doubt it, there's more to this than a desire to avenge the loss of our lads, or what happened to Ro," said Mike, the 2IC.

"I can see the reasoning for going after Donaghue, it is perfectly reasonable for us to have got onto him from the McStephoin deal. However, taking him out will, I fear, remove the easiest route we have to the top dog."

"This is what you were saying to the Boss Friday. I think I can see what you're getting at, if we develop a plan to get Paddy the pusher and seek some sort of approval from Whitehall. Oh yes, now I understand the way you're thinking, the timing will have to be spot on, if we time it right, he will have to warn Donaghue or lose the shipment and his bagman."

"All very true Mike, but there is a fatal flaw in the plan at the moment."

"Go on make me feel thick again."

"It depends on us asking the right department for approval, which will be a guess on our part; granted an informed guess. It is also based on the rather dangerous assumption matey. Can't afford to lose the shipment and will try to protect his operator."

"Oh dear; I hadn't thought; if his set up is big, the loss of a shipment of twenty kilos will be a flea bite."

"Ro. How much pure, uncut heroine would they get from a pick up truck carrying a half a ton or so of raw material, like the stuff they move down the road?"

"I don't know exactly Paul, but a lot more than twenty kilos."

"That's what I thought; we saw eleven trucks in four days."

"That is a hell of a lot," said Mike, "they would hardly notice the difference, so how can we hurt this lot?"

"Damned if I know. The boss was right about one thing; we should leave the actual drug busts to customs and excise, with help from the police."

"So, what do we hit?" asked B.J. "I agree with you Paul; the wanker, sorry Ro. The creature with strange preferences on the company he keeps should be our target."

"Revenge is not our priority B.J."

"I know you said this before skipper, but I disagree, it's a perfectly valid motive. There is also Ro to consider, with his contacts with the warlords he'll know we got her out. As long as she is alive she's a threat to him, for her safety, if nothing else we have got to get him. The other thing is, as long as he is there, the risk to us, every time anyone goes into the field will still exist. Operating against them is bad enough, it's worse if they are told when and how we're coming."

"I see your point, B.J.," replied Mike, "It is a bit of a problem."

"I've just had an idea. I know a target which will cause a panic. If we time it right, there is just a chance our friend in Whitehall might get careless."

"Go on; share this flash of inspiration with us boyo."

"I'm surprised no-one else thought of it, it's so bloody obvious."

"Spit it out for heavens sake!"

"I know what it is Skipper," said Kenny. "Think back to our debrief from our first trip out there. The road! It's a vital link in their supply chain; Whitehall knows we know about it. Best of all there is no risk to Ro."

"Spot on Kenny, I might have known it would be you figure it out."

"Why is that Paul?"

"It was you spotted the trucks in the first place, and, more to the point it will give you a chance to play with something which makes a big bang!"

"Now hang on a minute, for a start no-one has said blow it up! Even if we do destroy it what makes you think it's going to be you sent to do it?"

"It's got to be us Skipper."

"Why?"

"We know were it is and how to get there. Kenny is one of the best there is with explosives; he's also a geologist so he can work out the best place to plant them."

"You're forgetting one thing Paul, just because Kenny is back with your gang at the moment, he still belongs to 'B' squadron."

"Blast, so he does."

Ro chuckled, "Nice try Paul, it's comforting to know not all of your con-tricks work quite as well as the one you pulled to get me talking to your boss."

"The lady definitely has you weighed up Paul."

"Well it was worth a try Skipper."

"Paul has got a point Major," said Ro, sounding a little unsure of herself. "I know how these people think, if Paul and his team were sent out to the area again they would soon know, and set alarm bells ringing."

"It is a very good point Ro."

"And an equally good reason for someone else to go," added Mike.

"I thought the idea was to get the bastard in Whitehall to show himself Mike. It's perfect, a target which will really hurt them, a target for them they can hardly refuse. The only difference is this time we're calling the shots, so we won't be walking into an ambush, we'll be laying the trap!"

"You are bloody mad!" exclaimed the 2 I.C. "It would be like sticking your head into a hornets nest!"

"Not if we do it right. Anyway, if our little gang are clicking our heels around here, the one we're really after might not make the connection. Then it will all have been a lot of effort for nothing; we'll only get one shot at this so lets get it right."

"Your devious lateral brain has no doubt come up with the basis for a plan of attack?"

"Now you mention it Mike I have got a bit of an idea. Try this for starters, next week the rest of the gang Kenny hangs around with are due back off leave. He knows the way, so why don't they fly out to the U.N. base, just as before. Once out there they can lay up somewhere, pick a spot so they can see both our old L.U.P. and the road. Keep radio silence, unless there's a serious problem.

My gang follows on the next flight, Mickey will be back by then; of course we'll have to let the M.O.D. know, who in turn will inform the relevant 'desk' in the foreign office of our destination. We contact Kenny's gang on our radios on a pre-arranged frequency, to find out what is waiting for us. We can lead a fighting patrol out from the U.N base, then blow out a section of the road, we'll let Kenny do his bit, with the rest of us covering him."

"While you are topping up your sun tan, I suppose you want us to get G C H Q to listen for a signal warning of your imminent arrival and lift whoever sent it?"

"That should do it Mike."

"You must have got a death wish is all I can say. Still, I'll suggest it to the boss, don't blame me if he sends you to the funny farm!"

To the amazement of the second command the boss seemed quite interested in Paul's idea.

"Send him over Mike, I'd like to talk this over with him. At first glance it's all a bit gung-ho, but he's a thinker, there's more to this than blowing up a road."

O.K. Boss, if that's what you want."

"Wheel him over in about an hour then Mike."

"See you later Boss."

The 2I.C met Paul as the young sergeant was headed back to the office; he had been in search of fresh supplies of coffee. This particular squad consumed more than most, it seemed to be their principle source of nourishment.

"What the hell do you lot do with it all; bathe in it?" asked the Major.

"I don't know what you mean; the last tin lasted nearly a week."

"You may be surprised to hear the boss wants to see you in an hour, his office; alright?"

"Told you it was a good idea, didn't I?"

146

"I wouldn't get too excited about it just yet; use the time to get an outline down on paper. We can kick it around, see if we can find any weaknesses in it before you present your draft."

The boss turned out to be quite keen on the idea. He agreed with the point Ro had made, the presence of Paul's gang would greatly increase the chances of provoking the reaction they wanted. About the only change made to the original idea, was the squad to which Kenny belonged would appear as a team of engineers. These had been despatched to survey a possible alternative site, one suggested by the Chinese. It all seemed plausible enough to work.

A week later the four members of 'B' squadron left on their part of the mission. It was all very low key, anyone watching would not have noticed. Kenny left in his own car, taking with him all the bits and pieces of kit the others would need for their trip. He met the others in his team at Lydd airport. To lessen the chances of anyone spotting the deception the others had gone to Chatham on completion of their leave. The Royal engineers had been only too happy to help, their depot provided transport to Lydd. The small team of 'engineers' joining the U.N. supply flight attracted little attention and aroused no suspicions. The flight was predictably long and boring, the only beaks in the monotony provided by the refuelling stops at Bahrain and a military airfield in Sri Lanka. They were welcomed at the U.N. base by a fresh faced young Major, Kenny recognised him as the helpful young captain from his first incident packed visit.

"Hello, Kenny isn't it?"

"Yes Sir, good to see you again; and congratulations on your promotion."

"Thank you, it's only a local rank, but it won't do my career any harm."

"What happened to old jobs worth?"

"You mean the previous C.O? Oh, he was quietly shipped out, nervous exhaustion was the official reason." He looked at two of the others in the little squad. "You two look a lot better than you did last time I saw you."

"Thank you Sir, and well done on the crown, suits you."

"You know where the mess tent is, feel free to avail yourselves of our luxurious facilities."

"Who are the civvies?" asked Kenny.

147

"Two of our friends from Whitehall, they're out here to evaluate our contribution to the U.N effort."

"Do us a favour Sir," said Kenny, "don't let on to them who we really are. If they ask, we are a survey team from the engineers' depot at Chatham, they can check with the C.O. if they want; he'll confirm it. If they believe anything else, it could complicate matters."

"Fair enough Kenny, we'll talk later."

Kenny went in search of the crew of the Hercules, the first one he bumped into was the Captain.

"Hello Sir, I wonder if it would be possible for you to do me a favour on the way home?"

"I should think so; what is it?"

"It's a rather important message."

"We won't be leaving until the morning, if it's urgent the lads here can call home for you."

"It's a bit delicate Sir."

"I'll bet it is, don't worry Kenny, I am fully aware of the fact you and your friends are not R.Es. I know two of your team, our Herc might be painted white, with its U.N markings, but we really belong to the squadron which ferries your lot around. They use us because ours are the only Hercs with the range to get here from Sri Lanka and back without a tanker, at least with an acceptable safety margin. I take it the presence of a couple of Whitehall warriors could upset your plans?"

"You are exactly right Sir. If I give you a phone number, could you ring it with a message please."

"I take it this is part of one of your 'dodgy' ops, and a normal call would risk a compromise?"

"I can't really talk about it Sir, but it is important."

"No problem, I've been around your crowd long enough to know the score."

"Thank you Sir," Kenny produced a note pad, from his top pocket; without thinking about it he turned the top page over before beginning to write the number.

"It's a neat trick," commented the squadron leader, "I suppose it's to stop any nosey bugger being able to tell what you've written, I'll have to remember that one."

"Quite, better safe than sorry." The message read, 'from Bravo one seven, W.W X2 @ X roads'.

The squadron leader looked at the message, "That's it?"

"That's it sir; oh and one more thing, it won't be who you expect on the phone. The message must be passed on directly to the C.O of the R.E's depot at Chatham, I don't care if he is on the golf course!"

"I'll take care of it as soon as we land in Sri Lanka."

"Thank you Sir."

Some how the team managed to avoid the civil servants, they were away as soon as it was light. The sound of the land rover starting up woke one of the Whitehall warriors. By the time he had pulled his clothes on and found both of his boots, the big 4X4 was rapidly disappearing into the haze.

"Oh blast! I wanted to talk to them," he muttered as he returned to his bunk.

The commotion he made getting dressed had woken his partner. "What's up?"

"Those bloody Engineers have buggered off before I had chance to talk to them. Now we'll get a bollicking for not being thorough."

"Oh for heavens sake! They're just some sappers here to survey a new site for this unit; apparently the Chinese have found a better location a hundred miles or so away. They have been sent to check it out and map the route. It was all in yesterdays signal."

"So; when our Lords and masters ask for the names what do we tell them? You know what some of them are like when it's the military messing around and getting sneaky."

"Oh for gods sake Giles! You're getting as paranoid as those doddering old twits on the fifth floor. Now go back to sleep!"

"There's another thing; why didn't we see them around yesterday evening?"

"Probably because all they could think of was sleep! They had just flown half way round the world; I should think they were knackered; I seem to remember we slept most of the first two days we were here. Now go back to sleep!"

"Well I still think it was odd; it was just as though they weren't here; then to leave as soon as it was light, very strange."

"No it's not, it may have escaped your notice, but it gets bloody hot later on. If they've just come from home, then they will really feel it. I'd say they were just being sensible. Now stop wittering on and let me get back to sleep."

Hardly had the civil servant managed to doze off again than he was woken by the Hercules starting its engines prior to beginning the homeward leg of it's weekly shuttle service to and from the remote U.N base.

The discussion in the land rover was, not surprisingly about the two civil servants. "I wonder what they did to get sent out here?"

"It must have been pretty bad, nicked the bosses brandy."

"Put salt in the sugar bowl maybe."

"Nah, scoffed the last chocolate biscuit."

"Never mind them," said Kenny, interrupting the banter; "pull over to the left a bit Lofty, it's where we found Cy and Terry."

"The bastards were in those rocks, we didn't see 'em until it was too late. Keep going this place gives me the creeps."

"Joking apart, did anyone bother to find out exactly why those two super sleuths are out in this remote neck of the woods?"

"What woods, I haven't seen a decent bush since we got here never mind a tree."

"Daft bugger," retorted Lofty.

"I did manage a word with the C.O, apparently they are evaluating the British contribution to the U.N operation."

"How will their presence affect our little foray? It could fuck everything up."

"Thanks to Kenny, the boss will know about them by the time he has his dinner."

"It will spoil the taste of his grub; how did you get the message out Kenny. Any radio message could be intercepted and compromise every thing, what did you use; a carrier pigeon?"

"I had a word with the skipper of the Herc and gave him a message to send to the C.O at Chatham, who will pass it on to the boss."

"It was still a risk Kenny, radios are notoriously insecure these days."

"I doubt anyone will intercept this one; alright, I know complacency is dangerous, but I am confident this one is safe."

"Go on, you're bursting to tell us, this should be good."

"He's phoning one of my cousins, who just happens to be married to the adjutant at Chatham. She'll be at home all day and lives barely a hundred yards from his office, I doubt she'll even try to figure out what it means, she's ex R. M. Ps."

150

"You devious sod, it's easy to see who you used to hang around with before you joined our gang; nice one Kenny."

"I know I should have discussed it with you beforehand, but I saw the chance and took it. With the pair of Whitehall warriors around I might not have got another chance."

"Fair enough Kenny, no problem with that mate. We're well clear of the camp now, so I suggest we find a comfy spot and lay up until it gets dark."

"Good idea mate, it wouldn't do to get spotted just yet."

Ten minutes later they were concealed in a deep, narrow gully barely wide enough to back in the land rover.

CHAPTER 14

The C.O was in early, he had a stack of paper work requiring his urgent attention. There was one document in particular which was perplexing, it related to the ongoing defence review. As with all such reviews, ways were being sought to slash spending on the armed forces. In spite of everything, the regiment was seen by some Members of Parliament on the select committee as a prime target for cuts, even disbandment.

One thing caught his eye; as an example of the profligate spending of the regiment, the report cited the supposed costs of no less than three attempts to rescue an individual who had been kidnapped in South East Asia. It later transpired, according to the report, all this fuss and great expense was over a hippie girl, a junkie as well! The costs of the operations ran into millions of pounds, it even included the training of the two soldiers who had been killed by the Chinese, as well as the widows pension payable to the dead Captain's wife.

If he did nothing else, the Colonel silently vowed, he would discover the source of this particular piece of skullduggery. Clearly it could only have originated from someone who still had links with the warlords, the problem was how to find the source, without giving away the fact they really did have Ro.

As usual, Paul was first into the office the team were using to collate all the information from Ro. The kettle was nowhere near hot enough to make the coffee when the 2 I C dashed in.

"Paul, have you seen Ro?"

"No, I doubt she's up yet; if she is, she'll be at breakfast. What's the panic?"

"You get yourself over to the Kremlin, on the double. I'll get Ro."

"Hold on Mike, take a deep breath and tell me what the hell has happened to reduce you to a state of panic!"

"I'm not panicking!" exclaimed the 2I C. "You watch yourself, there's a Whitehall official over there and he wants your blood. He seems certain you got Ro out and wants to know how, and what you've done with her. Now get going, I'll find her and keep her out of his way, alright."

"Thanks Mike; oh, one thing if she's asleep, be bloody careful how you wake her up. She will lash out and it could have fatal consequences if you catch the full force; she is very, very fast, there is no chance of dodging it or blocking, you've been warned!"

"You're kidding, that skinny little thing?"

"I am not kidding, she is lethal, read the reports."

"Thanks for the warning, now get going."

"One thing Mike, what the hell is a Whitehall warrior doing here at this time of the morning?"

"I don't know; other than the fact he's after your blood."

"He must have shit his bed to have got here by seven; see you later Mike."

As Paul walked in through the main entrance of the H.Q. building he was met by the company clerk, "the boss wants to see you sergeant."

Before he could answer the clerk, the adjutant appeared, "Ah, sergeant the boss."

Paul cut him off, "I know, the boss wants to see me, thanks anyway."

Paul knocked on the door of the holy of holies; the familiar voice of his boss came from the other side "Come!"

" You sent for me Boss?"

"He didn't, I did!" it was the civil servant who had answered.

"Mind if I get a cuppa boss," Paul asked the Colonel, "I haven't had chance to get one yet."

Before the Colonel had chance to answer the civil servant replied. "I mind sergeant!"

Paul looked at his boss and moved deliberately towards the coffee pot.

"Sergeant!" the grey man snapped, "you will stand to attention when I address you, you will also obey my orders! Is that clear?"

The Colonel winced visibly, unsure how Paul would react.

"Firstly, what rank are you Sir?" Paul asked.

"It is no concern of yours sergeant, now stand to attention!"

"Fair enough, then who are you, it is only polite to introduce yourself as you clearly know who I am."

"I am appalled by your lack of respect."

"All I'm saying is let me get myself a cup of coffee, then I will try to answer your questions." To the obvious fury of the civil servant Paul got his coffee, "Want one Boss?" he asked with all the innocence he could muster.

"I'm fine thank you Paul."

Paul then sat in the chair facing his boss; the civil servant was almost beside himself with rage. "I ordered you to stand to attention sergeant, do as you are told!"

"Military officers give me orders, not nameless individuals."

"Enough! What did you do with the girl? I demand you tell me; now! Do I make myself clear?"

"I told you the last time you were here chucking your orders around, I don't bloody well know. It's all in the reports, we didn't see any girl, there wasn't a female in the building I'm certain. I am also certain we hit the right place. I don't understand what all the fuss is about."

"Stop buggering me about you bloody cretin! Do you know who I am?"

"Nope; it's why I asked, as to what you are, I could make several suggestions!"

"How dare you; you insubordinate cretin!"

"It's twice you've called me that, I suggest you pick your words a little more carefully."

"Very well, you are a bloody liar! I know you got the girl out. You will be charged with conspiracy, probably kidnapping, murder and treason!"

"This should be good," was Paul's unexpected reply. "You'll have to tell the court where you got your somewhat erroneous information, so you might as well tell us now."

"The source of my information is classified, not for mere sergeants."

"Try telling me then, I'd be interested to know, and my security clearance is certainly high enough."

"You could well be implicated in the conspiracy Colonel. On my return to London I will see to it you are removed from your command!"

"While you are at it, get the lying git you claim told you we got the girl out, so we can prove we didn't."

"Sergeant, you have no idea how much trouble you are in."

"Listen to me you pin striped pillock, how the fucking hell can I be in trouble. My orders were to rescue an unidentified agent from a specific location. The only agent we found at the given location was the dead one we brought back. The actual wording of my orders were, if I remember, to ensure the agent does not pass on any information."

"You certainly did!"

"We certainly did; the only people who left the room were my squad, with the body of your agent."

"You are lying again sergeant, you also brought out the girl. I know this as an absolute certainty, now I demand you hand her over to me."

Paul turned to his C.O, "'scuse me Boss I do speak English don't I?"

"More or less," replied the worried Colonel, unsure of how much more latitude to allow Paul. Aware Paul had obviously been told to wind the civil servant up; indeed, he himself had been party to the idea, should the situation arise. The boss was not at all certain this was the situation they had planned for; however Mike must have said something so he would allow it to run for now.

"Thank you," he rounded on the Civil servant again. "I will say this slowly as you appear to have difficulty understanding English. If you call me a liar once more, I will take you outside and knock your fuckin' teeth so far down your throat you'll have to stick your toothbrush up your arse to clean them; did you understand, dickhead?"

"How dare you talk to me like that? Colonel, I demand you discipline this unruly soldier at once. He is a disgrace to the army. I want that woman; and I want her now!"

"Oh for fucks sake!" exclaimed Paul. "We didn't get her, we didn't find her where your lot said she would be. However, I may have a solution. My squad is due to return to that part of the world in about a week, to lead a U.N team to deal with a target we located on our first trip. The objective is to cut the drug runners main supply route; why don't you come with us, then you can try to locate this bloody woman and bring her home yourself. It's wild country, but we can protect you against anything they've got, unless the bad guys have got a tank we don't know about!"

"Stop being facetious sergeant, just hand the woman over and I will overlook this outburst, in fact I will forget the entire episode."

"You were there when our plane landed, did you see a girl on the plane? I know I was tired, but I think I just might have noticed if we had a female on board."

"I know, beyond any doubt you rescued her. Apart from anything else there were the medical supplies you obtained from the ship which refuelled your helicopter."

"What, a couple of bags of plasma?"

"Exactly, I've got copies of their manifests which prove they supplied your squad with a shot of morphine and two bags of plasma."

"It's the first thing you've got right. One of our support squad was hit, just as the chopper lifted off. The wound was painful and very messy, but as it turned out easily fixed by our medical team."

"I want to see the man who was injured, get him. Now Colonel!"

"It might prove a little bit difficult, as he is away on an assignment at the moment and is probably out of radio contact."

"How convenient for you," sneered the civil servant.

There was a knock on the office door, it turned out to be the Adjutant, "Excuse me for interrupting Boss, but you did ask me to let you know when they lifted Donaghue."

"I did indeed, how did it go?"

"They got him O.K. complete with the twenty kilos of pure uncut heroine. It must be worth a fortune on the street, which is the good bit."

"Go on, clearly there's more," replied the Colonel.

"It's just as well we provided a bit of back up for the customs boys, there were three bodyguards with him. One customs officer was wounded when they opened fire; our lads got two of the three, a known Provo and a yank, the other Provo got away."

"Is the customs officer going to be alright?" asked the Boss.

"Judging from the first reports he should be O.K."

"Splendid, what a good result to start the week. Twenty kilos of pure heroine off the street, the dealer and two armed thugs, all for the price of one not too badly injured customs man."

"It should have dented some bastards piggy bank Boss. It's a pity we couldn't find the evil sod behind it all. Maybe if we'd got the girl out she could have given us the link between the terrorists and the drug suppliers in the far east, there's got to be one."

"What do you think Sir?" asked the C.O.

"I still say your sergeant tells lies Colonel," replied the civil servant. "I have no idea how you did it, but I know you succeeded. I suspect the operation which has just been completed was mounted as a result of information she gave you. I know a Donaghue, a

156

respectable businessman, yet you say he was caught red handed with twenty kilos of heroine. How on earth did you get on to him?"

"Pure chance really, he turned up in a completely unrelated operation, then again in an obbo I was on. Then a captured terrorist suspect mentioned his name in a different context, 2+2 equals, etcetera, etcetera; the result you just heard."

"I still say the information must have come from the girl; as did the information for the other operation you alluded to a moment ago."

"I take it you mean the one I invited you to join," retorted Paul. The intelligence came from our first abortive attempt to bring your mystery agent home, it comes from what we saw when we were waiting for our passenger to show up."

"Too neat, it must have come from the girl."

"Paul, sit down!" commanded the Colonel.

"I told you what would happen if you called me a liar again, all you have to do is read the reports on the operation, then you will see how we knew about the target. Damn it there are even photographs of it included in the report. Not very good ones I'll grant you, but then I'm no great shakes with a camera. I'll remind you all this occurred weeks before we were sent on our rescue mission."

"You are the most convincing liar I have ever met sergeant. The Chinese informed us, a girl they had been looking after following one of their operations against the drug overlords was kidnapped by British soldiers, probably S.A.S. This happened the same night as you launched your raid, the one which resulted in the death of one of my agents; I suppose it is coincidence it was in the same area."

"I didn't know there was another team in the area that night Boss."

"Neither did I Paul."

"The only possible conclusion one can draw from this is you are lying to me again sergeant."

This time Paul was on his feet before the boss could stop him. "Paul! Don't you dare hit him!"

The colour had drained from the civil servant's face; it was nearly as white as the knuckles on the angry sergeant.

"I don't suppose it could have occurred to your amoeboid brain, the Chinese commander of the garrison could have been in league with the warlords, in the same way the next one to the north had been. What you have just told us is exactly what I would have expected him to say to save his own arse. Don't forget, they knew, not just the fact we were coming, but also the fact we had been recalled, albeit too late to stop us; but they knew. Explain, if you can."

"You caught the pair responsible."

"We caught a couple of minor gophers; nobody who mattered much. The one I'm bothered about is the poor bloody girl, Orientals have very original minds when it comes to inflicting pain. I hope, for her sake it was over quickly, the sort of treatment they can hand out doesn't bear thinking about."

"Colonel, for the last time; order your sergeant to hand over that woman, or at least tell me what he did with her. The consequences of not complying with this direct order will, I assure you, be very serious."

"You and I have both heard him strenuously deny any knowledge of this woman, it must be clear to anyone familiar with this long running saga the unfortunate wench can only be lost, presumed dead," replied the Colonel.

"Why do you insist on protecting this uncouth sergeant, why risk everything on a young upstart, only recently badged, he certainly hasn't finished his training with the regiment yet. Your attitude implies there is something much greater at risk, other than his freedom or your reputation."

"In the same vein, why should an office tea boy from Whitehall get up at the crack of dawn, travel all the way out here just to make our lives more difficult? Why indeed, should the same tea boy have an almost compulsive fixation on a missing Whitehall 'funny'. The only answers I can come up with are, either you were shagging her, or more likely her mother years ago."

"How dare you talk to me like that! I'll have you know I'm a permanent deputy under secretary at the foreign office, and a deputy controller of intelligence matters in the Far East."

"Bloody hell, they let him make coffee as well as the tea!" retorted Paul. "He still didn't say if he was daddy or sugar daddy, which do you reckon Boss?"

"Don't involve me with this one Paul," replied the Colonel, barely able to conceal a grin.

"You insolent young devil, how dare you cast such a slur on my character, you will rue the day you crossed me!"

"What are you going to do; send a couple of your shirt lifter friends down here after me?" replied Paul. "Don't let me forget to warn the local farmers to shift their sheep out of the roadside fields; the temptation would be too great for your shit stabbing mates to refuse."

"How dare you cast aspersions on my department, you are beneath contempt!" The man leaned forward over the C.O's desk. "You have not heard the last of this Colonel."

"I'm sure we haven't."

"Good day Colonel," as he stormed out of the door.

"It went well, you really surpassed your self this time. I'm not sure what to do with you." The Colonel was trying to read what Paul was writing on his note pad, a frown crossed his brow as Paul turned it round so he could see. All the sergeant had written was 'ssh!'.

Paul moved to the end of the desk the man had leaned on and dislodged something which fell to the floor, what ever it was made a sound like a coin falling.

"Oh dear!" said Paul. "What is this, a bug? Oy! Big ears! Next time dry your sweaty palms before you try to attach one of these. The glue is useless if it gets wet, fuckin' amateurs!" Paul deactivated the listening device.

"Oops; well spotted Paul, it could have been embarrassing."

"Couldn't it just. They would have found out what wines were on the list for tonight's mess do."

"Quite."

The radio in Paul' pocket crackled into life, "Got them Paul, two of them in an old Sherpa van, they came quietly enough."

"Stay with them for a bit Taff; we'll get back to you. Oh just a thought, leave those tapes running."

Someone else came on the air, it was Mick, the sergeant Major. "He's stopped at a phone box Paul, this could be good."

"Thanks Mick, stay with the slippery sod."

"Would you mind telling me what is going on, I am after all only the C.O. around this military mad house?"

"Mike and I had a little chat before I came over; we thought if they can play silly buggers, then so can we."

"How did you know about the bugging; one of your 'feelings' I suppose?"

"Sort of, but I had seen our less than civil servant talking to the driver of the Sherpa when I came back onto camp earlier, I'd been down to the news agents to get a packet of fags. You know the one near the bridge which opens at half past five."

"He could have been asking directions, what caught your eye?"

"Apart from the fact I knew him by sight; two shiny new aerials on a grotty old van, and the driver was squeaky clean, collar and tie. The other little thing was both of the drivers' arms were the same pale un-tanned colour, a regular driver has a brown right arm."

"You don't miss much do you?"

"Not a lot Boss, here, you'd better have this," he handed the C.O. another bug.

"Where did that come from?"

"Off the chair; it was obvious he'd been sitting in it prior to my arrival. I'll grant you I made a point of sitting in it simply to annoy him, his reaction was all wrong. So, when he wasn't looking, I ran my hand along the underside of the chair, voila."

"Any more little surprises?" asked the Colonel.

"Oh yes, I've saved the best one until last."

The C.O. groaned audibly. "Go on, what else did I miss?"

"The other bug of course."

"What other bug? You've found another, where for heaven sake?"

"In your ash tray, it was the obvious place, right beside your phone. You don't smoke, it therefore follows 'matey' had been in your office long enough to smoke the cigar which had stunk the place out and filled the ash tray."

"So that's why you lit up, I knew you smoked but it's the first time I've known you smoke in an office, I wondered what you were up to. Out of idle curiosity where is it now, I presume you removed it?"

"It's in his top pocket, I dropped it in when I grabbed him by the lapels."

"That's why you told Taff to leave the tapes running, now he's using the phone and being taped on his own gear. You devious underhanded sod, but I like it, a very nice touch. Coupled with the performance you put on in the office they are worth a couple of days off, it was an act I presume."

"It was the idea Boss, upset him enough, he was bound to slip up."

160

Paul's radio crackled again, it was Taff. "Guess who dear Roland has just phoned? None other than Sir James, matey is certain we have got the girl; but he admits he didn't get anything at all. Apart from, and I quote 'ear ache from the bloody sergeant'. I think you got to him Paul, he's really pissed off with you mate, don't worry we're getting it all on tape."

"I take it you heard boss?"

"I did, it would seem your doubts about Sir James may be well founded."

"Hi Mike, our little idea worked, he went straight to a phone and called his boss."

"Great, we should be able to clean up some more of these sods. By the way, have you seen Ro? I can't find her anywhere."

"No, I thought you were with her," replied Paul sounding concerned, "you did check her room?"

"Of course I did, it was the first place I looked, it was all locked up and quiet. I also checked the canteen and the gym; as far as I can tell no-one has seen her today."

Paul was first to the door, he produced a key; after knocking a couple of times, he then shouted her name; getting no response he tried the key. "Well, she's in there, the dead locks are on, stand back." A well-aimed kick and the door flew open.

"What the hell?" exclaimed Paul as he saw the large blood stain on the sheets of the rumpled bed.

"Oh my God!" muttered Mike, "What on earth could have happened?"

Paul held up his hand, in gesture which meant shut up and listen, he thought he had heard a feint sobbing from the direction of the bathroom. The sight which greeted him stopped him dead in his tracks for a second or so.

Ro was kneeling in a pool blood, her arms locked across her stomach, her long brown hair trailing in the spreading blood. As he wrapped his combat smock round her, he heard her whisper "help me."

"Mike, grab the duvet for me, then get the medics, they'll need plasma drips and a shot of morphine. Go!"

The boss had heard the last bit, "Giving orders to Majors now are we, I think it's time to remind you, despite the latitude you have been allowed on this long running assignment, you are still a trainee

161

with the regiment. You do not give orders to officers, especially the 2 I.C."

"Mind the way Boss!" said Mike, returning with not only the duvet but a thick blanket as well. "Better still give these to Paul, I'll get those medics." Then he thrust the armful of bedding into his astonished C O's arms and fled in search of the nearest phone.

"What the hell is going on?" asked the perplexed Colonel. "Good lord, what is all this blood, what's happened?"

"I don't know, Ro is leaking all over the bloody place. I'm guessing her re-routed plumbing has sprung a leak, She's in shock, of that much I'm certain, she shaking like a leaf and in a hell of a lot of pain. I know the rule is try to avoid moving the casualty, the floor is cold and hard, lets try to get her wrapped up and on the bed. She's only a skinny little bugger, you and I can lift her easily, even in the position she's in. If we don't move her position we can't do anymore damage; just don't slip on all the blood. Come on Boss, this matters."

"Sorry Paul, it took a minute to sink in; it was all so unexpected, I'm not normally long cottoning on."

The two men gently lifted the girl from the bloody floor; she was barely conscious she whimpered softly as they carefully carried her to blood stained bed.

"Where are those bloody medics" growled the Boss "They are taking their time."

"They have got to come from the other end of the camp Boss, they'll be here."

Mike returned, "There's the rapid response paramedic on his way, a full medical team is following with the emergency ambulance."

"Well done Mike, you did tell them to hurry."

"I did Boss; I don't fancy a bollicking from Paul for being slow off the mark."

"Why not, I got one albeit, a mild one. I suppose I owe him an apology for the chewing out I gave him when I came in."

"Oh, I don't know Boss, what you said was all true enough, it's simply I was first onto the scene. In my judgement, for what it is worth, the situation demanded immediate action. It is no excuse for the way I spoke to the Major, I should at least have said please!"

"Idiot," chuckled Mike.

Paul was sitting on the edge of the bed, his arm round the quivering Ro.

"Hang on girl, the medics will be here any minute, what the hell happened?"

He had to put his ear as close as he could to her mouth to make out the feint, croaky words. Her rapid, shallow breathing increasing the difficulty in understanding Ro, "I feel as though I've been stabbed."

"Come on, try to lie down, the medics won't be able to do much with you like this."

"I can't," she panted, "something split, inside, I felt it go; God it hurts!"

"How long ago did this happen?"

"I don't know, I woke up in the middle of the night, my bed was wet, I tried to get to the toilet. The next thing I can remember is a crash, which was you kicking the door in."

The paramedic rushed in; "'scuse me, let me see the patient. Does anyone know what's happened to her?"

"She woke up in the middle of the night, apparently bleeding badly. She tried to get to the toilet, but collapsed and lay there for several hours, until we found her. Ro said it felt as though something inside had split apart."

"We'll get her to the medical centre, we have the facilities there for basic emergency surgery," he talked as he worked. "Here, hold this drip up."

Mike, the 2 I.C. simply did as he was told, he just looked at the Boss and shrugged, "It's just one of those days."

The medic suddenly realised who it was holding the drip aloft. "Oh, sorry Sir, if I'd have realised it was you, I would have said please."

The C.O. shook his head and walked towards the damaged door, he paused to examine the damage "It was quite a kick, both deadlocks and a Yale ripped clean out of the post. Mike as soon as you have finished here and got cleaned up I'll see you in my office, and bring the reprobate with you," indicating Paul

The medics didn't mess about, they took Ro to what served as the base hospital, they waited only long enough for the morphine to kick in. Their first problem was to deal with the shock, she was also getting very close to hypothermia, the effect of being on a tiled floor for several hours.

"Anything I can do to help?" Paul asked.

"Apart from let us get on with our job, not a lot sergeant, we'll let you know if there's any news alright."

Within a few minutes of her arrival at the medical centre, the senior doctor decided the only chance she had got was an immediate operation to stop the bleeding. In the end they called a specialist from Cardiff hospital, after a brief conversation, the surgeon put some instruments in his bag and left for the T.A. centre at Newport, there a helicopter was waiting to fly him to Hereford.

The problem turned out to be one of the major blood vessels, which had been damaged by her treatment at the hands of the warlords. The American surgeon had tried to save as much of her internal plumbing as possible. In the event one section of a large blood vessel had been burnt worse than he had thought. Instead of the two ends knitting together as they healed, the tissue continued to deteriorate, eventually it became so necrotic the stitches tore out and it nearly killed her.

This is not denigrating the work of the American surgeons who had done a remarkable job of re-plumbing, much of it by necessity had been improvisation, from such dreadful and severe injuries.

Paul sat in the Boss's office listening to the tapes made of the civil servant. To really rub it in, the regiment even used the Sherpa van which was supposed to have been monitoring the C.Os office. It was a race day, and whom did Roland meet in the V.I.P tent? None other than Sir James, the head of the section for which not only Roland but also the two already locked up civil servants had worked.

"Are they still monitoring him?" asked the boss.

"Yes Sir," replied Paul, "trouble is he hasn't really said anything to incriminate Sir James yet. It's clear enough Sir James is aware of what is going on, but there's nothing anywhere near enough to post as evidence. Slippery bastard isn't he, how are we going to stop him Boss?"

"I'm not sure we can Paul. For what it's worth I agree with you, he's rotten, proving it is a different matter. Dear Roland, on the other hand, I think with a little care it should be possible to remove him. He admitted, on tape links with the Chinese. If we can find the one he named and prove he's part of the drug runners' organisation then we've got him."

164

"I think I can help you there Sir," said Paul, "I'm pretty well certain he's the brother of the one Ro killed. I'll have to check my notes to be absolutely sure, but I'm sure he's the one she named as the head warlord. I can even show you, on the map where he lives; it is a virtual fortress by all accounts and heavily guarded by militia."

"Assuming you are correct, then what to we do about it? Sure, it means we can remove Roland the rat, but it won't help us to get any of the top ones at this end. To be honest with you Paul, I don't think we'll ever find out who is really calling the shots."

"You're probably right Mike, but if we could hit Wan Fat Tit mark two, and lift Roland it might rattle the cages of some evil bastards. I don't suppose we'll get any of them, but we can let them know we know, if you see what I mean."

"Not really; but he could have a point Boss, it just might shake them enough to make them 'retire'. The longer we keep up with this charade, the greater the risk to our guest. I think we should wrap this up as quickly as possible."

"I agree with you Mike, I think the risks out-weigh any gains, unless of course, our sergeant has any more bright ideas?"

"We're not going to get much more from the bug, the power has started to drop, the battery is probably getting flat."

"O.K., we'll lift bloody Roland, detain him in the guard room, until we can make more permanent arrangements."

"Do we involve Sir James in this Boss?" asked Mike

"What would be the likely out come if he was made aware of the fact that we had their conversation on tape?"

"It's a good point Paul; if he thinks we've got enough on Roland to safely lift him, Sir James can hardly be seen to support him, can he?"

"I think he's got two options Boss. The first one, he can get even more spiteful towards the regiment; he'll only do it if he feels safe. To avoid it, we must let him know we were listening to him and Roland, make it look as though we did a deal with Roland."

"It could get Roland killed Paul," observed Mike. "What's the other option, in your opinion?"

"It is just possible he might do a runner."

"You're hoping, he's virtually fire proof Paul."

"O. K" said the C.O. "I'll prepare a file on Roland and make the necessary arrangements for him to be admitted to the retirement

165

home for uncivil servants. Mike, nip over to 'B' squadron lines, find your name sake, then the two of you get down to the race course and escort dear Roland to his new residence. Give my compliments to the R.S.M; I want him personally to take charge of the escort. Two cars, three in each car, side arms will be carried."

"One thing Boss, how will we find him in the crowd?"

"Find Mick, he's got one of our short range radio's, he'll guide you in. Oh, don't forget to remove the bug from his top pocket when you lift him, preferably in front of Sir James; it should rattle his cage!"

For once there were no hitches, and Roland was delivered safely. Sir James was obviously concerned at the arrest of one of his deputies, but didn't make a fuss; his face was, as Mike reported later, an absolute picture when the bug was removed from Roland's top pocket.

The surprise came the following morning with the announcement of the resignation of a top civil servant. The statement was brief; terse even. A spokesman for the press office at number ten simply gave a single sheet of paper to the gathered press men, with a short typed note to the effect 'Sir James, a permanent under secretary at the foreign office had resigned for personal reasons.' That was it, the press asked many questions, but received no answers. They all knew whatever the man's official title; he was in fact a senior ranking officer in 'the security services'. The media smelt a scandal; the story rumbled around for a few days, got nowhere, then vanished, along with Sir James.

On hearing the news the Boss's only comment was, "not what we expected, but it will do for now."

Paul was due to leave in the afternoon, with his squad to join the U.N flight. Their role was simple; they would act as guides for a fighting patrol of U.N troops. This would be the force which would cover the team already there, when led by Kenny they would blow up vital sections of the 'secret' road.

Paul went to see Ro; he was shocked to his boots when he was shown into the room. It gave a whole new meaning to the expression as white as a sheet.

"Is she going to make it?" he asked the head nurse.

"She's hanging on; the consultant from Cardiff says there is nothing more he can do. I'd taken her medication to her several

166

times since she's been here. I never realised how badly she had been hurt, the poor little thing, how ever could anyone be so cruel."

"She's a tough one, if anyone can make it, she can."

"She will need to be tough, her chances are pretty slim to be honest. The injuries are terrible but the real problem is septicaemia, blood poisoning to you. We think we may have got the right combination of anti-biotics to counter her infection; she's so weak. I know she means a lot to you sergeant. We'll do our best, you can come and see her when you like."

"Thanks, I'll see you later," then added 'I hope' under his breath as he left to join his mates.

CHAPTER 15

"There's been a change of plans lads," said the Boss as he walked into the briefing room, "You'll be leaving from Brize on a R.A.F Herc with your panther; the U.N. plane will pick you up in Bahrain."

"Don't you just love a last minute change of plan?" muttered Taff.

"One other little bit of information you may be interested in; it appears there are two civil servants at the U.N camp. Kenny got a message through to us, so it didn't come as a total surprise. From the little I have been able to discover they are there to assess the effectiveness of the British contribution to the U.N operation."

"Give us some good news Boss."

"It won't be raining out there Taff."

"Thanks Boss."

"You're quiet Paul, anything wrong?" asked the C.O.

"Nothing anyone can do anything about, I'll be O.K. but thanks for asking Boss."

"Come with me, we have got time for a quick chat before you leave. There is no way I'd let even our most experienced members leave on a mission with something preying on their minds, so you have got no chance until this is straightened out, right?"

"Yes Boss."

"Right," the Colonel sat behind the desk in a handy vacant office; he indicated Paul should sit in the other chair. "Spit it out, it is not like you to let things get to you, so it must be bad."

"There are three women on this earth I care about. One is my mother, it seems she's got cancer to go with her crippling arthritis. My wife, she wants a divorce, she's playing away, again! Then there's Ro, with hindsight it might have been better if I hadn't gone to see her. Have you seen her Boss?"

"I must confess I haven't been to the medical centre the last few days, there simply hasn't been the time to do everything. I'm sorry to hear about your mother, would a bit of leave help?"

"I'm not sure it would, my house is in the same little village, I know I'll have to see the other half to sort things out sooner or later, but I'm not ready for it yet. Thanks for the offer though Boss, it's appreciated."

"What about Ro? How bad is she?"

"Hanging on, that's about all. She's heavily sedated, to the point she's totally out of it, I don't know how they managed to get so many pipes and tubes into one small body. She's literally as white as the sheets, to look at her you'd think she was made of porcelain, so thin it would break if you touched it."

"I'm seriously considering replacing you on this trip Paul. I am not convinced you are in any fit state to take on such a mission, much less effectively lead it."

"I can't do anything useful around here, all I'll do is sit and brood. What can I do if I go home, I can't help mum, the wife will just start shrieking at me; all it will do is upset the kids and make me feel worse still. I can't do anything to help Ro, even being there is pointless because she is totally unaware of her surroundings.

As far as I can see, this operation is just what I need, I've got a day and a bit travelling, ample time to sort my thoughts out. Then two or three days of problem solving on a job which has got to be done exactly right to get the effect we want. I know the whole thing should be straightforward, but I've learned from painful experience these are the very operations which can go tits up in the blink of an eye. Don't worry Boss, I'll be totally focused; if I need a reason, other than the fact friends lives depend on me, all I've got to do is remember how Ro looks."

"Well, alright you can go, but I am not happy about it, I'm going to send Mike with you. I know it seems as though I'm putting even more pressure on you, but think of him as support, a fall back position if you like. In fact he can put an ad hoc squad together, 'our' Herc can take you all the way. It will cure another problem as well, as there is at least one pallet of kit for the U.N which won't go on their Herc. This way they won't have to leave gear behind in Bahrain to make room for you."

"Fair enough Boss, do you want Mike's team to lead?"

"No, carry on just as we planned, his role is purely support; as you pointed out, this is just the sort of 'milk run' which goes pear shaped, it's still your operation Paul."

"Thanks boss, I'd better get cracking, we'll give Mike's gang a hand to get their kit together."

Typical of the Boss, he went to the medical centre to see for himself exactly what had left such a profound impression on the young sergeant. Over his many years of service, much of it with special forces, the grey haired Colonel thought he had seen

169

everything. The appearance of Ro shocked even this hardest of hard men.

Like many other on the base he had become accustomed to seeing the skinny, yet attractive young woman around the place. She always seemed full of life, although reserved and wary of anyone she didn't know, she had an infectious laugh. The other impression she left on an individual was an innate, if suppressed, sense of fun.

Apart from the monitors there was little to suggest she was even alive. The senior medic appeared, having been informed of the C.O's presence.

"Good morning Sir," he began, "Come to visit our star patient?"

"Is she going to survive? Would she be better in a proper hospital?"

"She is still alive Colonel, so she has a chance, as you can clearly see she is very poorly. As to your other question, there is little more anyone can do to help her; we can administer the drugs to help her fight the infection and keep her sedated. Any benefit gained by moving her would be very slight and greatly out weighed by the attendant risks in moving her.

The one thing puzzles me. What could have caused such injuries to her? I've heard tales of electrodes from the team who brought her back. I hasten to add, I had to force the information out of them, to enable me to treat her since she joined us. What I cannot understand is what caused such extensive internal burns, frankly there is no recognised treatment for such injuries; I feel so damned helpless."

"Damn it, just do your best Doc, if there's anything you want, let me know. In all my years I have never seen anyone with a totally bloodless look. No wonder Paul was shaken up, how long can she last in that condition?"

"Frankly Colonel she shouldn't be alive, but having said so, as difficult as it maybe to believe, she has improved. She is showing definite signs of improvement; the level of infection has dropped, quite significantly. So without wanting to foster false hopes, she has got a chance of surviving."

"Keep at it Doc, I'll be around if you need me."

"Bye sir."

By the time the C.O had finished his rounds the two teams headed for the Far East were almost ready to leave.

"I just thought I'd wish you all bon voyage, and a safe return. The others will join you at Kota Baru for the second stage of the operation in ten days time."

"Cheers Boss, at least we know what we're up against this time, we'll be O.K."

The trip on the Hercules transport seemed to last forever; the air crew swapped at Bahrain, as soon as refuelling was complete they were off again.. To the surprise of the R.A.F technicians, who had boarded the flight at Bahrain, most of the soldiers slept in their green sleeping bags, known as 'maggots'. Only the Major and one of the sergeants spent any amount of time awake, they were studying some photographs supplied by the reconnaissance flight.

"Do you think we'll need an alternative route Paul, are those militia really likely to be waiting for us?" asked the 2 I.C

"On past performances I'd say it was highly likely they'll have a go. The trick is to hit them hard from an unexpected direction; and the biggest problem then is keeping up with the sods. They're real scrappers when they are attacking, as long as things are according to their plans they are quite a handful. Surprise them and they run like rabbits on steroids."

"So this part at least should be a milk run?"

"I didn't say it Mike, but as long as we see them before they see us, it shouldn't be too hard. Kenny's gang will ensure there are no surprises for us, lifting dear Roland should have cut off their supply of up to date information. By the way Mike, when was the last time you went on an op?"

"Why do you ask? I do hope you are not insinuating I'm not up to this! Damned cheek, you might have been badged several months ago, sergeant, but you are still technically a recruit. In fact you have hardly begun your regimental training."

"It wasn't what I meant Sir, and you know it, this is a harsh environment we're going into and it can take a bit of time to get used to it, you'll see what I mean soon enough; it's deader than the empty quarter in the southern Saudi desert."

"Now you tell me! I was expecting jungle covered hills."

"Let's get a bit of kip, we can't do anything else until we talk to Kenny."

The Hercules made its usual abrupt landing, the soldiers, mostly still sleeping, had wedged themselves against wheels and the likes in preparation for this. Only Mike, the 2 I.C of the regiment was caught out, despite of the warnings he had opted for comfort rather than security. Luckily it was only his pride which was hurt.

"All right," he muttered as he emerged from his sleeping bag, "I asked for it. You were right Paul, over a year in an office has made me a bit rusty."

The welcome from the U.N troops was almost enthusiastic, more S.A.S could only mean something was likely to happen to break the monotony. True they patrolled much more, now the old C.O had been replaced, but action was rare as the militiamen tried to stay out of range.

Kenny had some interesting news, just as Paul had predicted, the pile of rocks they had used on the previous trip was now occupied by nearly thirty militia, equipped with at least eight pick up trucks. They made little attempt to conceal themselves; the regular patrols were quite open, often in daylight, several times passing within fifty yards of Kenny's team without seeing them. The militia would even drive around in bright moonlight, though never for more than a mile or so from the rocks, before the moon rose they would stay in their temporary base.

Within two hours of the plane landing the two teams from Hereford were on the move, almost half of the U.N garrison were going as well. The two civil servants approached the little group of officers, "What's going on?" asked the senior pen pusher.

"We are mounting a small operation to cut another of the heroine supply routes," replied the recently promoted youthful Major.

"Is it wise, who authorised this action?"

Mike was about to intervene on the young officer's behalf, when the young man rounded on the civil servant. "I authorised it, this is the exact purpose of the deployment. I quote from my standing orders, 'to interdict and destroy drug shipments passing through this area. Also to deny their transport passage through the area', this is precisely what I intend to do. If you would care to join us, do so by all means; if you do come along for the ride, you will leave your radios behind and will be under military command. I also suggest you see the quarter master and equip yourselves with combat fatigues, a helmet and a flack jacket. Now if you will excuse us we are a little bit busy."

"It was a bit of quick thinking Sir," observed Paul, at least we can keep an eye on them if they accept."

"It's exactly what I thought sergeant; if they stay behind, our provost detachment have been instructed to enforce radio silence, with vigour! The only exceptions are emergency help calls to us!"

Not surprisingly the two civil servants elected to stay where they were, although the junior one of the pair seemed a little disappointed.

"Seems as though you've got them well sussed out Sir," chuckled Paul.

The fighting column included all three 120mm field guns, as Mike's panther was pulling a trailer containing nearly half a ton of explosives Paul's team took the lead. The time spent preparing an alternative route on the plane, proved time well spent, by dawn the covering force were in their pre selected position, both the pile of rocks and the road in easy range of the guns.

"Any idea which chunk of road you are going to take out Kenny?"

"You see where it goes round the spur, right above the steepest part of the ravine?"

"No," replied Mike, "I can't even see the road!"

"Trust me; it's there. What are you planning Paul, wait until dark?"

"You are the ones who have been watching, have those guys in the rocks got infra red gear?"

"I don't think so, if they have the patrols don't seem to use it."

"O.K night it is, unless anyone has a good reason for going in daylight."

"Have you done a recon Kenny?"

"A bit more than that mate, I've already laid out the wire with detonators attached. All we have to do is carry the charges over there, stick a pair of detonators in each. I'll hook it up, set the timer, then we leg it back here."

"Why did you say 'carry' the explosives across; it must be nearly two miles to the place you pointed out, can't we drive over with the panthers?"

"Not without disturbing the guys in those rocks, sound carries a long way at night in this sort of terrain. If we go on foot our packs will weigh about sixty pounds each, should be a piece of piss for three miles."

"Three miles! With sixty pounds each; oh my aching back!"

"You're alright Mike, you'll be here on the radio," said Kenny. Paul and Taff can take the point, with me guiding them, then the twenty strongest U.N lads, in five teams of four. B.J and Mickey bring up the rear with a couple more of the U.N boys. Plant the charges, two at each station, get the hell out of the way, blow it, back to base in time for breakfast."

"What about those men in the rocks; won't they catch you in the open when you are returning to here?" asked Mike.

"If they look like causing serious grief, lob a few 120s at them. It should give them something to think about. If you do use the big guns send a couple of those Finnish trucks to pick us up" replied Kenny casually.

"What haven't you told us Kenny?"

"Would I lie to you Paul?"

"I didn't say you had lied, you daft bugger, how many mates have they got in 'them thar hills'?"

"A couple of hundred, give or take."

"And?"

"And the tanks, there are only three of them, they're ancient T55s."

"What time does the moon rise?"

"About half eleven, or a quarter to twelve; we've got the best part of four hours to do it."

"We'd better get our kit ready, then get some kip."

"One thing bothers me," began a sergeant from the U.N force; "We haven't got infra red gear like you lot, isn't there a danger of getting separated in the darkness. My lads would be alright in the moon light, but if we are to be spread out in little squads someone is bound to get lost."

"It's a good point, I hadn't thought of it."

"Neither had I," admitted Kenny, "but I've got the answer. A spare reel of wire! If I stay between you and Taff with your night vision stuff, fix one end to my belt, B.J takes the other end then everyone else uses their lanyard from their belt to the wire no one will get lost. We'll still be spread out over a hundred yards, each able to see the one in front, okay it's not ideal but it will do."

"I still say we should use the wheels," said Mike, "I can't see a valid reason to use these lads as pack mules."

"I can see your reasoning Mike, but look at it this way; with the vehicles we are certain to have a rumble, with all the attendant risk

174

of casualties. We are a long way from help for any poor sod who gets hit. If we do it Kenny's way and everything goes right, we shouldn't have to fire a shot. If we do get spotted, we'll still be better off as we'll have surprise and concentration of fire power on our side. We will also have the support of your group with your heavy weapons available if need be to call on. This is definitely a case of stealth rather than blasting our way in and out, save our powder this time, it might come in handy later."

Despite one or two minor frights the plan actually worked. A quick head count confirmed everyone was safely back. As soon as the moon came up the force got ready for the return journey. The now empty trailer was turned upside down on one of the ammunition trailers and secured. This freed Mike's panther to take the lead, the other two S.A.S land rovers would follow as rear guards; they would wait just long enough to confirm the success of the mission.

"Have a safe journey Mike, we'll be following soon, see you for breakfast."

"You take care you mad bugger; the boss will have my hide if anything happens to you."

One of the old hands in Kenny's section piped up; "Who's the Boss's blue eyed boy then?"

"You couldn't be more wrong old son," replied Paul.

"Those sergeant stripes count for shit out here," was the bad tempered reply.

"I am well aware of it; if it bothered me do you think I would have got past the first day of the selection course. There are two reasons the boss wants me back in one piece; for one, I have nowhere near finished typing up all the stuff on Ro, which has got to be me, as no one else can read my writing. The other reason is much more serious; my civilian trade is gardening, his wife knows this; guess who forgot to ask me to prune their roses before we were about to leave?"

"The Boss?" suggested Kenny.

"It's worse than it seems mate, apparently he forgot to ask me twice, and he'd been reminded."

"How did he know you had green fingers in the first place?" asked the grumpy trooper.

"From my file, I suppose."

175

"Sorry mate, I'm just pissed off with all the stress and none of the action. I couldn't see the point in having all the fire power and not using it."

"Like I said, in this case it was important to avoid us having any casualties, if only because we are so far from help. Don't worry Billy; you'll get all the noise you want with our next targets on the Boss's shit list. This was definitely the easy one, important because it will cut their only viable bulk supply route. Next up are the factories, refineries and distribution stores down south, they will not be so easy."

"I think I might have got you all wrong Paul, Kenny did say so; I'd got you down as a gong hunter."

"Cheers mate! Leave the bloody death or glory lark to the Para's; I'll settle for a few years of this, as long as I can easily maintain my fitness level. The day I struggle, I'm straight back to a R.E.M.E workshop, no problem."

"If it's how you feel, why did you bother in the first place?"

"I don't really know, all I ever really wanted to do was be a soldier; I'd got to know a little about the regiment since I'd been in, the chance came to have a go, so I took it. I suppose it was so I could learn a bit, I didn't think I'd got it in me to pass selection, just do my best and see what happens."

"Takes all sorts I suppose."

The little group lapsed into silence, waiting for the bang, at the same time keeping an eye on the pile of rocks, wondering when a patrol of militia would emerge.

Kenny looked at his watch, yet again. "Five minutes," was all he said.

"It was a bloody good idea getting the wire laid ready with the detonators in place, which must have saved us at least an hour."

"Just tryin' to help, I had an idea you'd do it the way we did, a big gang out in the open would have got a bit dicey in moon light."

"Good thinking mate, at least it gave us the option, I didn't fancy swanning around in panthers with heavy stuff around."

The soldiers sat on their land rovers, waiting to see the results of their efforts; they may have appeared relaxed to the untrained eye, but not for a second did they relax their vigilance. At least one, more often two or three were constantly scanning the area with the sophisticated infra-red gear they all carried; there was no way these men would be surprised.

176

Kenny attracted Paul's attention with a small pebble, "Check the road Mate; south bound, just coming out of the cutting."

"How long before those charges go off?"

"About five minutes."

"Oops!"

Right on cue, the charges detonated in rapid succession; from where the soldiers watched it was merely a series of not very bright flashes. They watched the clouds of dust rise, not unlike a volcano producing a moderate eruption; as yet no sound had reached them.

"It has got to chafe," observed one trooper, "I reckon the entire convoy ----."

His last words where lost in the thunderous roar of half a ton of C4 detonating, the noise augmented by several thousand tons of rock cascading into the gorge below.

"Nice one Kenny, time to hall arse. You lead, we'll watch your backs."

As the S.A.S teams took a last glance, they noticed two or three small, but growing fires in the gorge. Some of the smashed heroine trucks had caught fire. By pure chance the largest convoy so far to use the road was right in the middle of the section being blown. Fourteen trucks, laden with raw heroine fell, along with the road, into the abyss.

"Stick that in your dope stick and smoke it," muttered a trooper.

The two land rovers caught up with the main column a few miles short of the U.N camp. News of the success passed quickly along the line of trucks. There was a decidedly cheerful atmosphere in the mess tent as breakfast was served. The U.N soldiers felt they had participated in something useful for once. They were not worried by the prophecies of a revenge attack by forces loyal to the warlords. Even so they did heed the warnings and re-sited their guns before they went for breakfast. Although sceptical they also sent out two mobile patrols in land rovers, just in case.

Most of the men had finished their breakfast and were thinking of grabbing a little sleep when the sound of a heavy gun firing reached the camp. They heard two more heavy shots, followed by louder explosions before a sentry reported two land rovers approaching at high speed.

The shaken crews were unhurt, if badly rattled by the experience of being shot at by tanks, albeit ancient ones. The sergeant in charge of the patrol quickly gave details of the force heading towards them. Eight heavy trucks, full of troops; these were escorted by at least twenty 4X4 pick up trucks, many mounting heavy machine guns. To crown it all the three old T55 tanks Kenny's patrol had seen where with the attack force.

"Nothing to worry about," said the gunners, "just tell us when you want us to plaster them."

"As soon as you like," was Paul's reply. "The trick, I suppose is to let them get close enough to destroy those tanks, but at the same time keep them out of range of the Herc."

"No problem sarge."

It wasn't a problem. At least for the U.N troops; five minutes of hard work from the gunners translated into five minutes of hell for the would be attackers. One of the 4X4s charged straight at the U.N position, whether this was courage, bravado or a suicide attack; the result of a couple of well aimed bursts from the .5 B.A.Rs on the S.A.S land rovers stopped their mad charge dead in its tracks.

By lunchtime the S.A.S men were in their herc with their land rovers headed for Kota Baru and the next phase of the operation. There wasn't room in the Herc for the trailer they had used to transport the explosives, it had to be left behind.

CHAPTER16

To the surprise of the men as they emerged from the plane into the heat of northern Malaya, they were met by their Boss.

"Hello Boss, I didn't expect to see you out here," said Mike.

Without exception the one thing all the men off the plane wanted to know was "How's Ro?" They all brushed aside enquiries on the success of their mission the only thing they seemed interested in was the condition of the girl. The Colonel quickly came to the conclusion his own questions were a waste of breath until he got them an update.

"She was still alive when I left Hereford, still hanging on to life, was how the medics described it. I left orders to inform me of any change either way; but I'll call home and get an update otherwise we'll never get anything done!"

Paul and most of the others suspected the Boss wanted to know as much as they did.

By the time they had unloaded their land rovers, the Boss returned from the building being used by the large signals section brought to enable the Boss to co-ordinate the multiple operations to be mounted against the drug barons in two days time.

"Well? How is she?" Asked Mike.

"You know medics; in their parlance she is stable, and showing signs of responding to treatment; although she is still very weak. And before you ask, no she hasn't woken up yet. Just so as you know, I care as much as any of you about her. I am also deeply concerned by the effect she seems to have had on all of us. I know this is hard, but we must not allow our personal desire to extract revenge on her behalf, to cloud our judgement in the coming operations; is that clear?"

"Yes Boss" the men replied in unison.

The C.O didn't really believe them.

"Right, briefing in two hours. Sort yourselves out, get cleaned up and get some food, I'll see you later. Mike, with me."

The old base hadn't been as busy since the end of the Second World War. All sorts of planes were coming and going, not all of them British, teams were being dropped off all along the wild border areas of Thailand and Burma. Many of these squads would be working with local troops, although some would work alone. All was under the auspices of the U.N mandate to eliminate the warlords.

Paul's team were not very happy at the role allotted to them, they were to be the support team who's job was to secure the landing site for the helicopter which would recover the S.A.S team assigned to destroy the target designated 'F6'. This was a small, but productive underground factory used to process and refine heroine. As it was fairly certain the few people who worked there did so from choice, along with the remoteness of the site, it was decided to minimise the risks charges would simply be dropped down the ventilator shafts.

The teams would drop in an hour after dark from a high-flying Hercules, in much the same way as the team which had rescued Ro had done. In fact the operation had many similarities with the rescue, the principle difference being they only had to get themselves out.

"Well at least we will arrive in style," commented Paul.

"Don't think this is going to be an easy target, complacency is a dangerous enemy Paul."

"No chance of it Boss, the only casualty we suffered getting Ro out was one of our back up team. Granted it wasn't a serious injury, but it could have been; I have no desire to find out what it feels like, thank you. We'll let the other guy find out if you don't mind."

"Fair enough, as long as you realise this is not a 'milk run'."

"Nothing is ever straight forward against this lot Boss."

The drop wasn't as good as it might have been; surprisingly it was the more experienced team which had the trouble. Paul's team all landed safely, neatly in the clearing which was to be their extraction point. Two of the others landed seconds later nearby.

"Where are the other two?" Paul asked the Captain from 'B' squadron who was leading the raid.

"Somewhere to the East, I think they're in the trees down the valley."

"Great; B.J, you and Taff stay here and sort the chutes out. Mickey, grab your medical kit, let's go and find your lost sheep Skipper."

"I thought you and Taffy always worked as a pair, why the change?" enquired the Captain.

"We do, but if your lads are in the trees then we might need Mickey's medical skills. B.J is the communications wizard, so I guess it's got to be Mickey and me."

"Fair enough sarge, lets get going, I don't know how far they drifted off."

The first trooper was quickly found, he was retrieving his parachute from some bushes, cursing fluently, if quietly.

"Are you O.K?" asked the Captain.

"Just about, I'm a bit worried about Tommo though, I think he went into the ravine."

"How come you over shot so much?" asked Paul

"I don't know, do I; just one of those things."

Paul went to the edge of the rocks and scanned the area below, "Got 'im," he muttered.

"We'll have to abort this one, let's go get him," said the Captain.

"Hang on a tick skipper," said Paul. "To get to the target you've got to go back to the landing zone. Why don't you get cracking with your lads, take either Taff or B.J with you. They're good lads, take your pick; don't worry about Tommo; Mickey and I can get him out of there and back to the L.Z."

"Why don't you shut up and do as you are told, the man is hurt, he needs our help; I don't need a gobby recruit to tell me how to run my section."

"He's got a point skipper, if we get a move on we've got time to give them a hand to get Tommo out of the ravine, we'll have to go down to get his demolition charges, come on."

"We are aborting this mission, we've already got one casualty, I am not risking anyone else."

Paul ignored the Captain, turning to the other two troopers, "either of you two medics?"

"Tommo is our medic."

"Great! O.K borrow Mickey, one of you come with me in Mickey's place, let's get these charges and get on with it."

"You've made your point sergeant, I'll get on with it."

Between them the five men quickly fashioned a stretcher for the injured man out of a couple of saplings and his parachute. As soon as they reached the top Paul turned to the captain, "We can manage now thanks, get a move on and blow the shit pit sky high."

In spite of the shaky start, the attacking squad took B.J. with them dropped their charges down the ventilator ducts and legged it back to the pick up point.

Paul and Taff settled down to wait for the returning raiding party; they were nearly half a mile from the landing site, just where the path split. The path to Paul's left led down into a thickly wooded gully, the other to the landing site.

"I don't suppose you brought a 'smoker' by any chance?"

"Course I did Boyo."

"You star Taff, I'm moving position a bit, so it will give you a clear chuck with your smoke grenade."

"O.K make it snappy they'll be here soon."

Although they were being pursued, so far no shots had been fired. The squad who had attacked the factory appeared at a steady run, for a second it looked as though they would take the wrong path.

"B. J, this way; we'll cover your backs and be along in a few minutes, keep going."

As soon as the attack squad were safely away, Taff threw his smoke grenade as far down the other path as he could. The ground shook as the demolition charges exploded and destroyed the heroine factory. The two friends used this additional distraction to cover their rapid departure; to further compound the deceit a hastily chopped off bush was dragged into the entrance to the path.

Sure enough, the pursuers dived straight into the smoke filled gully; unaware they had lost the trail of those they sought to capture.

The realisation they had been tricked hit them when they heard the helicopter; by then it was too late. Forewarned of the casualty by radio the giant long range Chinook landed with it's tail ramp already down. The loadmaster was out in a flash, he and Mickey carried the injured 'Tommo' deep into the cavernous interior of the Chinook. By the time the demolition team arrived all the kit and roughly wrapped parachutes were already thrown into the chopper.

"Come on you lot, move it; we've been on the ground too long already!" shouted the loadmaster; the captain ran into the dark interior of the helicopter, tripped over a parachute strap and almost fell on the injured team member.

"All aboard, let's go."

"Wait, hold it! Paul and Taff aren't on board yet!" shouted B.J.

The loadmaster was beginning to close the ramp, "I said wait," B.J. repeated.

" Your Skipper says go. So we go O.K."

"Let me put it this way, mate, if this thing leaves the ground without Paul and Taff, then I'll personally chuck you out to wait for them, and you can tell them why the chopper left without them."

"What are we waiting for?" shouted the captain.

"For Paul and Taff, they were watching our backs."

"They must be dead by now; we must go. Now!"

"Hold it!" said the corporal from the other section; "B.J. is right, they are O.K there haven't been any shots fired at all yet. Here they come."

Taff ran to the helicopter, stopping on the ramp, he knelt, checking through his infrared site, covering Paul as he joined them.

"Now can we go?" asked the harassed loadmaster.

"Most definitely." Said B. J. "The sooner the better."

"You took your bloody time sergeant," snapped the Captain, "Your lax attitude jeopardised the success of the mission and the safety of the helicopter, its crew and the rest of the team."

"I reckon they all did bloody well skipper, they kept their cool, rescued Tommo. They must have done a good job covering us, we're all here not a shot fired at us or by us. The target is destroyed, you can see it burning, even from here."

"My report will recommend those two sergeants are immediately returned to their unit. He disobeyed my order to abort," the angry captain turned to Paul. "You would have attacked the place yourselves, even though I ordered my squad not to, wouldn't you?"

"It is why we came here, we owed it to Tommo and we certainly owed it to the person who gave us the location and lay out of the place. The information was so good it even allowed us to avoid the bloody guards. I cannot imagine a more textbook operation; damned nearly perfect intelligence, complete surprise; what more could you want. If you're typical of the skippers then get me R,T,U'd; you'll be doing me a favour."

Paul turned and walked over to Mickey. "How's he doing?"

"It's a bad break. His left shoulder is busted as well; he's stable. The I.V. will, or should stop any shock, the morphine should last until we get to Kota, if it doesn't, then I've got some more."

"Fair enough, you have alerted Kota about Tommo and his injuries?"

"Of course I have, you didn't think I'd forget did you?"

"Just making sure, I would have most likely forgotten to call it in, you know how forgetful I can be."

"Yeah, right." Replied Mickey with a grin.

The long serving corporal joined them, "how's he doing?"

"He'll be alright until we get to Kota."

"What I can't understand is how two of you overshot so badly; why did you deploy your 'chutes so early. I nearly hit one of you at about eight thousand feet."

"Skipper's orders Paul, his standing orders are always the same. The last one deploys at five thousand feet, the others at one thousand foot intervals upwards. It would have been Tommo you nearly hit, he was first to deploy."

"It's fuckin' crazy, I suppose there is some obscure logic in it, if it was a day time drop in open country, but at night in 'close' country, it's inviting disaster?"

"We've had this discussion before every drop; but there's no shifting his nibs, he's right and that's it, he won't tolerate any discussion."

"He's a bit of a plonker, that skipper of yours, how long has he been here?"

"He was only a couple of courses before you and Taff, he sort of snuck up on us, I think it must have been a case of 'Daddy' pulling strings."

"I might still be a 'sprog' around here, but I'll be damned if I'd put up with it; those kind of idiots running things get people killed. If he starts when we get back, dive for cover, because I will fly back at him, big time."

"It won't do a bit of good, we've tried, all we got was a bollicking, and he got worse than ever."

"Why not have a word with the Boss, he's alright, so is Mike, although he tends to play devils advocate, it's more to see how sure of your case you are than anything else. It took me a while to figure him out, but if you are certain you are right, he'll back you all the way. Sure, he'll try to knock holes in your argument; it doesn't mean he won't help you."

"I'll bear it in mind,, but things have to go to the squadron 2 I.C. first and he used to go to the same public school as our skipper."

"Oh gawd, not the old school tie brigade, see Mike or the Boss if you feel bad. I won't make any waves, but my gang will back you up, if he doesn't have a go at me first."

"Cheers Paul, you've got a good gang, 'sprogs' or not, don't get yourself in the shit over him he ain't worth it."

"We'll see, we've got a couple of hours, I'm grabbing a bit of kip, looks like the rest of my lot are already crashed out. It might be a good idea if you did the same, this ain't over yet."

Paul had hardly dozed off when the captain came back from the flight deck. He woke all the soldiers, "come on, on your feet; move!"

"What the hell?" Muttered Taff, as he was prodded in the ribs by a boot. "I suggest you are a bit more careful waking Paul, try it with him you could well regret it, he has been known to react badly."

The warning went unheeded. The captain pushed Paul with his boot, he never had chance to say anything; before he had woken up properly Paul had lashed out and swept the Captains other leg from under him. Paul was up in a flash, wondering what was going on, the angry captain scrambled back to his feet.

"What the hell do you think you are doing sergeant? You're on a charge; assaulting an officer."

"What the hell is going on?" Paul asked, "I presume something drastic has happened, from the fact you were on the floor it must have been you who woke me. What did you do, kick me I suppose?"

"You knocked me over! How dare you?"

"If you kicked me what else did you expect?"

"I did warn you he'd react badly," observed Taff. "Anyway what's the panic?"

"Weapons check, we must account for all ammunition issued to us."

"None of my gang fired a shot, as far as I know neither did any of your lot. Taff used one smoke grenade; apart from the demolition charges. Get back to kip lads." Then Paul lay down again, using a partially gathered up parachute as a pillow.

"Sergeant! On your feet, and stand to attention when you talk to me."

"Oh piss off, my lot are short of kip, and like I said, this isn't over yet, so you'd do well to get a bit of kip yourself; take it while you can."

"I'm reporting you to the boss when we get back."

"Good it will save me the trouble of reporting you, I can't lose. Either you get kicked out or I do, whichever way it goes my life expectancy increases, like I said I can not lose. Now sod off and get some kip."

The boss himself met the returning soldiers, they were the first ones back at Kota Baru, as their target had been one of the closest. He was concerned over the injured man, but relaxed when the medics waiting with him pronounced 'Tommo' would be all right after a bit. They were full of praise for Mickey, "you did a bloody good job son, I like the design of the stretcher, ideal for such a case."

"How the hell did he overshoot by so much in the first place, if he jumped before your squad Paul, yet all your gang landed together on the landing zone. I'm confused, can you explain please?"

"I was watching out for my gang, nothing to do with me Boss, but it looks as though S.O.Ps need looking at. Though they worked O.K. for my gang."

The boss gave Paul a sideways look, "go and find some grub, then get some kip, you are on again tonight; briefing at eighteen hundred hours."

"Give us a clue what we've got tonight boss?" Taff asked.

"Nothing very exciting; another underground store in southern Thailand, it's hard to get at from the ground."

"More trees to land in Taff," chuckled Paul

"It ain't funny boyo; it bloody well hurts"

"You should keep your short little legs together mate."

"Bollocks!"

"Them as well."

The boss grinned and shook his head. The team left for the mess tent; after they had eaten they drifted off in search of a quiet corner to grab some sleep. The boss noticed Paul wandering off towards the sand dunes near the end of the runway; he guessed he just wanted a little time alone to sort out his thoughts on his domestic and family problems. Judging from the conversations he had with members of the other team, Paul hadn't let his worries get in the way of the job in hand. He had half expected trouble with the captain in charge of the other team; doubts about him had been voiced before.

186

The Colonel sought out Taff, "I won't keep you long, I just wanted a little chat."

"Sure boss, what's wrong?"

"I was just curious, is Paul O.K? I mean this thing with his Mum, on top of the trouble with his wife; is it affecting him?"

"Sure he's worried about his mum, who wouldn't be? But like he said there's bugger all he can do to help; that's life; cruel but true. As far as the business with his wife is concerned, I think it's his girls' which bother him most. He'll be O.K he's the same cantankerous sod he always is when it matters."

"So he's focused on the job?"

"Totally, as ever."

"Thanks Taff, do you know where he is at the moment?"

"I think he went off to the dunes for a bit of space."

The boss wandered off in search of his troubled sergeant, at least he'd told Taff where he was going. He soon spotted Paul, he was peering through the coarse grass at something, it looked as though he was aiming at something with his rifle. He approached cautiously, not wanting to surprise Paul, he needn't have worried, as Paul casually asked him to join him, adding to 'keep down Boss.'

"I'm not even going to ask how you knew it was me; what's up?"

"I'm not sure, don't move the rifle, take a look through the sight."

The boss grunted, then spent a minute getting comfortable, "What are we looking at? Good god is it who I think it is?"

"Look on the boat"

"It's not possible!"

"So you agree, I'm not hallucinating?"

"What on earth made you look at that particular boat?"

Paul pointed out to sea. A long way out was a lynx, trying to look inconspicuous.

"What's the connection? Obviously there is one."

"Well it looked as though it was keeping tabs on the boat, which is, by the way, a hell of a lot faster than it looks. It certainly isn't the fishing boat its appearance suggests."

"A smuggler?"

"Without a doubt, keep watching. The pallet they are stacking boxes on will be picked up by a fork lift in a moment. Watch it when it goes back into the warehouse."

"Bloody hell; how many armed men did you make it?"

"At least ten, judging from the company he keeps, I'd say there was a good chance of more."

"Any chance of finding out what the chopper was watching?"

"Already done boss, it's Andy, the pilot who brought us out when we got Ro out. He confirms the boat is suspect."

"Any chance of getting some pictures of this lot?"

"Already done boss," he produced a small digital camera from a pocket of his combat smock. "This thing screws on to the sight, I got it from the technical section to try out for them. Apparently you can plug it in to a computer and get the pictures out."

"I didn't realise you were into all this high tech stuff Paul."

"I ain't. I just hate lugging loads of gear when there's something better around."

"The problem is we haven't got a computer here, so how do we get the pictures out?"

"According to the boffins we can plug it into a fax machine, dial up this number they gave me. You know the one we call the 'professor', according to him, the first picture will be emerging within a minute of us sending it to him, we'll see."

Back in the temporary head quarters they plugged their new toy into the fax machine. The 'professor' was as good as his word; in less than five minutes they had clear, well-defined pictures of shots one and five.

"That clinches it," said the boss, "As soon as most of the lads are back in an hour or so the place gets a visit. What I can't understand is what the merry hell McStephoin is doing here; as to Donaghue! It's him I take it?"

"Rather begs the question, who did customs pick up?"

"Any ideas on how to hit the place?"

"I don't fancy knocking on the door; they are likely to get spiteful," replied Paul. "However, I have got an idea."

"Thought you might have, come on let's hear it."

"The local unit have got several old Saracen armoured cars; use them as road blocks", he indicated three positions on the rough map. "Have some of our lads at each point, ready to jump on any one we flush out."

"So far it's alright, one little thing, exactly how do we flush them out?"

"The only weapons I saw them with, were A K 47s, why not have a couple of our snipers at the end of the field, where I was, with a couple of heavy calibre rifles. There is at least one Barret light 50 I've seen, there must be something else similar around, failing which use a B.A.R. the one on our panther is a good accurate weapon."

"So you are saying shoot it up from this side of the river, then jump on any who try to make a run for it."

"Seems the safest option to me boss, that shower of shit aren't worth the risk of one of our lads. Convince them, the only thing they can do is quit."

"We'll have to go in eventually."

"True, but better against half a dozen than all of them. The more we can take out one-way or another, before we do go in the better. We can always use a Saracen to open the doors; an A K won't penetrate their armour."

"We'll see what the unit commanders make of it at an 'O' group when they get back," said the C.O. "I'll get the two fit lads from your Op last night to keep an eye on them."

"I take it we're still on for tonight's raid Boss?"

"Absolutely, the selected drop zone is a bit tight; new boys you maybe but you have displayed a remarkable consistency in hitting small zones from high level. We believe the target is undefended, so there shouldn't be any trouble, infra red scans of the area have revealed nothing in the way of guards."

"That could mean no-one is around, which is unlikely, if it's the significant storage facility Ro said, then it's more than likely to be well protected."

"Then how do you explain the lack of contacts?"

"They're very good is the obvious explanation Boss."

"Having doubts?"

"No more than usual Boss; just allowing for the possibility all may not be what it seems."

"Go get an hour's sleep; and bloody well done spotting the lot across the river; bloody cheek, right under our noses!"

The raid on the warehouse ended up as an extremely noisy affair, the whole place burning almost to the ground, Luckily the wind blew the smoke out to sea; even so several fishermen were high as kites for a time.

Up until the fire started, things had gone well, six cars were stopped, mostly rammed by the Saracens; 'effective if a bit over the top' as the C.O was later heard to say. The boat tried to make a run for it, a couple of short bursts from the B.A.R on the opposite bank smashed the engine block. It then drifted on the out going tide straight to the pair of rigid raiders manned by some marines waiting for just such an eventuality

About a dozen die-hards tried to fight it out from the burning warehouse, five of them, all wounded were captured along with sufficient heroine to prove this was a Major source. Four Malayan soldiers were killed in the final assault, in spite of S.A.S warnings they decided they would be first into the warehouse. The waiting gunmen simply cut them down with automatic fire. In addition to the fatalities six more local troops and five of the S.A.S men were injured.

The real prize, Messrs McStephoin and Donaghue were captured in a reasonable state. As things like this had to be handled properly, the pair were handed over to the local authorities. They were convicted of all sorts of crimes by a local court and sentenced to many years in a Malayan gaol. The world and his wife wanted them extradited, not least the British, just when it looked as the legal moves to get them might succeed, the pair were sprung in a raid on a police convoy taking them to the final hearing. A total of ten police were killed in this attack, adding to the already terrible price paid in combating this menace.

The raid on the underground store was pretty much as planned, there were two guards, both asleep when Paul and the gang dropped in on them. To say they were surprised to wake up looking down the wrong end of a couple of M16s would be to understate things. They were handcuffed and brought back to Kota Baru; the supposedly secret dump was even larger than thought, it burnt for most of the week! There was one minor, almost predictable mishap; three of the squad landed almost on top of each other in the middle of the selected clearing. Taff managed to hit a sturdy bush, its thorns protected it even from goats, Taff left it a mangled heap of twigs, minus several of its protective thorns, now well embedded in the little Welshman's behind!

"Not a bloody word!" he growled.

190

"Sort him out Mickey, we're not short of time but don't take too long."

The medic managed to keep a more or less straight face as he removed the worst of the thorns, so Taff could move with reasonable freedom.

Once back at their base at Kota Baru they went through the usual debrief procedure. Someone said a solution must be found to the problem of Taff consistently undershooting drop zones, before they could come up with an answer they must find the cause.

As Taff seemed back to his normal cheery self, Paul decided to risk a wise crack.

"I reckon it's an aerodynamic problem, give him a very slightly larger 'chute; one which will slow him down just a little bit. There must be a formula for calculating the area of 'chute required, lets see." He paused, "The square root of weight, times the distance from ankle to arse gives us a low centre of gravity—"

"You piss taking sod; you wait, my turn will come boyo."

The boss put his head in his hands and smiled, 'his boys' were back on form.

The only thing left to do now was to take the head Warlord's fortified mansion near the Chinese border with Burma. In the first attack nearly two hundred Burmese troops launched what should have been a surprise attack, less than twenty returned to their base uninjured, such was the resistance.

Clearly a different strategy was needed. In the next attack the Burmese threw everything they had at the place. Three-helicopter gun ships attacked with missiles, two were shot down. Eight tanks supported over five hundred troops in the assault; these were assisted by twenty troops from Hereford. At the end of the day the place was a smoking pile of rubble. The last of the defenders killed in close quarter combat by the S.A.S. One of the soldiers died later from his wounds, three more were significantly injured. Over two hundred Burmese commandos lay dead, five of the tanks were twisted, blackened wrecks, their crews mostly dead.

As if the losses were not bad enough, the final twist was the warlord appeared to have escaped in his helicopter.

A report reached Hereford the day after the weary troops had returned; its source was the C.I.A. It stated a helicopter belonging to the warlord the Burmese had attacked, had crashed near the location of a major heroine factory in Cambodia. It went on to say,

191

all on board had died in the crash, and the fire had been so fierce it had not been possible to identify those on board.

Kuymer Rouge troops, loyal to Pol Pot, claimed to have found an undisclosed number of gold bars, including one of rare white gold and two bars of platinum. Pol Pot claimed title to the loot to pay for the action of his troops destroying the major heroine plant in the north west of that tragic land. The report also mentioned his troops had captured over a ton of almost pure heroine.

As Paul pointed out it didn't say the stuff had been destroyed.

"One hell of a result all round," commented the deputy director of special forces, who was addressing the general debrief of all those who had taken part in the operations against the warlords.

"My congratulations to all involved; in particular our very special guest, without who's courage all this would not have been possible."

There was a spontaneous out burst of cheering and clapping. For the first time he could remember Ro blushed!

Paul was sitting next to the wheelchair bound Ro; she still had a drip of some sort in her arm and was too weak to walk. The medics had finally relented and allowed Paul to wheel her across to the meeting. One of the senior medics sat the other side of the wheelchair watching her like a hawk.

"That's put the colour back in your cheeks gal" Paul said into her ear so only she could hear.

"You sod!" she whispered in her croaky voice.

She had noticed the Colonel walking, strangely somewhat self-consciously towards her; he motioned the medic to move.

"As you are all only too aware, awards and medals are an anathema to the regiment. Very occasionally someone does something so extraordinary we cannot let it pass without some sort of gesture, how ever empty or symbolic. This is, as far as I am aware quite unique in the annals of the regiment. It is my proud duty to present this incredibly courageous young lady with honorary membership of both officers and sergeants messes as well as a sandy beret. Never has a beret been so hard won. Madam I feel humble in your presence." The C.O stepped back and saluted.

The place went ballistic; it was nearly five minutes before some sort of order was restored. Everyone in the place wanted to shake her hand, pat her back, one or two stole a little peck on the cheek. All were very aware of the frailty of her condition and bore it in mind as they individually congratulated her. Paul was sure Mick, his sergeant Major lingered just a little bit longer than most, and was reluctant to let go of her hand; then there was the eye contact! As soon as they were finished the medic asserted his claim to her and whisked her back to the medical centre.

"Alright gentlemen," the C.Os voice "I propose we quickly run over the entire campaign in general terms; then take individual comments from you on any points we may have over looked or could learn from."

The meeting went on for what seemed like hours. One point became clear; a way was going to have to be found to heal the rift between the regiment and the shattered department in Whitehall with whom they were supposed to work. The Boss patiently worked his way around the room, allowing each man a few minutes to raise points; which from their point needed addressing.

Eventually it was Paul's turn. "There is one thing bugging me Boss," he began, "If we caught bloody Donaghue, and it seems certain it is him festering in a Kuala Lumpar gaol, then who the hell did customs lift?"

"As far as they are concerned they got the right man, I'll get pictures of both, then you can see if Ro can throw any light on it. For the record, the one customs have got is still refusing to speak, he is maintaining total silence."

"Doesn't it indicate a degree of training of some sort Boss?"

"To have maintained it for so long? It is a good point, one worth looking into."

"Strikes me there's more of a link between assorted Irish based terrorist groups and the international drugs trade than we thought Boss, was it being orchestrated from Whitehall, exactly who is behind it?"

"What's your point Paul? Are you suggesting we try to push the campaign further up the chain?"

"I assume you don't think we got the real ring leaders either."

"Will we ever know? Is it our place to find out?"

"Fair points Boss, it's getting bloody difficult to know who to trust outside of the regiment. It seems almost as though one lot uses the other to take the pressure off. We start to hit one lot then another lot kick off, we get sent to calm them down. Before we do more than scratch the surface we get ordered to the other end of the earth to put the lid on another 'revolutionary' group of nutters."

"We do seem to have clocked up a lot of miles of late. One of our political masters commented a week or so ago, 'the unit as a whole was buzzing around like a swarm of bees who had lost their nest'."

"The only link I can see is most of these groups have in common is their principle source of income, which appears to be producing and distributing drugs. Just a thought, would we have more effect on the assorted terrorists, if we concentrated more on their fund raising activities?"

"Good thinking, we'll look into it. I think we have covered just about everything," said the deputy director. "There is however one other thing I would like to mention. It is not regimental policy to discuss those who have been amongst us, and then later returned to their parent units. In this instance however I feel there are valuable lessons to be learnt in looking at the reasons for the most recent case.

Some how our system failed us and an officer was allowed to run his squad in a way which did not conform to standard operating procedures. It is difficult to draw the line between initiative and simply changing the way we operate to suite an individual's perceived idea of how we ought to do things. Conventional discipline around here is lax, our detractors would say too lax, it is possible they may have a point.

This problem only came to light because the officer to whom I am referring, wished to place a probationer on a charge, because this sergeant was attached to a different squadron the matter was referred to regimental headquarters. Subsequent enquiries revealed a lamentable state of affairs; this regiment has no place for arrogance and take notice, it will not be tolerated. As of now any complaints will be dealt with, without reference to rank by the adjutant or his deputy, a post which will be filled within the next few days. Squadron commanders will meet in the C.O.'s office after this meeting. We will put this entire incident behind us and move on. Thank you for your attention gentlemen."

"Right, I think we have covered anything, formal detailed debrief will begin at 0900hrs tomorrow, dismissed"

For the next few weeks Paul and his squad spent their time either being trained or training others in the use of the new Heckler and Koch.

Most evenings he managed to pop into the medical centre to see Ro, who was slowly but surely regaining her strength. She was surprised at the scope of the operations launched, on the basis of the information she had passed on to Paul. Gradually she began to get out and about again, at the Boss's insistence she and Paul had to go through her entire debrief in minute detail. 'Just to make sure we haven't missed anything'.

It must have been around the middle of the third afternoon they were going through yet another folder when Paul casually passed Ro a photograph.

"Oh; Mr. McStephoin, where was this taken? Looks hot."

"Kota Baru, it's one of those new digital cameras, I took it through the sight on my rifle"

"It's a really clear image, I'm impressed."

"Recognise him?"

"It's Donaghue."

"That's what I thought," replied Paul.

"Well, it is definitely Donaghue, I am absolutely certain of it; the picture is so clear there is no doubt."

"O.K then who is this?" he slid the picture of the man customs had arrested across the table to Ro.

Just for a split second Ro's veneer cracked, fleeting it may have been, but Paul noticed, "I don't know him," said Ro. Paul gave her a side ways look; "I have never seen him before, why should I know him, I don't know every heroine dealer in Ireland."

"Now I'm worried," said Paul. "All the hours I've spent talking to you and I have never seen you rattled. There have been numerous occasions when I know damned well you have been, how shall we say, economical with the truth. This is, I'm sure, the first time you've told me an out right lie, why for heavens sake?"

"What makes you think I'm lying?"

"It's not the point, the point is something obviously shook you, to the extent I noticed. Oh sure, I've seen you surprised, but I have never seen such reaction before. Who is he Ro? Tell me the truth please; the expression on your face, as fleeting as it was told a story of its own. He was someone special to you perhaps, is it someone who knows who you really are and could blow your new identity?"

"Stop it Paul; I told you I don't know, now can we leave it?"

"Ro; we've got to sort this out, the sooner the better. Because of you we have been able to take out all manner of arseholes. Damn it

195

you helped us to catch this guy; all right, agreed we thought we were going to catch Donaghue. This guy collected and paid for twenty kilos of heroine which was headed for the provos, the money from which would have paid for guns and explosives which would have killed lord knows how many people. He had a couple of their worst hit men with him, thanks to him one got away, I don't care how you look at it, this sod is bad. I'll bet he is, or was one of your lot who's gone 'native'."

Ro just sat, not speaking, whether she was sulking or thinking things over Paul wasn't sure.

"I don't believe you," she suddenly said, "I think you're fishing, trying to identify someone you just happened to see in an unusual situation."

"You are exactly right, we are trying to identify him; and the unusual situation was he had a case full of pure heroine in one hand and a 9mm Hi-power in the other. He shot one cop and hit a couple of others who were only saved by their body armour!"

"You are certain, there were no mistakes?"

"Absolutely certain, like I said, the only thing we don't know is his name, you clearly do, we need to know Ro. If he is a good guy trapped in strange circumstances, tell us, it is possible we may be able to help."

"Its alright I'll tell you who he is, it does make some sense, although I trusted him. He's a French narcotics agent, he is supposed to be liaison officer between the F.B.I and the U.N department running the operation I was part of. His name is Philippe Le Fervre."

"Oh shit!" Exclaimed Paul, "No wonder people in high places wanted you dead."

"I don't understand?"

"I don't really; but I have heard the name before, twice before. Sir James, the one who suddenly quit and vanished, it was his wife's maiden name. At least it was her name before they married; she was a rich, French divorcee. I get the distinct feeling a bit of digging in that direction might prove interesting, but later."

"I think what you are proposing is very dangerous Paul, the establishment will only put up with just so much stirring; it doesn't matter how bad the things dug up are. You know how they react to the least criticism."

"I know all that Ro, what I don't understand is your reticence to identify Le Fervre."

"Can you accept it was down to a misguided sense of loyalty on my part."

"I'm going to have to accept it, you're never going to tell me the real reason, are you?"

"Some things are best left, Paul; please trust me on this."

"Alright if it's the way it is going to be, I suppose I haven't got much choice, have I?"

"You're not happy are you?"

"No Ro I am not; you lied to me, now you won't tell me why. I'm guessing he knows who you really are; it's the only thing I can think of which would account for your reaction; unless there's a skeleton in your cupboard and you'd rather it stayed there!"

"He wouldn't know me if I walked up to him and kissed him! It's the truth, I promise."

"It's something I suppose, but now it makes less sense than ever to me. I'll see you later, I must let customs know who they have got banged up under the wrong name."

"I'll see you this evening then?"

"If I don't see you before, depends on what I dig up in the mean time, behave yourself for once; see you later."

Ro might have spent most of the afternoon asleep, Paul spent most of it with the intelligence section. What he learnt was quite disturbing, to the extent the officer in charge called in the Boss at quite an early stage.

What was emerging would shake the very foundations of the intelligence community in Whitehall.

It all revolved around Sir James; his wife was indeed a divorcee, she had been married to a French businessman, with distinctly dodgy connections. The first surprise was the Le Fervre picked up by customs was her son from her first marriage. The second was the discovery of her maiden name; it was Donaghue! It was her brother in a Malayan gaol awaiting extradition proceedings. The reason no one had seen a link was the normal checks on these things centred on Irish connections. The fact the grandparents had moved to Jersey, and stayed there, meant they had been missed some checks. All this in spite of the fact the family were major financial contributors to Sinn Fienne no-one seemed to have noticed; but then such checks were the province of a department Sir James had help set up.

"Nothing like keeping it in the family," said Paul.

The boss turned to the young sergeant, "You say nothing of this to anyone, in particular to Ro. This will no doubt go much deeper; you may end up getting called in front of some civil service committee over this Paul. If I can I'll keep you out of it, we'll try to convince them the discovery of the links was down to chance. This will get very messy."

"Point taken Boss, and thanks, I'll just tell Ro it's been sorted and leave it at that. If she can blank me then I can return the favour."

"Something is bugging you about all this Paul, get it off your chest."

Paul told the boss about Ro's reaction to the photo and her subsequent attitude.

"Strange; any ideas?"

"Only one, and we've already established I was wrong with my guess, so I've no more idea than you have as to what it was all about."

"A cause for concern perhaps?"

"Damned if I know boss, all this intrigue is doin' my bloody head in. All I ever wanted to be was a soldier; stuff all this secret squirrel crap, from what I can see most of it is a waste of time, not to mention bloody dangerous. It all seems to be about protecting their own little empires, not to mention their own arses."

"I think you can say we agree Paul. Get back to Ro, and not a word about what we've found out; O.K"

"Fair enough boss, she's full of surprises, just when you think she's told us every thing she's going to, she drops another bombshell opens up a whole new can of worms. See you later Boss.".

In the evening, sitting at their usual table eating their tea, Paul and Roana were exchanging their usual small talk and banter. Paul, as always, was trying desperately to extract any tiny snippet of information which might give a clue to her past life and hence identification. Typically he was getting nowhere. Mick, Paul's Squadron Sergeant Major approached, something about his

198

demeanour made Paul curious, the normal self-confidence was, he decided, definitely missing.

"Mind if I join you Paul?"

"Feel free, you need to ask?"

"Cheers," he arranged his plates and cups and placed his tray against the table leg. "I've got a favour to ask you Paul." He fidgeted, almost uncomfortably.

"Spit it out for heavens sake mate, what can be so terrible it's reduced our illustrious P.M.C. to an apoplectic nervous wreck?"

"Would you mind if I asked Roana out?" blurted Mick, "I wouldn't ask but -."

"Mick, ask Roana. she's the one you want to wine and dine and heaven knows what else, I'm sure you don't fancy me."

"Damn right I don't," replied the embarrassed S.S.M. "It's just, well, we sort of assumed you two were an item."

"Well you assumed wrong mate. Yes we're friends, good friends but it's all - O.K"

Roana looked at Paul, a gleam was in her eye which Paul couldn't remember seeing there before.

"I'll see you two later," he picked up his tray and joined Taff and some other Mates.

"What's 'appening there, you get blown out?"

"With any luck," replied Paul. "She's a remarkable person, and yes I like her a lot but, and this is a big but, I don't fancy her. Mick on the other hand is totally besotted. Thinkin' about it, I think she fancies him. Time will tell."

Later the same evening Paul and Taff sat in a corner of the mess having a quiet pint.

"Looks like Mick and Ro are getting on alright," commented Taff.

"The only worry is if Mick's ego will stand it, it's the third time in a row she's won at darts; she won six straight games of pool as well."

Half an hour later a taxi pulled up outside the camp gates and collected a happy couple headed for one of the best restaurants in Hereford. The rear lights had hardly faded from view when Paul and his team were summoned to the C.O.'s office

"Got a job requires your special talent. Grab your kit, your weapons and case-less ammunition. I'll meet you on the plane at

199

Lynham with your back up then I'll brief you on the problem. Take your side arms as well, three whiz-bangs and a C.S. each. - Go!"

Somehow or other, operations and training commitments contrived to keep Paul and his team overseas for nearly a year. Within days of his return to the U.K. he ended up in hospital, injured in a routine exercise which went wrong, resulting in a medical discharge. He didn't see Roana or his Sergeant Major again. He often wondered what had happened to them, but knew better than to ask.

CHAPTER 17

Those who have travelled, it will be obvious our home country is indeed an island, not a very big island at all; so it shouldn't be too surprising when from time to time a face from the past is unexpectedly encountered.

One morning, a very pleasant summer morning, Paul was sorting parcels in the warehouse into their various piles for the drivers, when there was such an occurrence. One of the parcels was labelled 'to be called for' and had been carefully put to one side. A battered old Fiat car rattled to a stop near the open access doors of the warehouse and a skinny but attractive woman in her thirties emerged. Paul went to meet her in response to his boss's request of 'sort the geezer out'. His appearance at the doorway was greeted with a squeal of delight.

"Sergeant Paul," with which she hurled herself at him, arms around his neck and legs firmly locked round his waist. The drivers, for the most part, were hanging out of their cabs making all sorts of derogatory, even slanderous comments; totally unaware of the reasons for the enthusiastic greeting.

In his own way Paul was, for once, at a loss for words. "I say, steady on Ro."

Moving to a discrete distance, they talked quietly for a few minutes. It emerged Mick had proposed after their meal at Hereford and they had married a couple of months later. All attempts to locate Paul to be his best man had failed, by the time Paul was contactable again Mick had left the army. Now they were living barely ten miles away.

Paul and Mick were both still nominally members of 21 T.A. regiment but because of disabilities, both were non - operational. Somehow both became involved with P.O.P.As. (pissed off parents association). The favourite pastime became handing over drug pushers to the local plod. Through 'Popas' they kept in touch with many old friends.

Ro, it transpired, was nowhere as well as Paul had at first thought. She was, despite appearances, a very sick lady. Gradually her condition deteriorated, her medication slowly became ineffective and she was admitted to a government 'special hospital' in the 'home counties'. It soon became apparent there would be no quick fix for her condition so Mick left his business in the hands of his manager and rented a cottage to be near his ailing wife.

By this time Paul had set up his own small business, he'd a van of his own which was, as he put it, the perfect match for him; old, past its prime, it smokes too much but was willing as hell once it got going. One of the local firms run by a friend of his, asked him to deliver a special load for them one fine Saturday morning. "No problem Mate."

The delivery completed he headed homewards, on impulse he turned off the M25 a couple of junctions early and went in search of Mick, his old Sergeant Major. As he knew the address it didn't take long to find his old friend. "Hi Mick. Just thought I'd pop in and nick a coffee seeing as I was passing."

"Come in Mate, good to see you."

"Where's Ro?"

"Still in dock."

"Oh dear, how is she?"

"Don't know Paul, they won't let me see her."

"You what?" exclaimed Paul. "What do you mean they won't let you see her, they can't fucking stop you."

"Seems as though they can. All I get is 'She's undergoing therapy, you'll be informed of any change in her condition'."

Paul took a drink from the mug Mick thrust in front of him.

"Cheers! Bloody hell Mick!" he exclaimed, "Now I know who taught Taff, pass the sugar."

"Bloody ingrate," was Mick's swift rejoinder.

Paul stirred in as much sugar as would dissolve, then added a bit more for luck. "What would you say to the idea of us going to see your missus?"

"Great, but we won't get past the gate!"

"Wanna bet?"

"They won't open the gate!"

"If they don't the old Merc. Will!"

"Paul!" exclaimed Mick, well aware what a maverick his friend could be. "They're M.O.D. cops on the gate; you know what they can be like."

"Then they're Civil Servants, and they'd bloody well better be civil and serve."

"Oh dear, you're going to try to bust her out, aren't you?"

"Only if we have to, come on let's go. I reckon I know the way." A fifteen - minute drive through the leafy lanes of Hertfordshire brought them to a fork in the quiet back road. Paul was about to take the left hand fork when Mick stopped him. "Wrong way Mate, the other road."

"You what?" replied Paul sounding shocked. "The rest home for Civil Servants is down to the left."

"I know, they moved her to a special secure unit two weeks ago, I haven't seen her since."

Bloody hell Mick, why didn't you let me know? You do know what goes on in the shit pit down here I take it?"

"No idea Paul, but it sounds as though you do, and it don't sound good."

"Damn right it ain't good, it's what could loosely be called an interrogation centre; it's deniable; well out of order, and illegal by all conventions. On top of it all, this is where the arseholes involved in her capture and the drug running were banged up."

"You're kidding. I'd heard of such a place, and the bastards have got my Ro in there? Oh shit."

"Shit indeed Mate! You haven't still got a cannon have you?"

"Not on me, why?"

"Me neither, never mind we'll 'borrow' a couple of the guns on the gate," was Paul's casual reply.

"You're mad."

"Not half as mad as the cranks who run this place."

Paul stopped the van very close to the solid looking iron gates, as well as a large built in mortise lock there was a chain looped through the bars which had a pad lock attached. Fixed to the gates was the standard, 'Restricted, Official Secrets M.O.D. Property' notice.

A quite large M.O.D. policeman wandered over. "Move away from the gates," he commanded.

"Why?" enquired Paul, "They open inwards. We've come to see my mate's wife, she's in here."

"There's no visitors allowed, so you might as well bugger off," replied the officious cop.

"So you won't let us in?"

"No chance."

Paul got back in the van, engaged second gear and hit the throttle as he let out the clutch. The gate locks resisted for a second or so then they flew open flattening the startled cop in the process. Mick was horrified and amazed at the speed with which Paul had knocked the van out of gear, yanked on the hand brake and baled out, leaping on the M.O.D. policeman before he had chance to recover

By the time the other policeman on duty in the gatehouse had opened the door to see what the fuss was about, his oppo. was sound asleep on the grass and his M.P.9 was in Paul's hands and levelled on the second officers mid rift. "Drop the gun," commanded Paul, "Very, very carefully."

The shocked officer complied.

"Right, get the sack of shit inside now – move!"

Within a minute both the policemen were securely handcuffed to a stout rail inside the guard post and gagged.

O.K. Mick, let's go see your Missus," Paul commented casually as he passed Mick the second guard's M.P.9

Paul stopped the van right outside the main doors, pointing straight towards the exit driveway, passenger door as near as possible to the imposing portal of the old country house.

"Oi, you can't park there!" shouted the approaching M.O.D. cop. "Can't you bloody well read?" he indicated to the little wooden sign stuck into the grass verge. "Let me see your pass."

"Sure," replied Paul casually. "Here's my pass," as he swung the M.P.9 muzzle to within an inch of the man's nose.

"Oh shit!" muttered the officer as the colour drained out of his face.

Mick took the officer's gun. "Inside."

They entered the hall, the man now recovering his wits a little. "You're not Irish."

"Ten out of ten," replied Paul, "We've come to see a lady called Roana, you don't happen to know which room she's in do you?"

"No."

"Well would you be kind enough to find out, please."

"What are you two? Terrorists, Whitehall Funnies?"

"Neither actually, anyway is there a difference? For what it's worth, we have no intention of hurting anyone and we only have the lady in questions health and well being at heart."

A man in a white coat, covering military shirt and trousers, appeared. "What's going on here, who are these men constable? Why are they inside? You know the orders."

204

"Taxi service to take one of your patients home doc!"

"I don't know who the hell you are, or how you got in but get out – now!" snapped the doctor.

"Bollocks," muttered Paul. "We've come to collect one of your guests, a lady by the name of Roana, now take us to her."

"Certainly not, how'd you know she's in here? Come to it, how did you know where here is? Where is your authorisation? Let me see your I.D s," continued the white-coated officer. Paul's fragile patience snapped. In one swift movement he'd rammed the muzzle of the gun into the startled mans face and had him pinned against the wall. With his left hand firmly grasping the mans' throat He then, with no apparent effort, lifted the larger man clear off the floor.

"Now listen arsehole, take us to Ro - now, or choke."

"All-all right," came the strangled reply.

Paul released his grip, "Lead on Mc Duff, move."

Both the doctor, and the M.O.D. policeman were pushed in front of Paul and Mick along the main corridor, the place seemed deserted. Both were very conscious of the M.P.9s pointed at their backs. The doctor stopped opposite one of the doors, he then indicated Ro was 'in there'.

Paul tried the door. "Key?"

"No I can't allow it," replied the doctor.

"It wasn't a request," Paul snarled, holding out his hand.

"Absolutely not. Her treatment is far from complete, this is an issue concerning National Security."

Paul took one step forward, his left hand shot out and the doctor collapsed and was violently sick. Paul snatched the key ring with such force it ripped off the belt loop on the man's trousers from which it had been dangling.

The M.O.D. policeman moved towards Paul. "Right that's enough." He was confident these men wouldn't shoot and he was bigger than either and well trained. Not well enough. He never even saw the blow which laid him out cold.

"Steady Paul, we're in enough shit as it is, don't add murder."

"You wouldn't worry too much if you knew the real purpose of this hell hole Mate, in fact it's as well you don't."

The lock turned and the door swung open.

Mick was horrified at the sight which greeted them. A bare, windowless room lit by an over bright un-shaded bulb, his frail wife, in a gown but no covers fixed to a very basic bed with very secure leather straps. There was a drip in both arms and several sensors were taped to her head.

"What the fuck have they done to her?" Mick almost choked. "The bastards."

"They're that Mate, and more, all in the name of National Security."

Paul worked one side of the bed removing the drip carefully, he happened to check the bag, 'Saline +++' "Plus, plus, plus what?" he asked no one in particular.

"Paul, what is this shit?" asked Mick.

"Fuck knows, empty it out and stuff the bag in your pocket, the real docs will need the info to treat her properly."

As Paul freed her arm the heavily drugged woman lashed out at him, he was half expecting it, as a result he was just, and only just, quick enough to grab the skinny wrist.

"Ro, Ro! It's all right. It's Paul, Mick's here as well. You're going home, come on girl, wake up."

"No, no - no more, no - more."

"Come on Mick, let's get out of here."

Mick's powerful arms enveloped his wife as Paul removed the last electrode from her head.

"Sadistic bastards," cursed Paul as he kicked over the equipment trolley, his reward was a shower of sparks. Ro had now realised the man carrying her was indeed her husband and had stopped struggling.

"Come on Babes, we'll soon get you home."

Paul grabbed at the door handle. He was certain it should have been on the left. He didn't stop to check he just kicked it with such force the door flew across the corridor, taking part of the frame with it. This had the unfortunate effect of once more laying out the unfortunate doctor, who had just about regained his feet.

They made their exit un-molested; Paul opened the van door so Mick could put Ro in first. As Paul walked round to the driver's door he was confronted by two men in civvies each with a 9mm Browning levelled at him.

"Hands on the bonnet - move!"

"You're taking the piss!"

The first Mick knew of the problem was a 9mm Browning flying past the windscreen followed by a body. Almost immediately there was a shot and a cry of pain. Though not un-related the second was not a direct result of the first. His concern decreased as a man was pushed past the van, his arm bent at an impossible angle up behind his neck, still wailing with pain. His troubles were far from over as he was propelled, with some venom, straight into an extremely weedy fishpond. Mick watched in horror as Paul picked up the mans' automatic weapon and dismantled it, throwing the component parts at the man who was floundering with a broken arm in the pondweed.

"You bastard!" exclaimed Paul. "Shoot at my bloody van would you? Here catch," he threw the main body of the weapon at the floundering man.

By now the other guard was beginning to stir, although he was still in the way of the van. Paul half lifted, half dragged the still groggy individual to his feet only to hurl him into the pond. His pistol quickly joined him, again in pieces. This guard made a final futile attempt to grab Paul. He stumbled out of the pond and lurched at Paul who promptly hit him so hard he returned to the pond he'd just left.

"Bloody wanna - be's," muttered Paul as he climbed back into his van. "Right, let's get you pair home!"

He paused briefly at the gate, using just his right hand he released the magazine into the ground, a quick flick of the wrist ejected the 'one up the spout'. The weapon landed in a particularly prickly berberis bush! Mick simply unloaded his 'borrowed' weapon and dropped it.

"You alright Mick?" asked Paul, sounding concerned.

"You Sod!" replied his old friend. "You scared the shit out of me. You're mad, they will be after us like a swarm of angry bloody wasps. We're going to be in all kinds of shit over this."

"Not half as much as they are headed for. Don't worry Mate, give me a minute to make a phone call. Ten minutes after arriving back at Mick's rented cottage, a large Jeep Cherokee pulled up and another old friend climbed out.

"Hi B.J., found us alright then?" Paul asked casually.

"What the hell have you been up to?"

"You sure you want to know?"

"Hello Mick, what's up?"

Mick related the events of the past month, ending with an obviously nervous brief account of the previous hour's happenings.

"Oh dear!" sighed B.J. "Still they had it coming, just keep your heads down, leave this to me. I'll get this sorted." Then the big man returned to his jeep. He moved his jeep so it completely blocked the drive. He made a couple of phone calls. Half an hour later a military ambulance turned up with a two-car escort. "Right Mick, off you go with your Missus. This time I promise you, she'll be looked after properly, by people who care. We'll sort things out here, you'll be OK now Mate."

The medics carried a barely conscious Roana past Paul to the waiting ambulance. "You'll be alright now, these are the good guys."

"This is getting to be a habit, rescuing me." For the first time he could remember, Ro began to cry. "Why couldn't you have failed or killed me in the crossfire. Damn you for being so good at your job!" Then she passed out.

Paul turned to his friend, "Give me a gun B.J. and let me go back and give those bastards their just desserts."

"Calm down Mate, they'll get sorted in a bit, I've already started things moving."

"I'll tell you B.J. it really hurt, no one should be treated like that, ever since we brought her home she's had to hide as though she's some sort of criminal. Dammit she deserves to be a national hero, it's a bloody scandal!"

"I agree with you Paul, now calm down and bugger of home, we'll sort this out, I'll be in touch as soon as it's sorted, O.K?"

"Alright Mate, sorry about dragging you into this mess but I couldn't see any other way," he replied a bit sheepishly.

"There wasn't any other way, as usual you got it right when it mattered, even if you did go a bit over the top with a couple of the guards.

"I know they were only doing their job, but they should have taken the hint."

"It's alright mate, it's over, relax. Go on scram, and bloody well done."

"Cheers mate, I'm gone."

POST SCRIPT

This story is dedicated to the memory of an extraordinary lady, who for the purpose of this book I have called Roana. What happened to her as described here is in essence true. "They" can no longer hurt her, she died just before Christmas 2001 aged a mere 48. "Mick" her devoted husband wasn't there when she had a heart attack. Despite his age he had been recalled to serve his country in some capacity following the events of September the 11th. In a fit of generosity the powers that be allowed him a whole day off for her funeral. This is how we reward our heroes.

So who was 'Ro'? Well, we never did really find out. The nearest we ever came was a girl whose parents were both 'civil servants' and were killed, probably by the warlords, they were on a 'trekking' holiday in Thailand. Their daughter was at school at the time, one of the better schools for young ladies. She took her 'O' levels then vanished, she may have spent two years as a student at the Sorbonne University, studying Oriental languages, the student in question then vanished again. This may have been 'Ro'; there again it may not, we will never know. If it was then at least she had her revenge.

Was it all worth it? The lives lost removing the warlords; the expense to the U.N and other governments was probably even greater than the value of the heroine destroyed. As to if it made any difference, probably not. Heroine was by all accounts in relatively short supply for a few weeks, and therefore more expensive, this resulted in an increase in street crime and burglaries to match the higher prices. Had the pressure been maintained on the warlords then some long-term gains may have come of it all. But as is the way of these things, it was decided by the great and the good to withdraw U.N funding for the operation, so the forces were withdrawn and the operation declared a success. In less than a year heroine traffic in the area was back to the pre-operation levels.

We know what happened to Ro bless her.

What of the others? Taff, my best friend, was killed in circumstances never satisfactorily explained. 'B.J.' went on to become a senior officer, on the rare occasions I see him I can't quite bring myself to call him 'Sir'. Kenny, Mickey and the others all had long careers, having avoided being on the chopper which went into the South Atlantic during the Falklands War, killing many of our peers. Having survived the trials of life, most of them seem to be involved with survival schools or adventure training. Me? I got hurt in a stupid accident, just one of those things, and left the army before completing my training.

All I ask is remember RO, a truly astounding lady.

RIP Ro a lovely lady.

Timothy Pilgrim.

AFTER THOUGHTS.

Talking with some old friends in the course of researching this book, one thing became increasingly obvious to us. The effects of the actions described in this book spread much wider than any of us had realised at the time.

The sheer destruction wrought on the warlords' evil empires was obvious, though I fear transient. The removal, one way or another of a small clique of very un-civil servants, seemed in itself a major achievement and ample reward. The same could be said of the removal of a handful of senior Provos. The real victory was less obvious and a little longer in manifesting itself.

All this took place just as the Provos were gearing themselves up for an unprecedented terrorist campaign. No matter how large the arms caches seized by the security forces, it was a simple matter to replace them with new and better weapons. Money flooded into the terrorist coffers, it's money men protected as 'sources' by the 'bent' section within the security service; all this torrent of cash from the cheap, regular shipments of heroin, flowing from the golden triangle, direct to the terrorists.

Thanks entirely to Ro, the protection was removed, as were the terrorists' front men who did the dealing, and their direct supplies cut off. Once the ring was broken, there was no way to restore it, as the protection was gone! The funds shrank to a relative trickle, as a result the planned offensive, as bad as it was, never remotely approached the planned levels of violence. Starved of the bulk of their easy cash, the Provos eventually withered and fragmented to become the sorry, cowardly gang of thugs they are today. All thanks ultimately to one incredibly brave little lady: RO.